"In Cutter's thriller, a man under extraordinary financial pressure is pulled into a dark, criminal world. This is an engrossing work—the sinewy and lean prose produces a kind of spare poetry. An absorbing story, moving and uncompromising."
—*Kirkus Reviews*

"In a change of venue from the legal thrillers he is so well known for, Cutter takes us on a journey without lawyers but with plenty of intrigue and business that is as dirty as the famous 'dirty rice' in Arkansas duck country."
—*Steve Pruett, executive chairman, Cox Media Group*

"Buckle up for a page-turning ride as Cutter takes you on a tale of twists and turns, shocking discoveries, and family intrigue in the rice fields and flooded timber of Arkansas. Treachery, betrayal, family secrets, and murder. You won't be able to put it down."
—*Leland Bassett, chairman, Bassett Entertainment Group*

"Set on the 'finest rice ground in America' with the 'best duck hunting in the world,' Cutter's new novel *The Hangman's Blind* is a fast-paced mystery as well as a literary classic-to-be. In *The Hangman's Blind* Cutter delivers again, blending his keen observations on everything from bird dogs to good cigars and memorable bourbons with insights into why we value places sometimes more than people. There is truth in his fiction that cuts to the quick."
—*Glen Young, Bear River Literary*

"Well-crafted with clever turns of phrase, a raw Southern landscape, and a gritty cast of characters, *The Hangman's Blind* is a study in the dark floodwaters of evil swallowing the well-intentioned."
—Ben Beversluis, editor, The Grand Rapids Press, *retired*

"In the tradition of *Weeds, Breaking Bad* and Arkansas noir, Charles Cutter's *The Hangman's Blind* will keep you guessing until the very last page. A complex mystery by a talented and prolific writer."
—Bill Castanier, The Lansing City Pulse

THE HANGMAN'S BLIND

THE HANGMAN'S BLIND

A Dark Tale of Clear Skies and Flooded Timber

Charles Cutter

M·P·P
www.MissionPointPress.com

Mission Point Press

Published by Mission Point Press
www.MissionPointPress.com

Cover Design: John Wickham
Interior Design: Sarah Meiers

ISBN: 978-1-965278-34-5
Library of Congress Control Number: 2024926036

Printed in the United States of America

To Christi, Charlie, Tom, and Kathryn

"Hell is empty, and all the devils are here."

—William Shakespeare,
The Tempest

CHAPTER ONE

Sunday, January 25, 1998, Stuttgart, Arkansas.
An hour before sunrise.

Trip McClure ran the johnboat up the ditch in the dark. Cash, his black Lab, sat in the bow. They headed north, then northwest through the buckbrush, and then into the woods. He stopped at the Crooked Tree to make sure the baby food jars he'd hidden in the old tree were still there.

He tied up the boat at Mama's Blind where the ditch was cut in two by the Game and Fish levee that marked the boundary of state land and Belle Oak. His great-grandfather had dug the ditch all the way to Bayou Meto to draw water to flood his rice fields and to flood up his green timber. Thirty-three thousand acres of Arkansas Game and Fish land on one side of the levee, five thousand acres of McClure ground on the other. When Archie McClure bought it, nobody wanted it. Now, everyone did.

Trip was going to end it at eleven, here at Mama's Blind. He'd been a fool, and he knew it. It had gone too far, and he was going to end it today—one way or another.

He and Cash climbed over the levee to the boat he'd hidden on the Bayou Meto side. Cash jumped in. Trip started the motor, and they set off, running dead slow through the trees. The lower unit bounced off roots and sunken logs. The exhaust from the engine blew back on him, sweet and smoky.

They took the ditch as far as the triple tape, three bands of orange, glow-in-the-dark tape. He took his compass out of his coat, marked a course to the Beaverkill, just south of west. He hunted the Beaverkill by himself, except for one other time, and he was pretty sure he was the only one who could find it.

Trip coasted into the Beaverkill. He killed the engine and drifted over to the fallen tree that gave the hole its name. When beavers felled the hundred-year-old red oak, it tore down more trees with it, creating a break in the canopy the size of a small pond, big enough for ducks to drop down into the flooded timber and feed on the floating acorns.

Trip pointed at the fallen oak. "Cash, kennel." The black Lab jumped from the boat to the log and sat.

He poled into the woods and tied the boat to a tree. Then he slipped into the water, covered the boat with burlap, and grabbed his shotgun and shooting bag. He waded through the woods, the smell of wet timber and rotting leaves all around him. When he got back to the fallen log, Cash wagged his tail at him.

Trip leaned against the tree closest to the fallen log. There was some daylight in the woods, but the sun was still below the tree line. It was too dark to see the shotgun, the Parker over/under he'd stuck barrel first in the mud the last time he was here.

I'll get it later.

Trip reached into his pocket for the Ziploc bag that kept his cigarettes dry, found the joint mixed in with them. He rolled it in his fingers. His ears were ringing again, and smoking a joint was the only thing that helped, but this wasn't the time to smoke a joint. He took out a cigarette and lit it. He sucked the smoke into his lungs, blew it out, and smelled the burning tobacco as the smoke trailed off to the south.

I may have wanted this too much.

He had no business being here today, but it was the last day of duck season, and that's why he was here.

Trip heard wings over his head, looked up, and saw silhouettes above the trees. He took out his duck calls: the cocobolo single reed that Cad had made him, the Rich-N-Tone acrylic, and the Haydel DR-85, a fifteen-dollar plastic double reed call—the meat call that called in the ducks when nothing else would.

The ducks were call shy at the end of the season, so he had to be careful with them. He ran his hands over the calls, then put the DR-85 to his mouth. He called to them sweetly, ever so sweetly.

Trip landed the first bunch. Cash didn't break, but it was all he could do to stay on the log. His leg shook—the leg where the cottonmouth had bitten him.

Trip shot two drakes out of the second bunch. Cash fetched them both.

A dozen ducks flew over the hole. Trip could hear the wind rush over their wings as they circled the hole, a low whistling, like wind through bare branches. The circle tightened. Then it was a spiral, a swirling spiral falling lower and lower. A hen dropped below the treetops and landed in front of them. Three more splashed down on the other side of the hole.

There was another splash off to his right, but it wasn't the splash of a duck. He didn't turn toward it.

Another splash to his right. Cash turned his head to the sound. Trip didn't turn, not yet. He blew the call softly and landed the rest of the ducks. He heard the click of a safety. Cash's ears pricked up. Trip turned.

At short range, there is nothing more lethal than a shotgun. At fifteen yards, the pellets tear the face off a man.

It wasn't going to end at Mama's Blind at eleven. It was going to end here. Now.

CHAPTER TWO

Monday, September 1, 1997. Six months earlier.

"He calls so sweetly," Celia McClure said.

"Yes, Mama," Little George said.

"He calls so sweetly," she said again.

"He does, Mama."

"Little George, it is rude to ignore me."

"Mama, I answered you."

"Look at me when I speak to you."

"I am looking for doves."

"I want you to look at me when I speak to you."

Little George turned to his mother. "I am sorry I didn't look at you, but we're on a dove hunt, and I'm looking for doves."

Celia, Little George, and the rest of the hunters sat in lawn chairs on the east side of the millet field, the sun at their backs and in the doves' eyes when they flew in from the slough. Trip had planted the field for the express purpose of dove hunting. The doves had started flying at daybreak, swooping and darting into the millet. The shotguns poured number eight shot at them. Trip McClure's opening-day dove hunt was the most sought-after invitation in Arkansas County. The hunters, thirty of them, stretched across the east edge of the field. Friends and family only, except this year there were the two Memphis bankers.

Celia McClure had driven over from Memphis yesterday afternoon with Little George, her oldest, and J.D., her middle son. Trip, her youngest, had grilled them steaks last night. They were here for the opening day of dove season at Belle Oak, just as they had been for the past thirty years and the two generations before them. Her sons' wives refused to come, which was fine with Celia. Little George and J.D. had come under protest. "I need to be accompanied," she had said, "particularly since your father will not be joining us this year." She broke the twenty-gauge side-by-side and checked the shells in the barrels. She snapped it shut and mounted it to her shoulder. Then she laid it in her lap. "Little George, I want you to look at me when I'm talking to you. You know I can't turn my head without turning my whole body."

"I am truly sorry about your back."

Celia looked down at her shotgun, then at her son. "Your brother gets them on a string, and he has his way with them. He can make them do what he wants. He calls them so sweetly."

"Mama, it's September first. It's the opening day of dove season. That's why we're here. Duck season is three months away."

It was only 9:30, but sweat had already beaded on Celia's forehead. "He doesn't try to boss them like you do. He coaxes them. He pleads with them. He talks them into it."

"I don't see why this matters right now."

Celia ran her hands around the brim of her straw hat, wide-brimmed and hemp-colored. She took it off, pulled a white handkerchief from the breast pocket of her khaki shirt, and wiped her forehead. "My goodness, it's warm." She stuffed the handkerchief back in her pocket and put her hat back on. Her ponytail, black as night, hung down behind her back. Tall, still thin. Gray eyes, like Trip's. Her skin was lined from too much sun. An aging beauty but still striking. She had never forgiven herself for getting old. Big George hadn't cared, but he was gone.

"Little George," she said, "it matters right now because this is what I am feeling right now." She twisted in her chair, her back stiff from the accident. She thought it would always be that way.

"That's all well and good, Mama, but this is September first. It's ninety degrees and duck season is three months away."

"You're repeating yourself. I see your little brother over there picking up doves with Cash, and this is what I feel."

Little George was tall and broad shouldered, but he was starting to go soft. His long, narrow face floated around puffy cheeks, and he had the beginnings of a double chin.

"Little George, you look just like your father, except you eat too much."

"Thank you for those kind words, Mama."

"You're quite welcome. I just wish your father was here with us."

"Daddy is buried in Memphis."

"I know where he is. I want him alive. Here. With me. Here at Belle Oak."

Belle Oak was just outside Stuttgart. Three hours west and a little south of Memphis. Seventy miles southeast of Little Rock. On the Arkansas Grand Prairie, the finest rice ground in America and the best duck hunting in the world.

Tully, the seventy-five-year-old, portly cook who had served dinner in the formal dining room last night, appeared with a tray of drinks. Tully had worked for the McClures for the past fifty-five years. Celia had never seen him sweat or even look hot, not even today.

"Something cold to drink, Miss Celia?"

"Sweet tea, please. With lemon."

"And you, Mr. Little George."

"Sweet tea, Tully. No lemon."

"Yes, sir."

"Tully," Celia said, "make sure Trip gets something cold to drink. And some water for Cash."

"Yes, Miss Celia, but I expect that Mr. Trip will cool him off in the catfish pond."

"I expect he will, but you get him some water just the same."

"Yes, Miss Celia. Lunch will be in an hour."

"That will be fine."

Tully and his tray left for the next shooters.

"Thank you for bringing me to Belle Oak, Little George."

"You're welcome, Mama." Little George leaned toward Celia. "Mama, the only thing worse than being called Little George is being called Mr. Little George. There's no need for it. Now that Daddy's gone."

"It's not that important."

"I don't like it, Mama."

"Little George, there's a lot you don't like." Celia took a flask from the shell bag at her feet and took a drink. She looked around the field then took another.

She picked up a pair of field glasses and looked up the row of chairs, shooters in lawn chairs as far as she could see, J.D. and the bankers at the far end. "Shouldn't you be up there with those two bankers?"

"No, Mama."

"J.D. is a lawyer. You're the one that runs the business."

"I think we're at the lawyer stage."

"Hush. We are not." She picked up the field glasses again. She saw Trip with the shooters, standing behind the lawn chairs, Cash at heel on his left. J.D. fired twice from his chair. Then one of the bankers. Trip waved a Confederate flag to stop the shooting, then sent Cash to retrieve the doves, one by one, while the shooters drank their sweet tea.

"Trip shouldn't be using that flag," Little George said.

"It's a tradition is all. He asked me if he should get another flag."

"What did you say?"

"I asked him what kind he had in mind." She sipped her tea. "He said a white flag, which I told him was singularly inappropriate."

"Why not a skull and crossbones?"

"Little George, you lived for this dove hunt when you were a boy." Celia picked up the field glasses again. Trip came back to the shooters and put Cash back at heel. He gave Cash a line with his left arm. She watched the dog as he took the line, nose down. At thirty yards, he stopped, wheeled to his left. She lost the dog in the millet. He reappeared with a dove, ran back to Trip, sat, and presented the bird. Trip gave Cash another line and sent him again. "That is poetry."

"That is a good way for a dog to get heat stroke."

"You surely are negative today," Celia said.

"We do have a few things to be negative about."

"Maybe we do but not today." She took a long drink from her flask.

CHAPTER THREE

The birds quit flying at eleven, but the dove hunters stayed in their chairs, waiting for the wagon, it being a southern custom never to walk when you could ride. The back of J.D.'s shirt had soaked and matched the thatch of his chair. The two Memphis bankers next to J.D.—Trip had forgotten their names—dripped sweat like water squeezed from a sponge, especially the fat one. Trip hadn't wanted them to come. Opening day of dove season was for friends and family. The fat one could shoot a little, but Trip had given him credit for some of the birds he himself had shot.

He heard Jake on the little John Deere, finally. Jake came up from the shop, pulling the wagon behind the tractor. He stopped next to Trip, lit a cigarette, and climbed down. Baseball hat turned backwards, wet through.

"Done yet, Mr. Trip?"

"We were done an hour ago."

"Is that right?"

"Have you heard any shots in the last hour?"

"No, sir, but I thought you might get some flying back in after they watered."

Trip shook his head.

"I guess none did."

"I guess not." Trip glared at Jake who looked down at his boots. He had a toothy smile and a thick nose, bent ever so slightly to the right from who knew how many bar fights. Jake Lawless had a gift for fighting, especially when alcohol and married women were involved.

"There's water and drinks in the wagon, Mr. Trip."

"That's fine, Jake."

He's a decent farmhand when he's not in jail.

"Take the little John Deere down the edge of the field. I'll pick up the chairs as we go. Make sure that wagon does not move until everybody's sitting down."

"Yes, sir, Mr. Trip." Jake smiled, and the scar ran down his cheek like a knife blade.

They picked up J.D. and the bankers first, then twelve more including Big George's cousin and his two boys. Then Trip's neighbor, Pig Shelton and his five boys. More friends and family, then Mama and Little George.

The tractor ran north on top of the levee, west past the millet field, then south, rice on either side of them. After Trip had drained the water off the rice, the heads had drooped and turned brown. At the four corners, Jake turned west again. Rice on both sides here, too.

Jake had a washtub of ice in the trailer, filled with a case of Dixie and a case of Coke. Pig, upturned nose and porcine build, drank a Dixie right away.

"Rice looks good, Trip," Pig said.

"It does."

"When you gonna take it?"

"Soon," Trip said.

Jake turned back to them. "It's got to dry some more," Jake said. "Field's still too wet to get the big John Deere in."

"If it rains anymore, you'll never get it off," Pig said.

"We'll get it off," Trip said.

The way things are going, I've got to get it off, no matter how wet it is.

"This would have been a better year for wheat," Pig said. "Follow the wheat with soybeans. That's what we did." He swilled the rest of the beer and crushed the can in his mitt of a hand.

Trip smiled a big "I don't give a shit what you did" smile at Pig. Trip—Archibald Alexander McClure III—had gray eyes like his mother and blond hair, longer than the fashion and swept back over his ears. He had orthodontically straight teeth, but the cigarettes had given them a gray cast.

He squatted next to Cash and scratched him behind his left ear. Trip took a Dixie from the tub and tossed it to Pig, who missed it. The beer turned end over end as it sailed off the wagon and over the edge of the levee and down into the rice six feet below them. Cash followed it with his eyes. The dog looked at Trip. "Leave it."

"That's a waste of good beer," Pig said.

"It is."

"I'd a caught it, but the wagon hit a bump."

"I know it."

The wagon turned south again, two more sections to cross until they reached the shop. Fifty years ago, Trip's great-grandfather, the first Archibald McClure, had built a levee around the tillable ground to keep the farm from flooding when Bayou Meto backed up into the ditch.

The levee ran down the middle of the farm with cross levees at every section line. They were six feet high and wide enough for the tractors of the day to ride on top. Now only the little John Deere fit.

Trip had six sections in crops. Three miles east-west, two miles north-south.

When they were in rice, which was most years, they precision-leveled each section, but just to be careful, they pulled levees every quarter section. This year, everything was in rice except the eighty acres of millet for the dove hunt and the catfish ponds, a quarter section on the north side which Big George had tried when rice was down and catfish were up. He gave up on the catfish when they started coming in from South America.

Trip looked back to the west. His great-grandfather kept two thousand acres in green timber to the north and west. Everyone thought he was a fool for not cropping it. It was the best green timber in Arkansas, and everybody wanted it, which was why the possible failure of Belle Oak's rice was of so much interest to so many. That and the little problem of McClure Tug and Tow.

Trip tossed another beer to Pig. He caught it this time.

It took the better part of an hour to collect the dove hunters and drop them all off at the shop. It stood a hundred yards off the road—a long way by Arkansas standards, but Trip's grandfather, Archibald Alexander McClure, Jr., didn't want it to flood, and this was the highest ground on Belle Oak. It was a big shop by anybody's standards, a sixty-foot square concrete pad. A third of it enclosed by muddy green sheet metal. Workshop, tool crib and office inside. A twenty-foot roof so they get the big John Deere under it.

The sun beat on the roof. There was just enough breeze to keep the sweat from soaking through their shirts. And the beer was cold.

Trip had the doves breasted. There wouldn't be enough for all of them so he had barbecue, too. Macaroni salad and coleslaw to go with it.

"Trip, those were some kind of dove breasts," said the fat Memphis banker.

Trip nodded at him. Up until now he had pretty much managed to stay away from everyone he didn't want to talk to, which was pretty much everyone.

I think this one is Wheeler.

"How'd you get that tang in there?" the banker said. He took off his hat, a bald head to go with a pasty, white face. "I don't believe I've ever tasted that tang before."

"Jalapeño juice."

"Jalapeño juice." The banker wiped his forehead and put his hat back on. "How do you do that?"

"Drain off the juice of a jar of jalapeños. Let the meat sit in it for an hour. Grill it four minutes a side."

"That was the best dove I ever had. The barbecue, that was good, but you know, I'm from Memphis."

"I did not know," Trip said, who did know.

"Surely you know. We bank the barge business."

"I did not know," Trip said again who knew all about the bank and the barge business.

"Your name is on the guarantee, along with your brothers," the banker said.

"Is it?"

Little George and the other banker joined them. "Trip's just having a little fun," Little George said. "Trip, you let him be."

"I was trying to," Trip said.

"Trip, you know Wheeler. And Ty, too."

"I don't believe I do."

"Planter's Bank in Memphis," Wheeler said again. "We bank McClure Tug and Tow."

"He knows that, Wheeler. He's just on you is all," Little George said.

"Why would that be? After all the money we put out to you," Ty said, taller and thinner than Wheeler and with decidedly more hair.

"He's just quiet about business," Little George said. "We sure do appreciate it."

"We're glad to be here. Best dove hunt I ever been on," Wheeler said. "Those woods flood up for duck season?"

"Once in a while," Trip said.

"Every year," Little George said.

"There he goes again," Wheeler said.

"Every mallard in Arkansas County knows about these woods, especially when they're banging over at the Government Addition," Little George said.

"What's an acre of green timber worth around here?" Wheeler found himself a beer and took a swallow.

"Depends on if it draws ducks," Little George said.

"Say it does," said Wheeler.

"Then I'd say three an acre, maybe four."

"Hundred?" Ty said.

"Thousand," Little George said.

"That's more than rice ground," Wheeler said.

"It is," Little George said.

"Four thousand an acre for green timber?" Ty said. "That's a lot of money."

"It's not all about the money," Trip said.

* * *

Trip started up the four-wheeler and had Cash sit next to him. He knew the dog wanted to run, but it was too hot. They ran the four-wheeler north up the middle levee, back the way they had come from the dove hunt. He stopped at the end of the levee, drying rice behind him, wild ground in front.

A covey of quail whistled. His grandfather had hunted them on horseback with English Pointers. There were at least five coveys on the farm, but not enough to hunt.

I love it when they say "bob white."

They slid down the levee and stood at the edge of the weeds. He sat Cash next to him on his left. "Cash, snake." Trip gave the dog a hand signal, his arm outstretched in front of him. "Cash, snake," he said again. The dog started to walk in the direction Trip pointed. He stayed two steps ahead of Trip, looking back at him every now and then. The trick to the snake walk was Cash not chasing down snakes.

It was just the opposite. The dog's instinct was to investigate anything that had an odor or moved, both of which snakes had in abundance. Trip had to train Cash to do the opposite. When the dog came upon a snake, he was to sit and stay. Trip had tied a dead snake to a rope and pulled it through the weeds in front of Cash. When Cash went after the dead snake, Trip nicked him on his training collar. Then he said, "Cash, sit." Three sessions cured Cash of any interest in snakes other than to sit whenever he came upon one, poisonous or not.

As far as Trip was concerned, whether a snake was poisonous was incidental to his fear. Trip was deathly afraid of snakes, all snakes. He was grateful when Cash sat, whether or not the serpent was venomous. Cash and the snake walk was the only way Trip would be out in the weeds this time of year.

He was careful not to make a path. The weeds turned to buckbrush, and a quarter mile later, the buckbrush thinned out and they were under the canopy of the McClure woods. It was cooler in the timber, cool and dry, but it would start to flood up in November, rains permitting.

The woods opened up on a garden in a clearing. Row upon row of cannabis in full sun, the finest marijuana within fifty miles of Stuttgart. The plants stood seven feet tall. Trip walked up and down the row and smelled the sweet smell. At the east end of the marijuana patch, he stooped into the tin-roofed lean-to where he dried the plants. He ran his hands across the drying marijuana and ground some of it between his thumb and forefinger.

"Cash, I'd say this is about ready."

Trip took a cigarette paper from a packet in his pocket and rolled himself a joint. He lit the end and inhaled. He had shot too long without earplugs. This was the only thing that helped the ringing in his ears—and the worry.

"Cash," he said, "we'll have a good harvest if we don't get too much rain."

Trip sat in the shade of the lean-to and smoked the joint. Then he bagged the dried marijuana in the lean-to and took one bag for himself. He cut two of the standing rows and hung them on the drying rack in the lean-to.

He and Cash snake-walked back to the four-wheeler and rode up to the yellow house.

* * *

"I would not call this the Last Supper," Little George said.

Trip looked up from his plate, chewing slowly.

What exactly would you call it?

"Trip, I am speaking to you," Little George said.

"I know it." Trip reached for the gravy and poured it on his rice. He ate a forkful, then picked up the chicken leg and took a bite.

"You can't just make an inflammatory statement like that and then ignore me," Little George said. "Not to mention the rest of the family."

Trip's favorite summer dinner was fried chicken, rice, peas, and biscuits with chicken gravy. Stewed okra on the side. He lined up a row of peas with his knife and pushed them through the gravy-soaked rice onto his fork. He knew this reeked of Southern cliché, but he had done it this way since he was a boy. He had always done it this way, and it was always cooked up by Sally, Belle Oak's six-days-a-week cook.

"Trip is not ignoring you, Little George," Celia said. "He is engaged in his dinner."

I am ignoring him.

The five of them—Celia, her three sons, and Trip's wife, Parker—sat in the dining room of the yellow house, a single-story ranch a quarter mile from the shop that stood on high ground underneath the live oaks, fifty years old and just reaching their prime. It was the house that Trip's grandfather had built when he got serious about rice, and the house that Trip and Parker had lived in for the last fifteen years.

Trip looked out the east window of the dining room. Right through Little George, who sat directly across from him.

The dining room, built over the architect's objections, looked like an afterthought. It stuck out from the east side of the main house like a compound fracture. The north wall of the dining room had floor-to-ceiling windows as did the east and west sides. The windows lit the room even on the darkest days. The architect thought that building a house in a flood plain was foolish, especially one with floor-to-ceiling windows. But Archibald Alexander McClure, Jr. was not to be dissuaded. He said he wanted to bathe in the light and he'd sandbag the house if the floodwaters of Bayou Meto ever reached the dining room.

"Trip didn't mean anything by it, Little George," Celia said. "Did you Trip?"

"He most certainly did," Little George said. "He said 'last supper,' and he meant it."

"That's not what you meant now, is it? You're just making conversation, aren't you?" Celia said.

Trip looked up from his peas, rice, and gravy. "That is what I meant, Mama."

"Just what did you mean?" she said.

"If these two go and lose the barge business, they aren't going to take this farm down with them."

"This farm is no more than a duck woods. Never has been," Little George said.

"This farm pays its own way."

"Your guarantee is on the barge loan," Little George said.

"You can take that guarantee and shove it up your ass," Trip said.

Parker rapped his knuckles with her fork. "Don't talk like that at the table."

"This farm pays its own way," Trip said again.

"This farm hasn't paid its own way since Roosevelt was president," J.D. said.

"We made money last year." Trip looked across the table at Jefferson Davis McClure, the middle brother. Trip thought that the older he got, the more he looked like Jefferson Davis—dark, angular, and severe. Big George had so admired the leader of the Confederacy that he named his middle son after him. But his middle son had spent his entire adult life hiding his name with initials.

"It hasn't paid its own way since the crop loan," J.D. said.

"I paid off the crop loan when I sold last year's rice. And the money from the crop loan repaid a loan to the barge company that Daddy cooked up," Trip said.

"Do not talk about your father like that," Celia said.

Trip set his fork down and walked over to the china cabinet. He took out a leaded crystal tumbler and poured himself three fingers of Maker's Mark. He sat back down at the table and swirled the whiskey around in his glass.

"Do not drink while we're eating dinner," Celia said.

"I'd say this dinner is pretty well over, Mama." Trip took a swallow. It burned on the way down.

"This farm pays its own way," Trip said, for the third time.

"Not without government money," Little George said.

"No farm on the Grand Prairie pays its own way without government money," Trip said.

"The fact is, the barge business needs money and the best way to get it is by selling the farm," J.D. said.

"Get some more money from those Memphis bankers," Trip said.

"They were here because we can't pay back what we already borrowed," J.D. said.

Trip raised his voice. "The farm will not be sold for the barge business."

"Boys, boys, this is just a little discussion about the family business," Celia said.

"The barge business isn't being run for the family," Trip said.

Little George stood up. "What is that supposed to mean?"

"It can mean whatever you want it to mean," Trip said, his back to his oldest brother.

"Little George has done a fine job of managing the business, especially considering the mess he was left with," J.D. said.

"Little George couldn't manage a train wreck," Trip said.

Little George started for Trip. Parker pushed her chair back and stood in front of him. "I'll take care of this."

Parker had black hair, black like midnight, pulled back in a ponytail that showed off dangling silver earrings. They drew the eye to the sweep of her neck and her tall, thin frame.

She twisted her head to him. "Trip McClure, you are the host of a family dinner, and you will not speak to your brother that way."

This has gotten out of hand.

"Little George, I am sorry. You may remove my guarantee from your ass."

"We're going to sell this damn farm and the woods goes with it," Little George said.

"Not without my say so. I'm the farm manager in Big George's will."

"All it takes is a majority to vote you out," Little George said.

"There's four votes. You and J.D. need Mama's vote," Trip said.

"I will not be put in the middle. There must be another way to settle this," Celia said.

"There is," Trip said. "We can take a crop loan against this year's crop."

"Big George already did that. But nobody knows what he did with the money." J.D. bit his lip.

"A loan on this year's crop?" Trip said. He looked at Celia. "Mama?"

"I'm afraid he did," Celia said. She took herself to the china cabinet and poured three fingers worth.

* * *

Trip stewed for two days, then he and Cash climbed into the pickup and took I-40 east to Memphis and McClure Tug and Tow. When he got out of the truck, he felt like he'd run into a wall, the heat, the wet of the river, and the smell. Garbage, sewage, and dead fish mixed with diesel.

Trip ran his hand along the side of Little George's black Mercedes on their way to the office. "Cash," he said, "just how bad can business be?"

They walked past the receptionist and into Little George's office—what had been Big George's office. Little George sat at a once grand walnut desk, the shipyard, the docks, and the river out the window behind him. He had on a white shirt and striped tie. He'd sweated through his shirt in spite of the window air conditioner rattling behind him.

Trip sat down on a cracked leather couch facing his brother and propped his feet up on the coffee table. Cash lay at his feet. Little George glared at him.

I don't think Little George is glad to see me.

"I'm surprised you could find your way here," Little George said.

"I asked for directions."

"Since when do you give a shit about the barge business? Other than your check?"

Trip did not care about the barge business. He'd worked as a deckhand at the barge company during summer vacations while he was at Vanderbilt, the third generation of McClures to attend. He'd tried the barge business full time after college but gave it up.

Little George stood up, walked over to the air conditioner, and stuck his face in front of it. His tie fluttered. "With the invention of the telephone, you can get things done quicker than by driving all over God's half acre in an F-150," Little George said.

"We're not selling the farm," Trip said.

Little George turned back to Trip. "I don't want to sell the farm any more than you do."

I don't believe you.

"There's a crop loan to be paid back which I didn't know about, and the rice isn't even in yet."

"We need money, and the farm is where we're going to get it," Little George said, "If we don't sell the farm, the bank is going to take back our boats. And they're going to start with the *Celia Marie*."

Trip stood. "We are not selling the farm."

Cash lifted his leg on the coffee table. "Cash, no. Mark something that will do some good." The dog lowered his leg and followed Trip out of his big brother's office.

CHAPTER FOUR

Celia sat on the gallery of the family's Memphis home—a cavern after the three boys moved out, and a mausoleum now that Big George was gone. The red brick colonial in Chickasaw Hills, where Memphis's old money lived, was shaded by grand old oaks, with white pillars running the length of the gallery.

Trip had just left. Molly lay at her feet. She stirred her sweet tea with a long spoon, sweet tea with lemon and Maker's Mark. She took a big swallow.

She sat on the gallery for hours at a time, looking up and down the street, drinking her special sweet tea. She was careful with the dead soldiers. The odd one went in the trash. The rest she took with her on her errands and threw them away when no one was looking.

Celia thought that Mae, the cook, surely knew, but she wouldn't say anything. She'd worked for Celia's mother until she died. All the McClures drank, and Celia just couldn't up and quit when Big George passed. No one would expect her to do that. But Big George hadn't exactly passed. That's not what she'd call it.

Big George wasn't much with business, but he had kept the barge company going all those years. The boys thought the troubles started when he died, but the troubles had started long before that. The troubles had started with trucks and freeways, and she didn't know where they would end.

Trip had arrived without warning, just like he always did. He never called. He just showed up. He'd nearly caught her with the bottle. Not that he would have cared if she took a little nip now and then, but he wouldn't like her drinking all day. Not that he could say much. She knew the way to his marijuana patch. She thought everyone else in Arkansas County did, too, but nobody cared enough to do anything about it.

"Molly, that boy is a fool when it comes to ducks. I swear he'd rather hunt ducks than breathe. That will surely be the end of him." She stirred her sweet tea. "But he calls so sweetly."

Celia didn't want Belle Oak sold either. It wasn't just a piece of ground to her. That's all it was to Little George and J.D. But not to Trip or Big George or her. It wasn't the farm. It was the duck woods. The woods had a hold on Trip and wouldn't let him go. She didn't blame him, but he was a fool over it.

She sipped her drink. The whiskey burned her throat. She was near the bottom of the glass, where the whiskey, lemon, and sugar all hung up. It was the best part.

"You didn't have to do it," she said out loud. "We could have figured something out."

She scraped her spoon around the bottom of her glass and got a spoonful of whiskey and lemon-soaked sugar. "Big George, what did happen to the money from that crop loan? We could have fixed the barge company with that money." She licked the sugar off the spoon.

CHAPTER FIVE

"Mr. Trip, are you sure this is a good idea?" Big John said.

Trip waved the big man further to the west. "Right there," he said.

"There's snakes everywhere out here."

"I know it."

"That's why there's no good reason to be out here." Big John stuck his shovel in the dirt.

Big John was big in every way—six-foot-seven and three hundred pounds. He had a double chin and a big belly that made him look fat, but he was the strongest man Trip had ever known. The fat hung on him, but it covered muscle you couldn't see. Trip had seen him lift the back end of a pickup.

He had a big head with a full black beard. His hair hung over his ears and was pulled into a bushy ponytail.

Then there was the Walkman with the headphones, Big John's only touchpoint to the late twentieth century. He had six cassettes, which held every song Lynyrd Skynyrd had ever released. Those six tapes were Big John's entire music library. He played them over and over again. Sometimes he sang along with them. That was the only way to know what song was playing. Trip thought Big John had a pretty good voice.

But the big man didn't like being out here in early September, on top of the levee that divided Ponds Six and Seven on the old catfish farm.

"Dig right there," Trip said. "Right up against those willows."

"Mr. Trip, I sure don't want to."

"Cash checked it for snakes."

"That dog is fetching turtles."

"That's what he does after he checks for snakes."

Cash appeared with a turtle in his mouth, a snapping turtle the size of half a cantaloupe. The turtle was not pleased. It craned its neck around to bite Cash, but the dog held the turtle so that it couldn't bite him, this being a lesson Cash had learned the hard way.

When Cash was two, he'd picked up a honeydew-sized snapping turtle, which bit him on the lip. Cash yelped and let go of the turtle, but the turtle hung on, locked onto Cash's lower lip. The dog shook his head side to side, up and down, but the turtle, truly pissed off, hung on until it bit through Cash's lip, which bled and bled. Trip took him to the vet to get it stitched up. That was the last time a turtle ever bit him.

Cash dropped the turtle in a pile of a dozen other turtles: four sliders, two paints, one box, the rest snappers. The turtles, in various stages of escape, crawled away, only to be refetched by Cash who repiled them.

"How can he be on the lookout for snakes when he's playin' with that pile of turtles?"

"He'll keep a lookout. The turtles don't care for snakes either."

Cash had started by piling turtles and snakes, but the snakes liked being caught even less than the turtles, and he couldn't keep them in the pile. They slithered away as fast as he could drop them in the pile. They just didn't see the fun in it and bit him every chance they could. Cash had figured out that the only place to hold them was right behind their head.

The snake part ended when a cottonmouth bit Cash on the leg. Trip saved him with a panicky trip back to the vet. After that, Trip taught Cash the snake walk.

"Mr. Trip, we don't need no blind to shoot teal. All you got to do is stand at the edge of the willows and let 'em drop in."

"For three hundred a gun, we need to put the sports in a blind."

"Three hundred," Big John said. "No one in his right mind will pay that."

"I already booked nine."

"They can't be from around here."

Big John had worked for the McClures as a farmhand for thirteen years. He could dig or talk, but he couldn't do both at the same time.

Trip walked over to the big man. "We'll set the blind right here, sneak it right up next to the willows."

Fifteen years ago, Big George had taken the southwest section, which was perfectly good rice ground, and run a new levee through the middle of it. Then across it. Again and again, until he had built a tic-tac-toe of ponds inside the section. They made good money on the catfish until the South Americans got into the act and the bottom fell out of the prices. The catfish farm failed. Big George tried minnows, but he just didn't have the personality for it, minnows requiring a certain amount of care and attention that Big George just didn't have in him.

The ponds had mostly dried up, but the Arkansas clay stopped them from drying all the way up, and they were a haven for ducks and reptiles.

Cash disappeared, then reappeared with another turtle, redid his pile, then left again.

Trip, who could dig and talk at the same time, stuck his shovel in the levee and said, "We'll put three in a blind plus a guide on the outside."

"You can't call teal," Big John said. He started to dig.

"You can a little. The guide's mostly to just watch over the sports and get the ducks."

Big John stopped digging so he could say something. "I just don't see who's gonna pay to hunt teal in the heat and the bugs and the snakes." He raised the blade of his shovel. "Mr. Trip, you just be still and don't move." Big John took two baby steps toward Trip. Trip saw the cottonmouth, its jaws wide open, showing off its white mouth and its fangs. The big man drove the blade of the shovel into the snake, just behind its head, slicing it in two. The head fell on its side, jaws still open, eyes fixed on Trip. The tail writhed on the ground and wrapped itself around Big John's leg. He danced and screamed, but not to Lynyrd Skynyrd.

"Thank you, Big John. I think that cottonmouth meant to bite me."

"You're welcome, Mr. Trip, but I'd rather look for work than help you build these blinds."

Cash reappeared with another turtle, which he dropped. He snatched the headless snake from Big John's leg, shook it in his mouth, then flung it into the weeds.

Trip and Big John rode the four-wheeler back to the shop. Jake had the combine idling. Big John nodded at Jake and drove off without a word. Jake left the engine running and climbed down. He had on a white tee shirt that Trip thought remarkably clean for a farmhand. He had a pack of Marlboros rolled up in the sleeve of his shirt. He offered one to Trip.

"Trying to quit," Trip said.

"Like hell," Jake lit a cigarette. "Cottonmouth get to Big John?"

"He'll be back."

"Time to get the rice off, Mr. Trip. Past time."

"As soon as we get these blinds built."

"The rice is dry, but if we get any more rain, it won't be."

"Teal season starts Saturday, and I want those blinds in so the ducks are used to them by the time the season starts."

"You don't need blinds to shoot teal," Jake said.

"You do for three hundred a day."

Trip watched Jake's cheeks hollow as he dragged on his cigarette. If Big John was fat over muscle, Jake was just pure muscle. He had forearms like cables.

"Three hundred a day? Slick Withers don't get that, and he's been doing this for twenty years."

"Not here he hasn't. Nobody's ever hunted here without an invitation," Trip said.

"That's a fact."

Trip walked up to the yellow house for lunch, sweat running down his face.

* * *

Trip didn't like to eat in the kitchen. That was where the help ate. Parker knew it, but it was Sally's day off, and Parker was in charge. When he saw the kitchen table set for the two of them, he knew she had something on her mind. Trip took himself and his place setting through the butler's door and into the dining room. Eloise, one of Parker's cats, a perky little tortoiseshell, jumped in his lap. Trip scratched her behind the ears and she started to purr. Trip truly loved Parker, which was the only reason he abided her cats. It was all he could do to keep Cash from chasing them.

"Baby, if you're having lunch, it's in here," Parker said.

"Come on in here and eat here with me."

"I know what you're thinking, and I'm not mad at you. Not yet anyway."

Trip looked longingly at the Maker's Mark in the china cabinet. Parker had many fine qualities, but patience wasn't one of them. Whatever advantage he might gain by waiting her out would be lost if he poured himself three fingers of whiskey. He had just about given up when she burst through the swinging door.

She had on a black tank top and a short blue jean skirt. The dining room had a bit of a chill from the central air, and her nipples poked through her top. Trip couldn't help but stare.

"Don't look at me like that. It's freezing in here."

"Can't help it, baby."

"You only want to eat in here so you can ogle me."

"I don't like eating in the kitchen. It makes me feel like a farmhand."

"You are a farmhand, and you're not even going to have that job if you don't get the rice off."

"You're not the first one who told me that today."

"Your lunch is in the kitchen. I only came out here to tell you that. Eloise, you come with me." Parker picked up her cat and plowed back through the swinging door. The refrigerator door opened.

Eloise is about to get some baby food. Probably veal from one of those little jars.

He started to count out loud. When he got to seven, she burst back through the door.

"What number did you get to?"

"Seven."

"That's better than last time." She stood on her tiptoes and wiggled up on the corner table just to Trip's left side, her skirt riding up. He couldn't help but look up her leg and see her panties.

"Parker," Trip said in his most sincere but fraudulent voice.

"They're candy cane. But you know that, don't you?" She pulled her skirt down. "How about you tell me about this teal business." Parker sat just ladylike enough to be provocative.

"Do you think we could talk about the teal afterwards?"

"After what, baby?" she said.

Trip stood up and kissed her full on the mouth. She hopped off the table and he ran his hands up the backs of her legs and held her bottom, his hands against her candy cane panties, then inside them.

* * *

Trip ate his turkey and onion sandwich at the kitchen table. He looked outside and at the blue-winged teal flying over the rice. They had started to show up at the end of August, before the dove opener, at first just a few, then a few more. Now there were thousands of them, spread out all across the Grand Prairie. They were the first ducks to arrive and the first to leave. They'd be gone by October, maybe sooner.

They weren't mallards, the great prize of Arkansas duck hunters. They were bigger than doves but not much. They had a patch of blue feathers, a shade lighter than sky blue, on their speculum, the feathers on the trailing edge of their wings.

It's the most beautiful blue I've ever seen.

There were teal calls, but you couldn't really call them. You could put out decoys, but it didn't matter much. They came in or they didn't. You could hunt them if you knew where they wanted to be, and Trip knew where they wanted to be.

Parker looked over at him from the sink. "Mr. McClure, this teal hunt business may be the greatest lunacy I have ever heard of."

Trip took a swallow of his Dr Pepper with a wedge of lemon. She only called him Mr. McClure when she was powerfully displeased with him, which was not often, but which was now, and he was at a decided disadvantage in her kitchen.

"There's more teal on Belle Oak than you can shake a stick at, but all the teal in Arkansas County won't bring in enough money to save this farm."

"It's not the teal. It's the mallards. We get the word out with the teal."

"You and a duck club will never work."

"Baby, we can make money on the sports."

"Mr. McClure, you can barely stand me some days. How are you going to put up with strangers? Not to mention entertain them. Especially at your beloved Belle Oak."

"I can do it."

"What you need to do is start with the rice." She walked over to him. "Are you done with your lunch?" She snatched his plate, flew it into the sink like a frisbee, where it shattered.

After lunch, Trip lay down on the living room couch, a mahogany leather couch long enough to stretch out and take a nap. Parker came in and told him that, whether or not the next thing he did was get the rice in, the next thing he wasn't going to do was take a nap. Trip and Cash walked back to the shop where they took a nap on the cast-off couch in the office.

* * *

The next morning, Trip slid down into the rice from the big levee north of the shop. The rice reached his thighs. It had been taller, but now it was bent over with the weight of the heads. He broke one off and crumbled it into the palm of his hand. He licked the index finger of his other hand, touched a kernel in his palm and brought it to his mouth. He put it in his mouth and crushed it between his teeth. It had a little bit of a nutty taste, but what he was most interested in was the moisture in it. It was dry. Dry enough he wouldn't need to spend much on the dryers at Riceland.

But first he had to get it off. He climbed up on the levee and looked across the fields, acres and acres of brown grain. A full section right here. Six in all.

If they had all the grain buggies going and if nothing broke down, it would take them at least ten days to get it all in. If it didn't rain and if the wind didn't blow. Wind could be harder on rice than rain, much worse than rain.

The forecast was for calm and dry, but anything could happen. If he could get the blinds built and then bring the rice in, it could work. He'd turn Belle Oak into a duck club, make money on the sports, and drive up the value of the farm. Then he could borrow enough money to keep the barge business going. Teal season was small potatoes, but if that worked, he could score big on the sixty-day big duck season.

He knew it was a half-assed plan, but he didn't know what else to do, and he was damned if he'd let the farm go. Or the timber. And he still didn't know what happened to the money Big George borrowed.

Trip looked over at the Hangman's Blind. They all called it "Big George's passing." That wasn't the half of it. None of them, not even Trip, knew all of it, but Trip knew the most because he was the one who had found his father.

* * *

Seven months ago. The last day of duck season. Big George had gone to the Hangman's Blind with Molly to hunt the edge of Archie's field.

The Hangman's Blind, so named because it stood next to a cypress tree that grew on the woods side of the levee. A branch grew perpendicular to the trunk about fifteen feet off the ground. It was the damnedest thing. Everybody thought that would be the ideal tree for a hanging, if the need ever arose. Every duck season they flooded Archie's field and built the blind on the levee next to the tree.

Trip didn't think it was worth hunting there that day. The ducks had eaten all the rice, and they weren't using the field. Big George said he didn't care. He and Molly were going to hunt there anyway.

They'd had a good shoot in the timber that morning and weren't going out that afternoon. They didn't think much about it when Big George didn't come in for lunch. They didn't think much about it when they heard one shot at the end of shooting hours. Maybe Big George killed a duck at the very end of duck season. They didn't think much about it at dusk either. Little George and J.D. went up to the yellow house. Trip took the four-wheeler to the Hangman's Blind, Molly and Cash running in front of him, delighted at one more chance to run.

At the blind, in the dark, "Big George, you all right?" Trip said. "Daddy. Daddy, where are you?"

Trip saw his father's four-wheeler. "Daddy," he said again. He pushed open the door. There was his father. "Big George, what are you up to? It's way past shooting hours and time for a drink."

Big George didn't answer, but Trip could see him sitting on the bench, his back leaning against the wall.

"Big George," he said again. His father sat on the bench holding the Colt revolver, the one with the pearl handle. Trip fished the flashlight out of his coat and shined it on the pistol. His father's fingers clenched the pistol, and he had to unwind them from the pistol grip. He ran his hand along it. His father must have thought about it long and hard. He'd rubbed the mother-of-pearl down to the steel before he pulled the trigger.

He shined the light on his father, who could have been asleep, his head tilted back. Except for one thing. He had stuck the pistol in his mouth, pulled the trigger, and blown his brains out the back of his head. His face was at peace, but his brains were splashed on the wall behind him.

* * *

Trip drove the pickup up Arkansas 165, Cash riding shotgun. About a mile out of Stuttgart, he pulled into the Gator, a one-story cement block building with no windows, a flat roof, and a gravel parking lot.

Slick Withers owned the Gator. How he kept it open and stayed out of jail, with all that went on at the Gator, was anybody's guess. Slick, so named because of his slicked back, jet black hair, had a cash machine of a roadhouse. When he wasn't watering the whiskey at the Gator, he carried hunters. He had movie star good looks and was built like a wide receiver. Trip thought it a shame that all that was wasted on somebody so slimy.

Trip opened the glove box, made sure that the pearl-handled Colt was where he left it. He did not favor the Gator, but Church had insisted they meet here.

Trip, even as a smoker, was offended by the smoke. It hung just above the tables, pushed around by the ceiling fans. He nodded at the farmhands, the trainmen, the elevator men, the mechanics, and the factory workers from the refrigerator plant. At least it wasn't Saturday. The Duck Stompers weren't here, the country band who knew, at most, fifteen songs, but featured a big-breasted singer, their chief attraction.

The main attraction of the Gator, though, was the gator, a big old bull alligator named Burt. He lived in a six-foot-deep concrete pit in the floor. Rebar over the top kept Burt in the pit, but it didn't keep him from sticking his snout between the bars when he wanted a snort. Over the years Burt had developed a taste for Miller Lite.

Somebody must be getting paid off to let all this go.

He took a table by himself in the corner. He had gotten there early so he could talk to Church before he got too drunk.

Church showed up five minutes later, a beer in one hand, a shot in the other. He set them both on the table and pumped Trip's hand.

"Trip McClure, what are you doing sitting here all by yourself? I thought we was supposed to meet."

"We are."

"Well, then, why are you here when I'm over there? That's not sociable." Church stumbled when he sat down.

Trip thought Church, officially Walter Knox, had rounded out since the last time he had seen him. He was clean-shaven but the blue-black of his whiskers cast a shadow over the lower part of his face. He had wire-rimmed glasses and the pastiest complexion Trip had ever seen.

"I am delighted that I was able to break away and come see you," Church said.

Trip knew this to be one of the greater understatements, as Church loved a field trip, anything to get out of Hazen.

"How is it up there, Preacher?"

"It's busy," he said, "especially on Sundays." Church was the assistant pastor at Calvary Baptist Church and a part-time fireman. He shared the pulpit and the firehouse with his father, who refused to die and give up either one of the head man's job to his son. Church truly believed he had been called, but he truly enjoyed being drunk—not drinking but being drunk—which he couldn't do in Hazen, which was why he so enjoyed being called away.

Drunkenness notwithstanding, Trip wanted to try him out as a duck guide for the teal hunt. Mary Magdalene, his yellow Lab, did blind retrieves at a hundred and fifty yards. And Church could call like a hen mallard with a mouthful of grain, which made the ducks fly directly in and die right in front of him. That and the fact that he had infinite patience with idiots, a trait in short supply when it came to guiding sports.

Trip knew that right about now Church needed money. Part-time preacher work in a small congregation did not pay the bills. Trip also knew that since the fire at the firehouse, Church really needed money. He also knew that if Church thought that if Trip thought he needed money, he wouldn't guide for him.

Trip told Church he needed a few guides for the teal hunt and if that worked out, he'd need guides for the big duck season.

"Mr. Trip, I would surely help, but I am just too busy right now."

"Even after the fire?"

Church turned red. "Not as busy after the fire."

"What exactly happened?"

Church gulped his shot. "You don't know?"

"No," Trip lied.

Church ordered another shot.

"Well, the firehouse burned down."

"No," Trip said, who knew all about it.

"Indeed," Church said.

"Couldn't you put it out with the firetruck?"

"The firetruck was inside the firehouse."

"What happened?"

"Well, I got the alarm call. It was Saturday night, and I was in bed with Mrs. Knox. I jumped right out, stuck the flasher on top of my truck, and turned on the siren. Sure enough, the firehouse was on fire. It's that old garage in the middle of town. We were all standing there trying to figure out how to put it out." The shot arrived. Church downed it in one swallow. "Except the firetruck is inside, and we can't get in the firehouse to get it out." Church shook his head. "So, we can't put out the fire."

"What happened?"

"Whole thing burned to the ground. Pretty much ruined the firetruck."

"That is a shame," Trip said.

"It surely is."

"I don't want to take advantage of your hardship," Trip said, "but I could sure use a guide of your caliber."

"I am awful busy."

"Really?"

"I'm a fire inspector now."

This is too much.

"There are those who believe the firehouse fire was arson. But when I proved to them that Mittens—she's the firehouse cat—knocked over the space heater, that talk stopped right away. That's how I got this job as fire inspector." Church waved at the barmaid for another shot. "I'm awful busy, but I might be able to help you out."

CHAPTER SIX

Trip walked down the driveway in the shade of the live oaks. It was hot already, and it was on its way to getting hotter.

When he got to the shop, he saw Jake's legs stuck out from beneath the combine, splayed like the blades of a pair of scissors. Cash crawled under the combine. Trip heard him lick Jake's face.

"Morning, Jake," Trip said.

"This combine is as ready as a pecker on a wedding night."

It's a little early for that.

"We have to get over to Cypress Slough and finish that last blind."

Jake slid out from under the combine. "Mr. Trip, if we don't get this rice in now, we might not get it in."

"We'll get it in."

"Not if it rains or the wind blows."

The difference between signing the front of a check and signing the back makes all the difference in the world.

Trip flopped down the tailgate of his truck. Cash jumped in. He loved riding in the bed, and Trip let him do it if they weren't going far. Trip started up the engine. The air conditioner blew hot air at his face. Jake slid in, and Trip pulled out of the shop. The heat rose off the blacktop in waves.

"There's one cash crop that's better than rice," Jake said.

"And that would be…." Trip let his voice trail off. He thought Jake was going to say "sugar cane," but the Grand Prairie wasn't the place to grow it.

"That would be hemp," Jake said.

"Hemp?"

"Hemp, as in marijuana. There's no government subsidies, and you can't get crop insurance, but you can make good money on it."

"I never gave it any thought."

"You got yourself a nice-sized patch out past the levee." Jake shook out a cigarette. "I'd say that is a large patch for one man to smoke up by himself. I would say that is a commercial-sized patch."

The pickup slid on the shoulder.

"You best watch the road, Mr. Trip. We surely don't want to crash before we get the rice in." Jake punched in the cigarette lighter. It popped out and he lit the cigarette. "And before we kill teal." Jake took a long drag on his cigarette.

Trip lit his own cigarette and looked out the driver's side window.

The truth of it was that Jake was right. No one person could smoke up that much weed. Trip smoked a joint three or four times a week, mostly for the ringing in his ears, but it did help take the edge off. The real truth was that he made a fair amount of money selling it to the shoeshine man at Le Pavillon in New Orleans.

Once, maybe twice a year, he'd drive to New Orleans and spend the night at Le Pavillon, a tall, skinny, hundred-year-old hotel on Poydras, two blocks from the New Orleans Parrish Courthouse. Before he went to bed, Trip left his shoes in the hall outside his room, and the next morning they were shiny and new, and in Trip's case, the toes were stuffed with hundred-dollar bills.

A.L. Williams was at least eighty. He'd run Le Pavillon shoeshine for sixty years. Roly-poly but not jolly. He had black hair, which Trip thought must be dyed. A.L. wouldn't say what A.L. stood for, but the concierge said it stood for "Abraham Lincoln," A.L.'s parents one generation removed from the Civil War.

Five years ago, a joint had fallen out of Trip's pocket when he pulled out the roll of bills to pay for his room. A.L. happened to be standing there. He picked it up and handed it back to Trip without a word.

When Trip checked out, A.L. brought Trip's truck up. Trip thought it was odd that the shoeshine man was the valet, especially when he handed back the twenty Trip gave him.

"You keep this," A.L. said. "Bring me some of that stuff fell out of your pocket and I'll put more than this twenty back."

It had grown into quite a commercial enterprise. Trip grew it, dried it, and packed it in one-pound bags. He locked it in the tool crib in the back of his truck, drove to New Orleans, and parked in Le Pavillon's garage. When he went to bed, he put the key in one of his shoes and left them in the hall outside his room. The next day his shoes would be full of money. Simple as that. He wanted the money before the trouble with the barge business. Now he needed it.

* * *

Trip, Jake, and Cash built the last blind on the oxbow at Cypress Slough, on the northeast corner of Pig Shelton's farm. Trip paid Pig a thousand dollars for a lease. Pig said he didn't want money from a friend, but he'd changed his mind when Trip told him he was hunting for hire.

Crooked Creek ran southeast from Lonoke County to Arkansas County, where it emptied into Bayou Meto. Along the way it turned back on itself time and again, confounding its path to the river. In at least half a dozen spots, Crooked Creek had lost patience with itself and cut a new path to Bayou Meto, leaving oxbows.

Cypress Slough was a crescent shaped oxbow with cypress in the water and hardwoods on the bank. The teal dropped in here in September, big ducks later. They set the blind on the inside of the crescent, at the fat part of the slough. When they finished, Trip said, "Let's cut some rice."

* * *

The rice rose from the Arkansas clay, thigh high, in long straight rows, like soldiers, except that the heads, heavy with the ripe grain, bowed every which way.

It hadn't rained, and the rice had dried nicely. He wouldn't have to run it through the dryers in town after all. The rice was ripe, maybe overripe. He just needed a little time to take it off and get the teal hunt in. If he could make it to big duck season, he just might make it.

Jake started up the big green John Deere and turned on the blades at the mouth of the combine. They'd had some trouble with them, but they were working fine now. Jake turned off the blades, rolled the machine out of the shop, and clipped the front bumper of Cadwallader Widowmaker's 1972 black Suburban.

The bumper hung from the front fender like a hangnail. Cad sat with his hands on the steering wheel and looked up at Jake. Jake looked down at

Cad. Neither one moved. Finally, Cad raised his left hand and gave Jake the finger. Jake jumped down from the combine.

"This can't be good," Trip said to Big John. The big man, headphones on, didn't say anything.

Jake made for Cad, but just as he reached the driver's door, Cad opened his door and knocked Jake over backwards with it. Trip ran over to the Suburban and stood between them, one of them flat on his back, the other one getting out of his Suburban.

Cadwallader Widowmaker was tall, straight, thin, and seventy-six years old. He turned the finest single-reed duck calls in Arkansas.

Trip had hired him to drive the combine because he was the best driver he had ever known. It required an absolute feel for the rice. Too fast and you'd miss some of it, too slow and you'd burn too much time, not to mention diesel. Trip hadn't told Jake, who considered himself the best combine driver in Arkansas County.

Jake picked himself up. The sun lit up the thin white line of the scar that ran down the left side of his face. "God damn it, old man. I'm going to break your nose."

"Somebody already did that."

"You can't just ram around like that with farm machinery running," Jake said.

"I was parked."

"You ran into me."

"Boys," Trip said, "we have work to do. I'll take care of the bumper. Cad, you hop up in that cab and let's get going."

"I'm not driving no grain buggy while that old man endangers us on the combine," Jake said.

Trip had three grain buggies, oversized trucks that followed behind and to the side of the combine. The combine spewed the rice into the trucks, and the trucks ferried it to the elevator. With three grain buggies, Trip figured he could keep the combine going while the buggies circled between the rice field and the Riceland elevators in Stuttgart.

That is, if he could make peace between Jake and Cad. "Jake, I need your lead foot to get back and forth to Riceland."

"I'll be on my way." Cad climbed back into his Suburban.

"No, you won't. You drive the combine. Jake, you drive a grain buggy with Big John and me."

"I think I'll pass," Jake said.

"If you pass, it will be the last time you do anything at Belle Oak."

Jake unrolled the cigarettes from his shirtsleeve and smoked one down to the filter. Then he walked over to the Suburban and tore the bumper the rest of the way off. Satisfied, he climbed into the lead grain buggy.

They started in the southeast section. The combine looped the field. Rice poured into the trailing grain buggy. They ran the rice well into the night, headlights on, and the elevator stayed open for them. Parker brought them sandwiches. Trip called it at midnight. They started again at six the next morning and ran until ten the next night. When they got back to the shop, Trip passed around the Dixies.

"Same time tomorrow?" Cad said.

"No," Trip said.

"Why ever not?" Cad said.

"Now we rest the farm," Trip said.

"What for?"

"For the teal," Trip said.

"The teal?" Cad scuffed his boots on the concrete.

"We'll rest it two days, hunt teal for a week, then finish."

"You can't do that," Cad said.

Trip drank from his beer.

"One good wind and it will all go to hell."

"I'm hunting teal for hire. Then I'll finish the rice."

"You're a bigger fool than your father." Cad kicked at the concrete with his boot. "God rest his soul."

Trip tossed Cad another beer.

* * *

At 9:00 a.m. the next morning, Trip delivered coffee on a tray to Parker. She sat up in bed and propped herself up with pillows. Two of her cats jumped off the bed and ran away.

"Why, thank you, Trip."

For all her fine qualities, Parker did not wake up well. In the history of their marriage, Trip had delivered coffee on a tray to Parker in bed every day that he could, which was almost every day. He started his day at 5:00 a.m., got things going, came back and made her coffee. She just wouldn't get up until he delivered her coffee, even if it got to be noon.

Not that she was lazy. She ran hard well into the night. She just started late and started slowly, which made her first words of the day unsettling.

"I did not say you were a fool."

"You did," Trip said.

"That's not what I said."

"Everybody's calling me a fool," Trip said.

"I did not say you were a fool. I said that I thought it was foolish to stop cutting rice for a teal hunt."

"It's the same thing."

"It's not the same thing."

"You just don't want them staying here," Trip said.

"That's right, but that has nothing to do with being a fool." Parker took a sip of her coffee. Trip sat down on the edge of the bed.

Parker had grown up in Birmingham where her father owned radio stations. She and Trip had met at Vanderbilt. It had been love at first sight, more or less. Parker was a city girl who tolerated the farm because of Trip.

She said he only liked her because she was named after Trip's favorite make of shotgun. He said it must be a fine family that named their daughter after such a fine shotgun. She said it was a family name, but her father favored quail hunting with his twenty-eight-gauge Parker side-by-side.

Trip took a sip of Parker's coffee. "We'll just try it out."

"I don't care about the teal hunt, and I can hold up with your Vanderbilt boys, but if you lose the rest of the rice, you'll surely lose the farm. And the timber. Which is all you really care about."

"The rice is dry. It will hold even if it does rain."

"I hope so," she said. "Get off the bed. I've got things to do."

What Parker had to do was get ready for the first three teal hunters. Trip had persuaded her to let his friends from Vanderbilt stay at the yellow house. He rarely invited anyone to hunt ducks, let alone stay overnight. But these being difficult and foolish times, the beautiful Miss Parker had acquiesced, but not enthusiastically.

Trip could only manage so much company, even if one of them was his best friend. Parker welcomed company, even if they were men with shotguns, dogs, cigars, and whiskey. It was the foolishness she was worried about.

* * *

Trip met the guides at the shop at 4:30 a.m. on opening day of teal season. Big John, Church, but no Jake. Trip had four hunting parties lined up, and he was a guide short. He was sorely grieved at Jake and trying to figure out how to jigger the hunters to make it work when Cad showed up.

"I didn't say I was here to guide. I'm here to witness the greatest folly in the history of duck hunting in Arkansas County." He scuffed the concrete with his boot. "As long as I'm here, I might as well go on a teal shoot. If I don't have to walk very far."

He's a lifesaver.

"Take your group to Hangman's Blind. There's teal working the ditch on the slough side. Church, you take your bunch over to Cypress Slough at Pig's. Big John, you take the Fork Slough."

"There's more birds at the catfish ponds," Cad said.

"That's where I'll be," Trip said.

Cad lit his pipe. He watched the smoke blow off. "East wind and no dew. We best get in and get out this morning."

* * *

The hunters started to trickle in, two and three at a time, Trip's hunters being the last ones to show up. They were all Sigma Chis, all from Vanderbilt. The McClures sent all their sons to Vanderbilt, three generations worth, mostly because McClure Tug and Tow gave generously.

The three of them had climbed pretty far into the Maker's Mark last night.

They look a bit wobbly.

First among the hangovers was Everett Dixson, old oil money from Midland, Texas. He had a soft Texas drawl and had never met a hundred-dollar bill he didn't like. Bobby Halstead, quick on his feet, ran his daddy's beer distributorship in Atlanta. Jude Winter, grandson of Cassius Winter, the McClure's Detroit lawyer. He was a tall, spare Yankee, with black hair and a pointed nose. He was a litigator who loved the sound of his own voice, and he was Trip's best friend.

This morning none of them seemed too eager to hear anyone's voice or smell anything other than Parker's coffee.

"Trip, I would appreciate it if you would put out that cigarette," Everett said.

"Amen to that," Bobby said.

The three of them stood under the corrugated steel roof of the open-air part of the shop and just about as far away from Trip as they could get and still hear him, which wasn't very far because Trip barely spoke over a whisper. "Boys, it's past time to go. Those teal are going to fly early, and we've got to get in there about twenty minutes ago."

"Not until you put out that cigarette," Everett said.

"I didn't hear much from you about that twenty-dollar cigar last night, which Parker does not allow indoors."

"Yes, sir. I do appreciate the courtesy but burning tobacco doesn't seem to agree with me this morning."

Trip walked over to his truck and dropped the tailgate. "Cash, kennel." The dog jumped in and the rest of them got into the truck. Trip put the truck into four wheel and they climbed up on the levee. The truck bumped along the top of the levee, the beams of the headlights rising and falling, swinging left to right and back again, rice on each side.

Bobby rolled down the passenger window and threw up.

"Keep it outside and off the paint," Trip said.

"I don't know how anybody could have this much fun for three hundred dollars a day," Everett said.

"That includes your meals," Trip said. He pushed in the cigarette lighter.

"I take it back," Everett said.

Trip parked the truck under some willow saplings two hundred yards from the blind. "You boys stay here while Cash and I check for snakes."

Bobby came back to life. "I'll pay you six hundred to take me back to the shop."

Trip, flashlight in hand, skittered down the bank to the stake blind with Cash. "Snake," he said. Five minutes later he climbed back up the bank to the truck. "Just one. A bull snake."

"I am not going anywhere a snake has been," Bobby said.

"Amen to that," Everett said.

"Come on boys," Jude said.

"Take your guns and get in that blind," Trip said. "Cash will watch out for snakes. Don't load your guns till I tell you. There's forty acres of Japanese millet right in front of us, in about a foot of water."

Daylight came up in black and silver.

"There's one right there," Bobby said. "There's more to the left."

"Those are the decoys," Jude said.

The black and silver melted into an orange cast covering the pond.

"Load up," Trip said. "I'll call the shot. Don't shoot behind you or over anybody's head. There'll be plenty of birds right out front."

At first light, a pair of blue-winged teals sailed over the blind. The birds banked to the east, the sky-blue speculum lit up in the dawn. They splashed down fifty yards in front.

"Too far," Trip said.

They waited another ten minutes. A flock of green wings flew right at them. Cash quivered. At twenty yards they pulled up and started to drop in.

"Take 'em boys," Trip said.

His pals stood and fired. The birds flew away.

"Nice shooting," Trip said.

"They were farther than I thought," Everett said.

"If they were any closer, you could have clubbed them to death with your shotgun."

There has got to be an easier way to make money.

A single blue-winged buzzed by, right to left. The three sports fired. Seven shots from two over/unders and an automatic. Trip thought it was Jude who killed the bird.

Trip looked over at Cash who had marked the bird. "Fetch it back, Cash." The dog jumped out of the blind and launched himself into the pond.

"That is about the sorriest piece of shooting I have ever seen." Trip lit a cigarette.

"Please do not smoke," Bobby said.

"I'll stop when you start killing ducks."

Cash brought back the duck.

As the sun rose, their marksmanship improved. By 9:30 they had killed nine ducks, missed three times that many and seen hundreds. It was getting hot in the blind. "Another half an hour, boys, and we'll call it."

"We haven't got our limits."

"You'd have killed three limits by now if you'd drunk a third of what you drank last night."

A cottonmouth dropped its head down over the blind and looked out at the catfish pond.

"Holy shit," Bobby said.

The snake turned its head to Bobby. Trip saw Bobby's eyes bug out. The snake looked at Bobby with yellow eyes and pinprick pupils. It opened its mouth wide, white, like cotton. Everett and Bobby reached for their shotguns. Trip raised the barrel of his gun, hooked the snake, and flung it into the pond. The snake swam back at them, which ended the first ever for-hire teal shoot at the Belle Oak catfish ponds.

It never did rain that first day, dew or no dew. Trip wasn't worried about the dew. He had his eye on the storm out in the Gulf.

CHAPTER SEVEN

While Trip tried to make money to save the farm, Celia sat on her gallery, scratched Molly's ears, and drank her sweet tea with Maker's Mark, lemon, and a little sugar.

She had stayed in Memphis for the teal hunt, refusing to go to the farm if there were paying hunters there. The McClure dove hunt was another thing altogether. That was for friends and family, by invitation only, and she didn't think Little George should have invited those two Memphis bankers.

Celia thought Trip must have known something, naming that dog of his "Cash." The moneymaking abilities of the McClures had declined ever since the first McClure landed from Scotland. The first Archibald McClure on American soil couldn't get out of the way of money. Big George couldn't get in front of it. Maybe it was the times that changed, and the barge business was no good anymore. She sipped her drink. Big George had tried to make money.

"Lord knows he tried."

He borrowed money and bought new tugs. He hired new people. He bid on new contracts. It wasn't enough. It was actually more than enough. He just bet wrong. Every time.

Celia looked down at Molly. Her chin had gone gray since Big George passed, and she'd put on some weight. Her coat still had a sheen to it, though. In the sunlight she could almost see herself in it. "What you have is a broken heart. Now I'm being maudlin. You're a dog, and dogs love the one they're with." She took a swallow of her sweet tea. "But it sure seems like your heart's broken. Unless it's my heart I'm seeing in your eyes.

"Maybe Little George can turn it around and keep the barge company afloat." She laughed out loud at her metaphor. Molly turned her muzzle toward her. "I'm just talking old friend." She didn't fear for Little George. He'd land on his feet even if McClure Tug and Tow went under. She laughed out loud again. And J.D. had his law practice.

Trip was the one she worried about. Trip and that damn duck woods. He only farmed to keep the woods for duck season. And he never put much into farming until he had to.

"The McClure men and their ducks."

The truth of it was that she feared for Trip. She didn't think he could hold onto the farm. He was too delicate. Not physically—he was all muscle—but he had to quit that damn smoking. He wasn't delicate. He was fragile. Fragile in his head. She thought he was like one of those men in a Tennessee Williams play. "He's Tom Wingfield. That's who he is."

Trip had done just fine at Vanderbilt, as long as he made it down to Belle Oak often enough. Thank God for Parker. "Bless her Alabama heart."

But he couldn't quite make it in the world. He had surely failed at the barge business. One day he left Memphis for Belle Oak. And he never came back.

"Molly, he calls so sweetly."

Celia filled her drink from the pitcher. Molly was the one who came to tell Trip, and he was the one who found Big George. Celia was at the farm, but Trip was the one who found him.

A single shot from the Colt revolver with the mother-of-pearl handle. A single shot by his own hand. A single shot in the mouth and through the back of his head.

He must have thought about it for a long time because he'd worn down the handle where he had rubbed it with his thumb. Back and forth. Back and forth. He rubbed it until he wore the mother-of-pearl down to the steel.

He must have thought it over. There was some comfort in that. Precious little, though.

She didn't think Little George or J.D. knew about the pistol grip, but Trip knew. He kept the Colt in the glove box of his truck.

The boys thought it was about money and the barge company. It was about money, but it wasn't about the barge company. It was about what had happened New Year's Eve. That was why Big George took his own life.

"Molly, it was my fault. I might just as well have pulled the trigger."

CHAPTER EIGHT

Word had gotten out by the third day, and Belle Oak was full up for the rest of teal season. The hunt was going nicely without Jake, who as Big John said, "was still disappeared."

Trip kept an eye on the weather. The storm in the Gulf never made it to a hurricane, but it dumped a foot of rain on New Orleans.

He drove the Vanderbilt boys out to Cypress Slough. They walked in the dark, single file along a two-track, Cash somewhere out in front of them. There were woods on their left, a ditch and cut soybeans on their right. After about half a mile, they turned onto the path to the platform blind at the bank of the oxbow.

"This is a long walk to shoot a small duck," Everett said.

"It is," Trip said.

"Then why are we out here?" Bobby said.

"Because we just about shot off the farm. I've been resting this spot since opening day."

Trip watched them climb the ladder into the blind. He passed up the guns one by one. Trip climbed up, then Cash, who had taught himself how to climb a ladder.

They sat in the dark for half an hour. When the sun came up, the wind came up out of the southwest. The cool of the night died out at dawn, then the sky turned a hazy red. Trip watched a half dozen teal skitter across the slough, lift up, then land. They got back up, then landed again.

Those birds are nervous.

"I can see to shoot," Everett said.

"There's birds right there," Bobby said.

"We don't shoot birds on the water," Trip said.

Five blue-winged teals swept in from the west, but they flew by too quickly to shoot. A flock landed out of range and swam into the decoys. There must have been at least fifty of them.

The sun got higher, but the sky got darker. The wind started to blow, and the birds jumped up from the slough. They swarmed like bees then disappeared to the east.

Trip looked to the southwest. The sky was black. "It's time to go, boys."

"We just got here," Bobby said. A single teal dropped out of the sky. He shot and crippled the bird. It swam into the cypress trees across the slough.

"Fetch it back, Cash," Bobby said. The dog looked once at Trip, then jumped in after the duck.

"Cash, come," Trip said.

"Let him get the duck," Bobby said.

"Hear that freight train?" Trip said.

"I do," Bobby said.

"There's no tracks around here," Trip said. "That's a tornado. We have to go right now.

"Cash, come." The dog either could not hear or would not be called off. "Unload your guns and get out." The three hunters raced down the ladder. Trip followed, looked for Cash but couldn't see him. "Get back to the two-track and lie flat in the ditch. I'll be right along." He cupped his hands against the wind and lit a cigarette.

"Come on, Trip," Jude said.

"I'll wait for Cash. You get Bobby and Everett to the ditch."

The wind blew harder, a hot, fiery wind. A tree cracked and blew down in the oxbow. The hunters ran. Trip waited for Cash.

There was thunder and lightning right on top of him. It started to rain. No sign of Cash. The wind blew out his cigarette. He turned up the path and looked over his shoulder. Still no sign of Cash, the freight train closer now.

Trip started running. He saw the boys in the ditch and ran past them. The rain tore into his face. He made it to the truck just as Cash popped out of the woods with the teal. "God damn it, Cash. You come when I call you. Duck or not. And don't ever listen to anybody from Tennessee." Trip opened the door. Cash jumped in. Trip drove up the two-track and his pals climbed in.

The rain banged on the windshield, big, hard drops. When they turned onto the blacktop, it was dark. Trip turned on the headlights. The wind blew crosswise, harder now, and pushed the truck onto the shoulder. The tires on the right side spun in the gravel, and Trip had to slow down.

"God damn it, Trip," Everett said. "There's a funnel cloud." A black spiral hung in the sky.

"That one's by us," Trip said.

"There's another one. On your left."

There were funnel clouds all around them, like fingers reaching down to tear Belle Oak apart. Trip kept driving.

"Pull over till they go by," Everett said.

They made it to the blacktop road next to Belle Oak's rice. Less than a mile to go.

A funnel cloud dropped down in front of them. Trip yanked on the steering wheel and drove off the road into the rice. The tornado veered toward them and caught the tail of the truck, lifted it up in the air, and flipped it on its side.

* * *

Trip had no idea how long he'd been unconscious. He came to when Jude pulled him from the truck. He stood up, or tried to. He sat back down, his right arm hanging at his side.

It hurts like hell.

"I've got to get to Parker," he said.

"You can't get to anywhere," Jude said.

Trip tried to stand again. He sat back down. "Where's Cash?"

"He's around here somewhere. When the truck tipped over, I pulled you out of the truck and I laid on top of you. Cad came and got Bobby and Everett. They're both fine." He bent down and looked at Trip. "I'm pretty sure you broke your arm."

"Broke or not, I've got to find Cash and get to Parker."

They were about three hundred yards into the rice, the rice that hadn't been harvested and now looked like it might never be. The yellow house was off to the northwest, but Trip couldn't see over the levee.

Church showed up on the four-wheeler. "Mr. Trip, how exactly are you?"

"Where's Parker?"

"She's serving sweet tea and worrying about you," Church said. "You really should not play chicken with a tornado."

"She's all right?"

"Not exactly," Church said.

"What happened?"

"I think she will be quite put off with you tipping your truck over. And if your arm is broke, I expect that will put her off even more."

"What about the tornadoes?"

"Missed us all. Didn't even touch down except the one that ran you down."

The guides had had better judgment than Trip. They had come right in as soon as the sky got dark. The guides and the sports drank sweet tea at the shop. Parker fed them and then sent them home.

Church studied Trip's arm. He studied it, but he didn't touch it. He walked in a circle around Trip, eyes fixed on his arm. Then he stopped and walked the other way around. Around and around, one way and then the other. Every now and then, he pushed his glasses up the bridge of his nose. Finally, he said, "I do believe I see the problem."

"My arm's broken, you fool." Trip was sure that nothing in his life had ever hurt this much, and that if Church got any closer, Trip would strike him down with his good arm.

"Mr. Jude, you stand right behind Mr. Trip. No, right behind him. Just like that. Now, clasp your hands around Mr. Trip's chest, careful of his bad arm." Jude circled his arms around Trip's chest, leaving the bad arm free. "That's right. Just like that." He pushed his glasses up his nose one last time. He took two steps to Trip and stood eye-to-eye with him. "Mr. Trip, take a look over there." He pointed away from Trip's bad arm. "Look at them teal swirling over that knocked down rice. And here comes Cash."

Trip turned his head. Church nodded at Jude. Jude bear-hugged Trip. Church took one last step toward Trip. He grabbed his bad arm at the wrist. He stepped back and pulled Trip's arm as hard as he could. There was a popping sound like pulling the cork from a bottle of champagne. Trip screamed a scream that would wake the dead.

"Damn you, Church. Damn you to hell."

"I know you don't mean that, Mr. Trip. And look at your arm. It's not broke at all. It was just dislocated." Church smiled at him. "And now it's relocated."

Trip's shoulder still hurt like hell, but he could move his arm well enough to wrap it around Church on the four-wheeler. Church took him up to the yellow house. Cash ran alongside them. Jude walked back. They left the truck where it was, on its side, a testament to the teal folly. By the time they got to the yellow house, Trip's arm didn't hurt as much, but that was probably because of the Percodan that Church had given him.

* * *

Later that day, in the dining room with Parker, "Mr. McClure, just what are you going to do now?"

He turned toward her, his back to the china cabinet. "Mrs. McClure, I expect it is time to finish up the rice." He walked over to the china cabinet and poured himself three fingers of Maker's Mark.

* * *

Trip's arm hurt like hell when he'd gotten up this morning. Parker put it in a sling, and Trip thought it would be easier to drive the combine with one arm than a grain buggy. It turned out he couldn't drive the combine with one arm. He took some of Church's Percodan and took off the sling.

Trip looked behind him at the wavy lines of uncut rice left by the big green combine. Trip and Cad switched, which pissed off Jake mightily, who in the words of Big John, had "undisappeared" this morning. They cut the rice as best they could, but it had lodgings, bad lodgings. The heads, top heavy on the stalks, had been twisted and knocked over by the wind. Jake had set the heads on the combine as low as he could, but even when they cut the rice at the ankles instead of the shins, they couldn't get all the heads, and the combine took in more of the stalks. It made for slow going.

At the end of the day, Trip went to the office at Riceland to see what he'd made. "Johnson, this can't be right."

"It's right as rain," the elevator man said, a wiry little man with a skinny face.

"This can't be right. Not with all those buggies we brought in."

"It's good rice. Nice and dry. What there is of it."

"Weigh it again, Johnson."

"It ain't the weight, Mr. Trip. It's the rice. There's too many stalks. Hurry on up. It's eleven o'clock and way past my bedtime."

Trip turned on his heel and left. He climbed in the grain buggy next to Cash and drove back to Belle Oak. They had three more sections to harvest, but he'd never pay off the crop loan if this was all Riceland would pay. "Damn it, Cash. Damn that wind." He lit a cigarette. "Damn that teal hunt. Damn that fool teal hunt."

* * *

"Boys," he said the next morning, "there's rain in the forecast. We've got to get the rice off before we lose any more of it."

"We can't move any faster," Jake said.

"I know it," Trip said.

"What then?" Somehow Big John could hear over "Simple Man."

"We'll run it like yesterday, but we'll dump it in our bins and take it to the elevator later."

"That won't save much time," Cad said. He tamped down the tobacco in the bowl of his pipe.

* * *

It rained two days later, but by then all the rice was off. Trip went to see Theo Boxwood on the second and top floor of Second National Bank of Stuttgart. The First National Bank of Stuttgart had gone under during the Depression. The banker was a chubby man with pasty skin and a comb-over that started just above his left ear. Trip thought Boxwood always looked like he was recovering from a life-threatening illness. "I am so glad to see you." Boxwood stood up at his desk, walked up to Trip, and pumped his hand. "Do we have an appointment?"

"Not that I know of."

"I guess we do now." Boxwood sat down on one end of a burnt-red Naugahyde sectional that took up most of two walls. Trip sat down at the other end. Boxwood looked at Trip's muddy footprints and scowled. Trip smiled at the banker. He didn't like Boxwood, who knew it. "You get your rice in yet?"

Trip handed the banker a check.

Boxwood studied it and smiled again. "This covers the interest. What about the principal?"

"It's in my grain bins," Trip said.

"You got money in the grain bins?"

He is not a clever man.

"The rice is in my grain bins. I haven't sold it yet."

"What's it doing in there? Your rice is supposed to be at Riceland and Second National Bank of Stuttgart is supposed to be paid back."

"I wanted to get it off before it rained."

"You had a month to get it off. I hear it's got lodgings."

"Little bit. The bins are full."

"It's time to pay off that crop loan your daddy took out."

"Rice is going up. I want to hold it for a bit. How about you extend Big George's loan and take security in the rice."

"I already got security in that rice."

"How about you loan me a little more money?"

"How about you give me the teal money and I'll see what I can do."

* * *

Parker had a craving for sushi, and despite Stuttgart's being the rice capital of the world, Stuttgart had no sushi, at least none that Parker would eat. Trip thought sushi tasted like cat food, but he gave in.

He opened the door of Parker's Mercedes, the little red convertible. She had on a short khaki skirt, a black, sleeveless top, and strappy sandals. He lingered at the door, and she gave him a flash of her black panties.

Parker said Trip got anxious whenever he had to leave Belle Oak. Trip didn't see the point in leaving a place you liked if you didn't have to. He sat in the passenger seat and took a swallow of his Maker's Mark and ginger ale traveler.

Parker took Arkansas 135 west. She wound the Benz up to a hundred after they went through Humnoke.

At San Su, three blocks south of the capitol building, they sat with the chic of Little Rock.

"Baby, this dinner's on me, but I don't know who's going to pay for the next one," Parker said. She sipped on her sake.

"All the bins are filled. I'll sell it as soon as the price goes up."

"You may be able to fool Theo Boxwood, but those grain bins are only half full of rice. The rest is stalks." She took a piece of spicy Hamachi with her chopsticks.

"There's plenty of rice in there."

"You bought us some time, but Theo will figure out there's not enough rice to cover the crop loan."

"We have the teal money," Trip said.

"You said he took that."

"I kept some back."

"I knew you had some larceny in your heart." Parker smiled at him, then chewed a slivered piece of ginger. "Then what?"

"Then it will be duck season. We'll make it all back and then some."

"We'll never make it that far." The waitress came back to their table. "Would you please box this for me." Parker finished her sake. "I swear you're going to end up working on a barge or selling time for my daddy."

"We'll make it, baby."

The waitress handed Parker a Styrofoam box. "If this doesn't work, we're not even going to have leftovers." She handed the box to Trip.

CHAPTER NINE

Trip signed for the Notice of a Special Meeting of the Members of the Mc-Clure Family Farm Company, LLC. Big George had sent it Certified Mail, Return Receipt Requested. Trip knew what was in the letter without opening it. He'd thought twice about signing for it, but maybe, just maybe, he could win.

The four directors—Little George, J.D., Celia, and Trip—were officially on notice. The purpose of the meeting was to put Belle Oak up for sale.

The meeting was to be held at the company headquarters, the yellow house at Belle Oak. The vote was two for—Little George and J.D.—one against—Trip—and one abstention—Celia, who said she didn't want the family torn apart.

Trip told her that abstaining was the same as "a vote for a nitwit who couldn't float a bar of ivory soap in a bathtub."

Southern hospitality notwithstanding, Trip refused to feed them dinner. He was damned if he would serve a feast at his own demise. Parker over-ruled him and served prime rib with roasted baby potatoes.

* * *

The next morning, Trip and Cash drove down the road in front of the farm. His ears had been ringing ever since the meeting, and he couldn't get past it. He wanted to smoke a joint, but he had important business. He lit a cigarette instead.

Trip parked his truck just off the blacktop in front of the six by four-foot "Farm For Sale" sign. Little George hadn't wasted any time. He'd hired Grand Prairie Real Estate, and Amelia Rademacher had planted it there not more than an hour ago. He reached in the truck bed for the chainsaw. He pulled on the starter cord, but it didn't catch. He pulled again. Nothing. He pulled out the choke and yanked hard on the starter cord. It turned over, but it still wouldn't catch.

At that moment, the beautiful Amelia Rademacher drove up in her white Cadillac. "Let me get that for you." She picked up the chainsaw and pulled the cord, ever so gently. It kicked over, then started to sputter. She pushed in the choke and the chainsaw idled. "Here you go."

Trip crushed his cigarette underneath his boot. "Thank you."

"I do believe it was flooded."

Amelia was nothing if not good looking. She had been his high school sweetheart and had never forgiven him for not marrying her. She had straight blond hair, a turned-up nose, sunglasses the size of teacups, rose lipstick, and dimples on her cheeks. Amelia liked it when Trip kissed her on one of her dimples.

"Trip, just what is this chainsaw for?"

This is a good time not to say anything.

"Since there isn't a tree for half a mile, I assume that the chainsaw is meant for my little 'for sale' sign."

This is an even better time to not say anything.

"I sell more farms than anybody in Arkansas County."

"I know it."

"More than the next three put together."

"It wouldn't surprise me." Trip turned off the chainsaw.

"And, I'm going to sell this one. This little sign isn't what's going to sell it. And it's not the rice that's going to sell it.

"What's going to sell it is the duck woods." Amelia took the chainsaw from Trip. She pulled the starter cord and it started right up. She put it in gear and revved it up. The chain flew around the blade. "So, I don't really give a damn about this sign." She marched to the sign, crouched, her legs together in a ladylike fashion, and cut down the sign.

Amelia drove off. Trip got back in the truck and lit a joint. "Cash, maybe this will help my ears." He looked out in the field, past where the sign had been. It was October, and the first of the big ducks dropped into the swags. Where they really wanted to be was in the green timber eating acorns, but it was October, and the green timber was still dry.

Trip and Cash drove south—cut rice fields on their left, hardwoods on their right—to Bayou Meto Wildlife Management Area, twenty-thousand acres of green timber with the Bayou Meto River running right through it.

They turned right on a gravel road and into the hardwoods—mostly oaks, but also some hickory and ironwood—and into the twilight of the woods. Trip parked in the small dirt lot at Lower Vallier, next to the dark green Game and Fish trucks. He and Cash followed the path to the brown river water drifting past the banks, in no hurry to get anywhere.

That's a good way to be.

Two men in waders wrestled with a twenty-foot plank. One of the men dragged one end of it across the river. They lifted the plank to the top of the concrete pier on each bank.

"Not yet, boys," said a third man in olive wools and a trooper's hat. The two men laid the plank down on top of the piers, and they each fished a cigarette from their waders.

"I thought I might see you here."

"You did invite me, Captain."

"I knew you wouldn't miss it. It's just four boards, but then it's not just four boards to you, is it?" Captain Arcenault was a tall, lean man. There was a blue cast to his chin—a man who had to shave twice a day, and did just that.

Trip had known the Captain his entire life. His first name was Charles, but Trip thought it might as well be "Captain" since that's what everybody called him, including his wife. He'd been with Game and Fish for at least thirty years, and he'd been a captain as long as Trip had known him. He wrote tickets, arrested poachers, and rescued hunters. The thirty-thousand acre Bayou Meto Wildlife Management Area was his kingdom.

Trip picked up a stick and threw if for Cash. The dog ran after it and brought it back.

"He'll have to swim for it once these boards flood up the woods," Captain Arcenault said.

He looked over at his helpers. "Drop it in boys." The two men in waders dropped the first plank in. The man on the far bank came back and took the end of another plank across the river. They dropped in the second plank. The Captain turned back to Trip. "Game and Fish will likely make Amelia an offer."

"What kind of offer might that be?"

"That ground should have been part of Bayou Meto since the beginning."

"It's never going to be part of Bayou Meto."

"You're the last outlier, and it's time."

Trip threw the stick again. It splashed on Captain Arcenault.

"Miss Nancy would call that passive aggressive. Whatever that means."

"That means that Game and Fish isn't getting Belle Oak."

"Better us than a duck club. We'll give you a life estate." He reached down and brushed the water off his pants. They had a sharp crease, the sharp crease of a military man. His hat stayed on his head when he bent over. Trip had never seen him without his hat. He had no idea what color the Captain's hair was or even if he had any hair.

"If you're gonna carry hunters, you make sure you get a guide's license."

"Yes, sir, I will."

"I could've written you up for those teal hunters."

"That wasn't for hire."

"Don't make it worse by lying."

"What if it's just friends and family."

"Now you're being what Miss Nancy would call disingenuous."

Cash brought the stick to Trip.

"Don't throw it my way, or I will be truly pissed off."

"I don't think that's how Miss Nancy would put it."

"She's not here, and you watch that funny smell on your clothes." Arcenault turned to his helpers. "Okay, boys, drop in that third plank." They dropped the third plank in the slots. Slowly, ever so slowly, the river started to back up. It didn't seem to mind. The men dropped in the fourth plank.

The ground was so flat and the clay so hard that the boards and the levee would flood the woods for miles and miles, all the way to Belle Oak and beyond. When the rains came, the river would flood the bottomlands, the way it had before there were levees. When Arkansas was full of green-timbered river bottoms.

* * *

Trip, Cash, and Jake stood outside the Bunkhouse. It was left over from the migrant worker days of the rice business. Low slung with a pitched roof, pine slab siding, and two eighty-foot white pines in the front yard. "We've got six weeks to make the inside right," Trip said.

"That's not enough time, Mr. Trip."

"It is if we get to work now."

"We don't have a building permit."

"Get some boys and get started. No one will know what's going on way back here."

The Bunkhouse was south of the yellow house, a mile off the main road at the end of the rice fields and back where the woods started. If he could get it fixed up in time, there would be eight double rooms, three bathrooms, a bar, and a dining room. There would be a room for the guides on one end and a kitchen on the other.

"There might be enough time, but you don't have the money," Jake said.

"I'll worry about the money."

"All you have to do is sell that weed and you'll have plenty of money."

"I don't know what you're talking about."

Jake held an imaginary joint between his thumb and forefinger, sucked in and held his breath. He blew out the pretend smoke.

* * *

Trip and Cash rode down I-55 to New Orleans in the twilight. He ran with the windows down, and even with night coming on, he felt it getting warmer. He sucked in a lung full of marijuana, held his breath, then exhaled ever so slowly, just like Jake had mimed. Trip thought Jake's imitation a little too perfect for a nonsmoker.

They checked into Le Pavillon. Cash was welcome as long as Trip paid double the rate. He left his shoes in the hall for A.L. with a note to meet him in the bar at midnight. Trip's newly polished shoes showed up at 11:45 and Trip went down to the bar. A very old man sat with a younger woman next to the piano player, a woman with henna-colored hair and a voice that didn't need a microphone. After each song, the very old man passed a slip of paper and a twenty-dollar bill to the younger woman who passed it to the piano player. She put the money in her tip jar and played the request, this one a melancholy version of "Strangers in the Night."

A.L. came to the entrance of the bar but no further.

"Come on in, A.L."

"No, sir. I can't. The help is not welcome in here."

Trip walked over to A.L.

"Mr. Trip. I am truly sorry, but that is too much for me to dispose of."

"Any ideas?"

"No, sir, unless you want to ride on out to Metairie. There's a man there might be able to help you."

At four in the morning, Trip opened the door of the single-story white, brick building. A red neon sign that said "Paison" lit the doorway. As soon as he entered, a big hand grabbed him by the arm, led him to a table, and sat him down. There was a bottle of Maker's Mark and a glass full of ice in front of him. The man with the big hand sat down at the table behind Trip. Sitting across from Trip, an olive-skinned man in an open black silk shirt, a gold necklace tangled in the chest hair that grew out of his shirt. The man reached across the table and shook Trip's hand.

He's a caricature of himself.

"Carlo DeMarco," he said. "You must be Johnny Walker."

"Why, yes," Trip said, who had told A.L. not to give his real name. Trip thought A.L could have been slightly less creative.

"This is my cousin," DeMarco said. Trip turned around, but he couldn't make out the face that went with the big hand. They were the only ones in the bar, and Trip was sure he had walked straight into a drug deal full of all the characters and props in a gangster movie.

I'm a fool.

"Drink up, Mr. Walker," DeMarco said. "Mr. Williams says you are fond of Maker's Mark. In spite of your name."

Trip took a swallow. DeMarco certainly didn't talk like a gangster.

"He also tells me you are a planter short of cash but long on a certain substance."

Trip took another swallow.

DeMarco reached under the table and brought up a packet of cash, neatly wrapped. "Here's twenty thousand dollars. That should get you started. Bring Louis what you have in a week." He nodded at the man with the big hands. "Don't bring it here. Check into the hotel and A.L. will tell you where to take it. We'll settle up then."

Trip stared at the money. They were hundred-dollar bills. Nice and crisp. Just like in the movies.

"Drink up, Mr. McClure. It's past my bedtime," DeMarco said.

Trip finished his drink, felt the burn, and hightailed it out of Paison.

Trip found Cash curled up in a ball in the driver's seat. The dog looked up at him, licked him once on the lips, and went back to sleep.

"Cash, there's a time to stay and a time to go, and this is a time to go." Trip slid the dog across to the passenger seat.

Two blocks later, Trip pulled into a 7-Eleven. He counted out nineteen thousand dollars. "He shorted us, Cash. The son of a bitch shorted us. Maybe that's the vig, but this is more than we had five minutes ago, and now we've got enough to get the Club House ready for duck season." Trip stuck the bills in the visor above the windshield. He turned north to Belle Oak. A mile further north, he pulled into another 7-Eleven and lit a cigarette. "Cash, what exactly are we doing. I mean, just what are we doing here? I am now involved in a drug deal." Trip flicked the half-smoked cigarette out the window and turned the truck around. He drove into the parking lot at the Paison. He banged on the door. No one answered. Back in the truck, "On the other hand, we are a bit down on our luck, and we could surely use the money." Trip drove back to the Le Pavillon. It was six a.m. Except for the lights on Poydras, still pitch dark. Trip parked on the street and went into the lobby.

"Did you forget something Mr. McClure?" the concierge said.

"I forgot my shoes."

"Let me go find A.L."

"No, that's all right. Just tell me where he is."

"I'm afraid I can't do that," the concierge said.

"Why ever not?"

"We don't believe it a good idea for the guests to be privy to innards of the hotel."

"The innards." Trip handed her one of his fresh hundred-dollar bills.

"Take those stairs down two flights. Third door on the left. Knock three times."

Trip went down two flights of stairs, then knocked three times.

"Come on in."

There was A.L., sitting at a desk. At least a dozen pairs of shoes surrounded a fifth of Maker's Mark. A.L. drank from a half-full glass. He set it down and started on a pair of black wing tips.

"Business must be good, A.L."

"White folks ain't the only ones who like good whiskey." A.L. drank a little more. "Not the only ones who can afford it these days, either."

Trip thought he had started this out wrong, like the spoiled white boy that he was, and a spoiled white boy with a problem. "A.L., I appreciate what you did, but I don't want any part of drugs."

"You don't? I thought that's exactly what you wanted, 'cause that's exactly what you asked me to do."

"I thought it over. You give this back to him." Trip handed A.L. the wad of cash. "It's all there except he shorted me a thousand."

"Must be the vig." A.L. started back in on the wing tips.

"Here's the money, A.L."

"Can't do it, Mr. Trip."

"Why not?"

A.L. snapped his shoeshine cloth. "Two reasons. First, with Mr. D., a deal is a deal. Second, I already got my commission, which I don't intend to give back." He snapped his rag again and went back to the wing tips.

* * *

Trip felt better when he crossed the state line at Vicksburg. Even though he'd grown up in Memphis, Arkansas was home. He was five when his grandfather Archie had taken him to Belle Oak for the first time. They had taken a tractor out on the levee in an early November drizzle. His grandfather had just flooded up the rice. Trip had stood at the edge of the levee and looked down at the ducks in the muddy water. He slipped and slid feet first, six feet down into the flooded field. He remembered how cold the water was, but mostly he remembered his grandfather looking down at him. His grandfather lit a cigarette and looked down at him in the flooded rice. He smoked about half of it and then said, "See if you can haul yourself back up here. Otherwise, I'll come fetch you." Trip grabbed the weeds on the bank and pulled himself back up the levee.

His grandfather finished his cigarette and flicked it into the water. "I've been to Georgia, which I don't care for, not to mention the Georgia boys, who I don't care for at all, but Georgia mud is nothing compared to Arkansas mud. There's nothing any slipperier. Anywhere." He boosted Trip back on the tractor, and they rode back to the shop. His grandfather never said another word about it.

Trip got up early the next morning and ran into Stuttgart to buy what he needed to redo the Club House.

When he got back to Belle Oak, he found Parker in the kitchen. She gave him a suspicious hug. "Trip, honey, do not believe for one minute that I don't know what you do in New Orleans."

"Baby, I have always been true to you."

"I know it."

"I just go and play cards, and this time I won big."

"How much?"

"A thousand shy of twenty thousand."

"Mr. McClure, every time you are a little short, you disappear to New Orleans and come back with a little money. How can you always win?"

"Lucky, I guess."

"Nobody is that lucky. What you do is sell a little weed. That's what you do."

"No, I don't."

"Don't lie to me. I know what you do, and I know where your patch is."

"I don't sell it, baby. I just smoke a little. For my ears."

"This farm isn't worth going to jail for. It's just a farm." Parker looked out the window. "But it's not the farm, is it," she said, not asking. "It's the duck woods."

Trip tried to put his arms around Parker's waist, but she stepped away from him.

* * *

Trip grabbed the scythe from the shop and rode the quad out the levee. He let Cash run ahead. Trip slid down into the weeds and set off on foot. It was surely too cold for snakes, and he wore knee-high rubber boots.

When he got to his marijuana patch, the plants were gone. Not cut. Not harvested. They were gone.

Uprooted. There was no sign of them anywhere. Not even a hole in the ground. He ran to the center of the patch. Dirt. There was bare ground where the plants had been. He circled the field. Once. Twice. Three times. It was like they had never been there. He kicked away the leaves, saw where the holes had been filled in and where the leaves and weeds had been spread out to cover the holes and make his patch look like nothing more than a clearing.

Where was his shack, the drying shack? What about that? Gone. It had been torn down and carted away.

"Now what? I've got nothing for DeMarco. I'll give him his money back." He kicked at the dirt. "But I can't. I spent it on the Club House."

Not all of it. He had maybe two thousand left. He lit a joint, stared at it, then flicked it into the weeds.

CHAPTER TEN

Celia, paintbrush in hand, stood on the bow of her namesake, a fifty-foot tug with twin diesels.

The pride of the McClure Tug and Tow fleet, the *Celia Marie*, barely three years old, was to be repossessed by Planter's Bank today. The first casualty of the fleet, and the way things were going for McClure Tug and Tow, the first of many. Celia had already taken off the eponymous life rings and stowed them in the trunk of her silver Benz. She was, over the protest of Little George, about to paint over her name.

The day was clear and bright, especially for November, but the wind blew hard from the north, straight down the river.

This will blow the ducks down to Belle Oak.

Little George stood on the dock and shouted over the wind. "Mama, is this necessary?"

"I will not have those awful bankers take this beautiful tug with my name on it. Especially after we invited them on the dove hunt."

"Mama, it's just a boat."

"The *Celia Marie* is more than a boat. She is much more than a boat."

"It's a boat with your name on it. That's all it is."

"That's why we're losing her. Because you think she's just a boat."

"We are losing her because the United States of America has built a fine interstate road system, and we can't compete with trucks."

"Trucks can't haul coal and grain. This tug is named after me, and that makes it personal." Celia, dressed to the nines in a belted black dress, heels, and a string of pearls, dipped her paintbrush into the can of black paint.

"You know better than to wear high heels on a tug."

She reached over to the rail and took a drink from a cup next to a stainless-steel thermos.

"Isn't it a bit early for that?"

"It's coffee."

"What about the ice cubes?"

"Hush up. This would not be happening if Big George was here."

"If Big George was here, this would have already happened." Little George looked down at his feet, then up at his mother. "Unless he was here with the money he borrowed from Second National. But we don't know what happened to the money. And no one knows why he did what he did. Except maybe you."

Celia slapped the paintbrush over her name on the starboard side and splashed paint on Little George.

"Damn it, Mama. You got paint on me."

"Good." She drained the cup, filled it back up, and marched to the stern. She bent over the side and painted over her name on the transom.

I know exactly why Big George borrowed the money. I just don't know what he did with it.

She took another drink.

Otherwise, the phone calls would have stopped.

This wasn't the time to tell Little George or anyone else about it. Maybe sometime. But not now. What good would it do? If she had the money, she could save the *Celia Marie*. But that would have meant she wouldn't have done what she did. And Big George would still be alive.

Little George followed her to the stern but stayed well away from her and her paintbrush. He brought Celia's thermos with him and took a drink.

"Little George, you stay out of that."

"Do you need it that much?"

"No. I just don't want you to get my bad habits. It runs in families, you know."

"Thank you for thinking of me." Little George took another swallow from the thermos. "If we had sold the farm by now, we wouldn't be losing this tug."

"We can't lose too many more, or we won't have anything left to tug and tow."

"According to Amelia, Trip has already cut down three of her signs. Selling the farm is the only way to save the business," Little George said.

"If he can make a go of duck hunting, we can keep both," she said. "He calls so sweetly."

"He does, Mama, but calling sweetly has very little to do with saving the farm."

"Fiddle faddle." She threw the paintbrush as far as she could. It splashed into the river and sank into the choppy water.

CHAPTER ELEVEN

Trip ran back to the quad, which confused Cash who had rarely, if ever, seen Trip or any Southerner run. A Yankee might run like that, but not a Southerner. Trip gunned the quad. It fishtailed as it slipped in and out of the muddy two-track on top of the levee. When they got back to the shop, Trip jumped into the truck and they made for Stuttgart.

Jake is the only one who knew about my patch. Except Parker.

He found Jake at the Gator. "Bit early to start, isn't it?"

"The Gator opened two hours ago, Mr. Trip." The bar was half full, but it was already full of smoke.

"Come outside. We need to talk."

"We can talk right here."

"No, we can't."

"I've got some news for you, Mr. Trip."

"I'll bet you do."

Jake looked at him sideways. "Let me finish my beer." Jake tried to drink the rest of the beer, but Trip grabbed him by his collar and jerked him to his feet. The farmhand splashed what was left of the beer on the front of his shirt and dropped the mug. It would have shattered on the floor, but Slick had switched to plastic mugs long ago. Trip had Jake in front of him still holding his collar, Jake on his toes. Trip kicked open the door and kicked Jake outside.

"Where the fuck is my weed?"

"Mr. Trip, don't you ever do that again."

"Or what?"

"Or I'll carve you up like a turkey on Thanksgiving."

"Where's my weed?"

"I had to get rid of it."

"Get rid of it?" Trip said. "Get rid of it?" he said again.

Jake unbuckled his belt and unzipped his pants. Calmly, ever so calmly, he tucked his shirt back in.

"Where is the weed, Jake?"

"Sheriff Dewitt came out to the Club House and started asking questions."

"What kind of questions?"

"Questions like he knew all about it. Don't worry, I put him off."

Damn it.

"He don't know where it is," Jake said.

"He doesn't know because it's not there."

Jake smiled at him. The scar on his cheek stretched. "That's the good news."

"The good news?"

"The good news is, I cut it and made it look like it was never there. That way you can't get in trouble."

Trip looked down at his boots, then at Jake. "Where is it now, Jake?"

"That's the beauty of it, Mr. Trip. It's nowhere."

"Nowhere?"

This is terrible.

"Nowhere," Trip said again. "Did you burn it?"

"No, sir. I wouldn't do that," Jake's scar stretched further across his face.

"Then where is it?"

"I sold it for you, Mr. Trip."

"You sold it?"

"Yes, sir. And I've got the money right here." Jake reached into his pocket and hauled out a wad of bills.

There's cash everywhere.

"Here it is." Jake handed him the money. "It's all here. Except what I drank, which is about forty dollars, which I figure is what cutting it was worth."

Trip looked at the fistful of cash in Jake's hand. It looked like it was all in twenties.

"How much is it, Jake?"

"Take it Mr. Trip."

"How much is it?"

"Almost fifteen hundred," Jake said. "Fifteen hundred less the money I paid myself for harvesting your crop."

"Thank you, Jake." He stuffed the cash in his jeans.

* * *

Trip sat in his truck and lit a joint. It started to drizzle, not a real rain that would flood up the woods. He drove back to the shop and backed the pickup up to the trailered johnboat. He lifted the tongue of the trailer, wheeled it to the truck, and dropped the end of the hitch on the ball. He drove on the main north-south levee, one hand on the wheel, the other scratching Cash behind his left ear. "Cash," he said, "it's only been a couple months since the dove hunt, but a lot has happened in the last couple of months."

The levee was getting slippery so he kept the truck in the ruts as best he could. A mile later, he turned left and ran half a mile west to the landing, on the ditch side of the levee. He slipped the truck in reverse and started to back the trailer down the ramp. The truck slid on the muddy ramp. He stepped on the brakes, but the truck skidded backwards.

"Damn it, Cash."

Trip put the truck in four-wheel drive and started back up the ramp. All four wheels churned in the mud. The wheels spun forward, but the truck slid backward, off the ramp, and into the ditch. The trailer jackknifed and ended up in three feet of water, along with the truck.

"Cash, when exactly do you think things are going to turn around?"

They crawled out the back window to the truck bed. Trip climbed down and stood in the water. He'd had enough foresight to wear rubber boots so at least his feet were dry.

That's about the limit of my foresight.

If he opened the door, water would pour into the cab. The engine block was under water, but probably not the spark plug wires. He didn't think he'd ruined the truck—at least not yet. The johnboat, tied down to the trailer, struggled to float up and off. There was about six inches of freeboard. If he didn't untie the boat right away, it was going to fill up with water.

He stepped on the bumper. From there he stepped into the boat. Water poured in. When he released the stern straps, the stern shot up and knocked him into the water.

Now I'm good and wet.

The water sloshed to the bow, pushing it down. More water poured in.

Trip splashed to the bow and released the brake on the winch. The bow lifted. A foot of water slopped around inside the johnboat. Trip found the cut-off Clorox bottle in the bilge and started bailing. When he finished, Cash jumped from the truck bed into the johnboat. "Why a dog that likes the water as much as you won't jump in a foot of water is beyond me." Trip lit a cigarette. "Maybe you think that water doesn't belong inside a boat. If that's it, you're right."

The johnboat didn't look like it was any worse for wear, as long as the engine started. The truck and trailer were a different story. He'd have to walk back to the shop and bring out the Little John Deere. If he had any luck, the engine wouldn't be ruined. A little more luck and the inside wouldn't be too wet.

Despite what he should do, Trip pumped the ball on the gas line of the engine. He pulled out the choke and reefed on the starter cord. The engine kicked to life. He unhooked the bow from the winch, shifted into reverse, and backed off the trailer. He ran a half mile west, dead slow, to the end of the levee, then half a mile north, first through weeds, then through the buck-brush, until he reached the timber. The ditch cut to the northwest, and the water in the ditch started to peter out.

The boat grounded about three-quarters of a mile before they got to the Game and Fish levee that held in the floodwaters of Bayou Meto and marked the Belle Oak property line.

Trip looked up through the trees. "Cash, this would be a good day to be in the timber if it was sunny, which it's not. And if there was any water in the woods, which there isn't. And if the season was on which it's not. Other than that, it's all good." Trip got out of the boat, waded to the side of the ditch, and stepped up into the woods.

"Cash, Snake." Trip walked through the woods, at the edge of the ditch, Cash in front. It was probably too cold for snakes, but with the way things were going today, he wasn't going to take a chance.

He thought he could figure out what to do next if he started out doing something simple, like launching the duck boat. He hadn't counted on being too distracted to see that the ramp was slick. He had fifteen hundred dollars, less what Jake had drunk up. And no weed. And no prospects for any. He was pretty sure the Italians were going to want their weed soon.

"Everything I do makes things worse."

Trip followed Cash alongside the ditch until they reached the levee. He climbed to the top, the Bayou Meto timber in front of him, the Belle Oak timber behind him. To his left, Mama's Blind, built into an opening in the canopy on the Belle Oak side of the levee.

His woods were still dry. The rains hadn't brought up the water yet. There was about a foot of water on the Game and Fish side of the levee. "Cash, the boards at Lower Vallier are starting to do their job. We just need the rain to keep coming." He kicked at the leaves on top of the levee.

The levee cut the ditch in two, the ditch his great-grandfather had dug from the river to the farm before Game and Fish built the levee, the ditch that brought the river water to the farm to flood up the rice and the Belle Oak woods.

Trip dropped back down the Belle Oak side of the levee. After Game and Fish built the levee, his grandfather built a gate to let the water through, which was strictly illegal. Breaching a state levee was a felony. Arkansans had strong feelings about their levees, their water, and especially their ducks.

Game and Fish had never found the gate hidden inside the levee. The McClures had dug their ditch first and what was right was right. Trip dug out the mud, pulled out the rocks, and lifted the gates. Water poured into Belle Oak.

They took the boat back to the sunken truck and trailer and walked back to the shop for the Little John Deere. It took the rest of the day to get the truck and trailer out. He could have finished sooner if he'd had some help, but he didn't want to have to explain his foolishness.

Trip spent a quiet evening with the lovely Parker and just enough Maker's Mark to take the edge off.

* * *

The next morning, after he made sure Jake and Big John were hard at work on the Club House, he met Theo Boxwood for coffee at the Mallard, a single-story, white frame diner on the edge of town. Boxwood waved him over to a window table. Water streamed down the glass. The waitress came over and poured Trip a cup of coffee.

"How 'bout this rain?" Boxwood said. "More like a drizzle."

"How 'bout it."

"Drizzle won't flood up the woods."

"No, sir, it won't." Trip knew where Boxwood was headed, but he wasn't going to follow him there.

The banker slurped on his coffee. "Trip, I am concerned about your rice."

"Why ever for?"

"Because I am concerned about my collateral."

"It's all right there," Trip said. "In my bins."

"I know it." Boxwood motioned to an unseen waitress for more coffee. "That's just it. It's in your bins."

"That's where it's supposed to be."

"I think I'd feel more comfortable if it was in the bins at Riceland."

Trip didn't say anything.

"I think it would be better, don't you?"

Trip lit a cigarette.

"Please don't do that." Boxwood waved his hand back and forth. "You know that's not good for you, don't you?"

Trip looked at the cigarette, pulled hard on it, and dropped it in his coffee. It hissed when it went out and floated in his cup.

"Thank you. I think," Boxwood said, put off by the floating cigarette. "How about if we truck it into Riceland."

"Who pays for that?"

"You bring it in yourself. Then there's no cost," Boxwood said.

"There's fuel and labor and then storage."

"That's not much."

"Theo, I'm all paid up through the end of this month."

"Then what?"

"Then I'll sell it."

"And?"

"And pay you off."

The waitress refilled the banker's cup. Boxwood made a great show of the accoutrements—pouring, spooning, stirring. "I'm just not comfortable with that rice in your bins."

"I am."

"You think it over." Boxwood slurped on his coffee, eyes closed.

* * *

Trip walked past his truck. Cash gave him a sorrowful look.

"Cash, I have a few things to think over."

He knew full well why Boxwood wanted his rice at Riceland. They'd weigh it. Worse, they'd grade it, and when they figured in the chaff, Trip would be way short. He knew it, and it looked like Boxwood knew it too. But if Trip could get his hunters in, he could make up the shortfall by the time the loan was due. Even if he did all that, he'd still be short the marijuana money. There just wasn't enough to go around.

"Well, if it isn't Trip McClure," boomed a voice. "You're just the man I was looking for."

Trip, jolted from his painful reverie, looked up and found he had wandered all the way up to the County Courthouse. And who should be skipping down the steps but Dewitt, the Arkansas County Sheriff, the head man of local law enforcement, and just the man Trip didn't want to see.

Trip grinned at the double-named Sheriff Dewitt. He had a *basso profundo* voice, but he was barely five feet tall, and he was as big around as he was tall. He had a round face, a round nose, and round eyes. His family, the Pine Bluff Dewitts, had fared poorly in Pine Bluff for generations. It was one thing after another, including the arms, legs, hands, and fingers lost by the Dewitt men at the lumber mill. Dewitt's parents finally gave it up and moved to Dewitt, another duck town, though much smaller than Stuttgart. It was fifteen miles southeast of Stuttgart, near the confluence of the Arkansas and the Mississippi. The Dewitts' fortunes changed in this smallest of towns. The senior Dewitt actually found safe, steady work as a clerk in the hardware store, and his wife sired a son. So overjoyed by their newfound happiness, they named their son Dewitt, after their new hometown. They never gave it a second thought, and to his credit Dewitt didn't either. The voters elected him sheriff time and time again, and the fiftyish sheriff ran the county with the zeal of a man who had found his calling.

"I was out to your place the other day."

"Yes, sir." Despite his grin, Trip didn't want to have anything to do with Sheriff Dewitt today.

"What do you think I found?"

"I surely don't know," Trip said, who was afraid he knew exactly what the sheriff had found.

The sheriff had stopped three steps from the sidewalk, which put him eye-to-eye with Trip. "I'll bet you don't."

Trip started up the stairs.

"You just stay right there." Sheriff Dewitt had a nicely pressed, dark brown sheriff's shirt with a very shiny badge that took up most of the left side of his chest.

"I've known McClures a long time and found y'all to be more or less law abiding."

"We try to walk the straight and narrow."

"Don't you sass me, young man. Now look here, you are in a world of hurt." He wagged his finger at Trip.

Trip shoved his hands in his pockets and tried not to look guilty.

"That's right. You just follow me right up these steps. Now, march."

Trip, for once, did as he was told and followed the diminutive sheriff up the courthouse steps.

So, this is where it ends. Busted on a dope charge.

At the top of the steps, the Sheriff held open the door for him. Trip sulked through.

"Turn right, second door on the left," the sheriff said. "You are not above the law."

He must know more than Jake thought he did. Maybe Jake told him.

"You march right in there and get yourself a building permit right now. And I'll forget I ever saw that nitwit Jake out there pounding away. You McClures are not above the law."

CHAPTER TWELVE

Celia and her Benz dropped down off I-40 onto State Highway 11 at Hazen and drove through the flattest ground in Arkansas, farmland cut by ditches and creeks. Gray woods at the back of the fields framed the horizon.

She drove through the same drizzle where, five miles to the south, Sheriff Dewitt had just ordered Trip to get a building permit. The wipers swept over the windshield, just often enough to scrape the glass clear of the ever so patient Arkansas drizzle. Celia kept her own special rhythm with the wipers, sipping her sweet tea on every fourth pass.

Two miles north of Stuttgart, she turned west on 165. She slowed down when she came to the Big Ditch. The woods ran right up to the road here. There was a two-hundred-foot bridge across the man-made irrigation ditch that, like all ditches in Arkansas County, emptied into Bayou Meto. If only she and Big George hadn't been on this road and crossed this bridge that night.

Five miles down the road she pulled into the four corners of Humnoke and turned into Connor's, the Shell station known for its fried chicken. She sat down next to the window at a formerly white, plastic booth.

An average-sized man came in and sat down across from her. Celia thought he looked average in just about every way. He was of average height and average weight. He had on khaki pants and a checkered tan shirt underneath a brown jacket. Actually, he was average in every way but two. He had greasy, black hair and thick, black glasses over big, black bulging, frog eyes.

Are those glasses a disguise?

"Mrs. McClure?" said the greasy-haired man.

"Perhaps," she said.

"I thought so."

"I didn't say I was."

"You didn't say you wasn't."

"And who might you be?"

"Can't say."

"If you can't say, then we have no further business." Celia wiped off the table in front of her with a napkin.

"Do we have business?" the man with the thick glasses said.

"I'm sure I don't know."

"You ain't here for the chicken, are you?"

"What is your name?"

At that moment, a waitress in blue jeans showed up at the table. "Cullen, how are you?" She looked at Celia then back at the greasy man with the thick glasses. "You know this nice lady?" Not waiting for an answer, "The usual?"

Cullen dismissed the waitress with a wave of his arm.

"Don't you shush me."

"The usual," he said.

"Fine," turning to Celia, "How 'bout you, ma'am?"

"Sweet tea, please."

"How about some chicken?"

"I don't think so."

"You sure? The fried chicken here is pretty special."

"All right. I'll have a thigh with a side of Pennzoil," Celia said.

"What?"

"Nothing for me," Celia said.

"I guess I won't figure on your tip to help get my VCR out of layaway." She walked over to the kitchen, a fryer next to the cash register.

"So, it's Cullen."

"Might be."

"I would like to know the name of the person trying to blackmail me."

"I ain't trying to blackmail nobody."

"What would you call it?"

"It's not me who's doin' it."

The waitress arrived with Celia's sweet tea and the biggest glass of Coca-Cola she had ever seen. "Here you go, Cullen." She plopped the Coke down in front of him, spilling some of it on the table.

"Lola, you watch out. You just about dumped that on me."

"If you drink all that, you'll have to pee all afternoon." She put a straw in front of each of them then left.

"So, Cullen," Celia said, "is 'Cullen' your first name or your last name?"

"Might be," he said.

"This conversation is going no further until I know your name. First and last."

Cullen stared at Celia. He pushed his glasses further up the bridge of his nose. He ran his hands through his greasy hair.

I may be ill.

Finally, he said, "Dubose. Cullen Dubose."

"Well then, Cullen Dubose, are you or are you not trying to blackmail me?"

The average man put his lips to the glass and slurped off the top half inch of the Coke. "I'm here for a client."

Celia didn't believe anyone would hire Cullen Dubose, if that was his name, for anything, blackmail included. "Well then, what exactly does your client want?"

"You know what."

Celia unwrapped her straw and sipped her sweet tea. "This is how a straw works, Mr. Cullen," she said. "Like this."

"This is going to cost you more, you keep this up."

"What do you want?"

"I don't want nothing."

"Really?" Celia tried to see his eyes through his glasses. "I think you do."

"You know what I want."

"And what would that be?"

"All God's children need money."

"For what?"

"You know, for what."

"Illuminate me."

Cullen Dubose looked around the diner.

That's a bit dramatic.

There wasn't a soul in the diner except the two of them. Plus Lola, who was over at the fryer. She waved at him. "Almost ready, hon."

Dubose slurped on his Coke. "You know damn well what I seen."

"Do not curse in my presence."

"Sorry, ma'am," he said, suddenly deferential. "I am here to get money and bring you peace."

"My late husband already bought peace." Celia looked out at her Benz.

"He bought some peace. He bought peace for a while." Dubose picked up his Coke, thought better of it, and set it back down. He unwrapped his straw and drank through it. "I am sorry about your husband."

"You should be," Celia said. "You caused it."

"You caused it, ma'am. I only saw it," Dubose said.

"I thought you said you had a client."

Lola showed up with a plate full of chicken and set it down in front of Dubose. "Here you go, Cullen. Fried gizzards. Just the way you like 'em."

Celia cringed at the mountain of deep-fried chicken gizzards.

"I've been saving them up for you." She took out a bottle of Louisiana Hot Sauce from the pocket of her apron. "Anything else?"

"Got all I need, Lola."

"More sweet tea?"

"No, thank you."

Lola disappeared into the back room.

"What did you see, Mr. Dubose?"

Dubose popped a gizzard in his mouth and rolled it around with his tongue. "These are hot."

"Please don't talk with your mouth full."

Cullen swallowed the gizzard whole. "You want some whiskey for that sweet tea?"

"I most certainly do not."

"Quit, did you?" Dubose drowned a second gizzard with hot sauce and popped it in his mouth. "That's not what I saw on the way over."

"I have no money for you."

"You got all them tugs and that big farm and that duck woods. You got to have some money for me."

"Not anymore."

"That's what your husband said, but he found some."

"Just what did you see?"

"You know what I seen."

"It was dark," Celia said.

"It was dark. Slippery too. The bridge over the Big Ditch is always the first thing to ice up."

"How can you see through those glasses?"

"My eyes is fine," he said, angry now. "You keep my eyes outta this."

"I have no money for you."

"And your boy is about to carry hunters for hire. That'll get money. How about some of that money?" He ate another gizzard. "That boy sure can call."

"You keep my son out of this."

"It's too late for that." Cullen squirted hot sauce on the gizzards. Some of it splattered on his glasses. He took them off and wiped them with his napkin. His eyes were tiny black pinpricks.

CHAPTER THIRTEEN

The rain began like it meant it, not a downpour, but the steady rain that came up from the Gulf in November. No wind, just rain, a gray sky and rain, and Trip was going to start pumping up the rice fields.

He and Big John skidded out to the power unit at the big reservoir in Trip's truck. He started up the Allis-Chalmers that sat on top of the levee under a sheet metal roof. The diesel pounded away. It drowned out the ringing in Trip's ears, but it wasn't pulling any water out of the reservoir.

He was going to pump a foot or so of water into the rice fields for the ducks. Since the first days of rice on the Grand Prairie, ducks ate and loafed in the cut rice when the rains came and flooded the fields. Now all the rice men had reservoirs that pumped water in and out of the fields, first for the rice, then for the ducks.

The big reservoir was a diked-up quarter section full of water with dead timber on the southwest side. Trip's grandfather had dug a ten-foot hole in the northwest corner for fish and stocked it with bream, crappie, and large-mouths. The catfish had found their way in. Bluebills, redheads, and canvasbacks spent part of the winter on the big reservoir.

Trip smoked a cigarette under the sheet metal roof and watched the hip-booted Big John wrestle in the mud with the intake hose. Big John was sure it was plugged up. He had his Walkman in his pocket and his earphones on his head.

I wonder if the rain is going to short out Lynyrd Skynyrd.

Trip crushed out his cigarette.

Doesn't look like Big John is worried about it.

The big man lifted the intake hose from the water. He pulled the screen off the hose and looked inside it. The hose sucked Big John's face in. He wrestled it and tried to pull it off his face.

He looks like an elephant fighting with his trunk.

Trip shut down the diesel. The suction quit. Big John jerked the hose off his face and fell backwards into the water. He sputtered to his feet. "Now why'd y'all do that for?"

"Because you were about to die."

"I just about had it, and now I'm wet."

"You were on the way to wet. I just sped it up."

Big John got to his feet, grabbed the hose, and reached in up to his elbow. He twisted, turned, and pulled. Out came the fattest water moccasin Trip had ever seen.

"This here was the problem," Big John held the snake by the head. Trip jumped back even though he was twenty feet away.

"Don't worry, Mr. Trip. The snake was drowned."

"How'd it get in there?"

"I think it lived in there and ate what got sucked in."

"Snakes can't live underwater."

"This one did." Big John threw the snake up next to Trip.

Trip jumped out from under the sheet metal roof and into the rain. "God damn it, Big John."

The big man jammed the screen back on the hose, dropped the hose back in the water. "You can start her up again, Mr. Trip."

* * *

Trip and Cash dripped on the rug in the foyer of the yellow house.

"Trip McClure, you stay on that rug with Cash." Parker tossed him a thick, blue bath towel. Trip dried his face and mopped his hair.

"That towel is for Cash. Dry him off so he doesn't catch cold."

"Labrador Retrievers don't catch colds."

"Make sure you dry his tail. You always forget his tail."

Some days she cares more about Cash than me.

"Take off those clothes and take this towel to yourself while I go run you a bath." Parker handed him a brown towel with a rip in it. Trip undressed and wrapped the towel around his waist.

This should be Cash's towel.

Trip walked to the bathroom. Parker was bent at the waist filling up the bathtub. He stopped to admire her bottom, squeezed into a pair of blue jeans.

She turned to him. "Mr. McClure, why are you wearing a towel?"

Trip dropped the towel, sank into the tub. Parker sat on the edge. "Baby, all this duck club business. And what not."

When she says "what not," I never like what comes next.

"This duck club idea of yours is a bad idea."

"Baby, we're already full up for the first week."

"The Club House isn't done, and you are not fit to manage a hunting business, let alone entertain a bunch of drunks with shotguns."

"If you keep booking hunts and getting deposits, we'll make it until I get it figured out."

"I thought you had it figured out."

I did until Jake sold my weed.

"And don't splash me." Parker wiped a drop from her eye.

I hope that's not a tear.

"Little George is going to sell Belle Oak out from under you," Parker said.

"No, he's not."

"He will, and I don't want him to, but I don't want him not to as much as you do," Parker said.

I don't know what she said, but I know what she meant.

"I lived somewhere else before I lived here."

It wasn't a tear.

"And another thing, you take care of Cash."

"I will, baby."

"I don't want him to catch a cold." She looked around the bathroom. "Where is he?"

"I let him out on my way in here."

"Out? You just dried him off. Where is he?"

Trip looked out the bathroom door and through the sliding glass doors to the patio where Cash was sitting in the rain.

"Where is he?"

Cash loved the water, and he didn't care if he got wet from the bottom up when he went after a duck or from the top down when he sat in the rain. Cash loved the water, and he liked to sit in the rain. Like now.

"I'll go find him," Trip said.

"You stay in the tub. I'll go find him."

This won't be good.

He counted to three and sank down into the tub, his head underwater.

"Trip McClure, you are a fool." She stormed off.

Trip burst to the surface and sucked in a mouthful of air. *At least she left.* Cash ran in, followed by Parker.

"He was on the patio, sitting in the rain. I swear, you are going to kill that dog."

Cash shook himself head to tail. Arkansas mud splattered on the walls. He jumped in the tub with Trip.

"Damn it, Trip McClure," she said. "Damn you and your follies."

* * *

Trip picked the Vanderbilt boys up at the Little Rock airport and took them all to Wings Over the Prairie. It was opening night of the festival that celebrated the opening of duck season.

The Stuttgart city fathers closed downtown to all motorized vehicles. Tents were pitched. Booths popped up. Stuttgart's population doubled when it hosted the world's duck- and goose-calling championship, the best duck gumbo cook-off in the universe, and the Miss Duck Capital of America Beauty Pageant.

Duck call makers, a cottage industry if there ever was one, set up everywhere, the quacking and honking background music for the weekend. Bands, mostly country, some southern rock, played all over town.

Mostly, though, Wings Over the Prairie was a colossal drunk.

This was why Trip kept as far away as he could. It was too much for his senses, especially his ears, but his pals had insisted.

Once, long ago, he had entered the world duck-calling championships with one of Cad's calls, the single reed cocobolo he still used. He breezed through the preliminaries, cheered on by his mother. "He calls so sweetly," she said to anyone who would listen and everyone who wouldn't.

Trip lost interest as the contest went on. Duck calling in the timber, the sloughs, and the rice was much different than on the main stage in Stuttgart. In the field, Trip knew what to say and when. He read the ducks by their wingbeats and their own calling.

On stage, though, a routine was required, the duck-calling version of scales and arpeggios. The duck call is a musical instrument—hail call, greeting call, feeding chuckle, comeback call, greeting call again—all of which bored the bejesus out of Trip who was the quintessential meat caller.

He struggled in the semis, quit, unquit, and won the world championship with an inspired routine in the finals, featuring the most beseeching comeback call ever heard in Arkansas County. He never entered again.

But the Vanderbilt boys weren't there for the championships. They dragged Trip along for the women and the booze. Trip parked in Theo Boxwood's private parking place behind the Second National Bank. Everett produced a fifth of Maker's Mark that proved to be too much temptation for Trip. He led them to the high school gym where the gumbo cook-off was well underway.

"No booze in here, boys," said the rent-a-cop, a bloated, worried-looking fellow.

"Hector, how are you?" Trip said.

"Just fine, Mr. Trip. Just no drinking in here except from what you buy from the kegs."

Hector gave him a worried look.

Trip handed him a twenty and took the whiskey to the bar where draft Lone Star, the official sponsor, was, for obvious reasons, served in plastic cups. Trip drank the beer, poured three fingers of Maker's Mark in his glass, drank it, and did it again.

A bit more relaxed, he took the boys over to the gumbo chefs, row after row of pots and pans and paper Dixie cups.

"Here you go, Trip," said a husky voice in an equally husky body. The man handed Trip a Dixie cup with two spoonfuls of gumbo.

"Thank you, Sherm."

And that's how it went. Dixie cup by Dixie cup, beer by beer, three fingers by three fingers through the smoky gym, where smoking was strictly prohibited, all to the not-so-melodious sounds of the Greenheads, Stuttgart's most popular country band. They made their way across the tic-tac-toe of the rubber floor mats that covered the hardwood until they came to the booth of Versal Jonas, duck gumbo chef extraordinaire, the long line due to the Andouille sausage, crawfish, onion, okra, and chilies he used in his gumbo.

It was here, standing in line, after keeping company with who knew how many beers and how many fingers of Maker's Mark, that Amelia Rademacher found him.

"Why Trip McClure, how are you?" She hugged him, and he felt her nipples press against his chest. He smelled her perfume, sweet and flowery, with a tincture of sweat.

"Amelia," Trip said, trying not to be aroused. "How are you?"

"I am just fine. Especially now that you're here."

His friends all had eyes for her, but she only had eyes for Trip. Amelia, the daughter of a planter, the wife of a planter, the most successful realtor in Arkansas County, and an Arkansas beauty, was on the loose.

"Trip, it is so nice to see you," she said, a variation on a theme.

Trip smiled.

"I hear you have a duck club this year."

"I do," Trip said, trying not to be too engaged.

"You'll take all these other boys' business. What with your woods and your calling."

"Yes, ma'am," Trip said, drinking from his plastic glass.

"Don't you 'ma'am' me," she said, pouting just a bit. "Trip, why don't you go and buy me a beer."

"I would, but I don't want to lose my place in line."

"These boys will hold your place."

Jude nodded at him. Trip started over to the keg.

"Wait for me. I don't want to stand here with these boys." She grabbed his hand. When they got to the keg, he bought them each a beer. He drank his and bought himself another.

"Trip, I am so hot." Amelia made a show of fanning herself. "Let's get some air."

I'm pretty sure I know where this is headed.

"Amelia, aren't you trying to sell Belle Oak?"

"Not right now I'm not. Just one breath of air." She burst through the double steel doors. They slammed shut behind her, Trip still inside.

"Well," he said, in a drunken, self-satisfied way, "that takes care of that." Except that it didn't. There was a deafening pounding from the other side of the doors. Trip grinned and opened the doors. "Yes?" he said, stupidly.

"You come out here right now. You know better than to leave a lady by herself in the dark."

Trip shuffled through the double doors. Amelia marched off. Trip stayed put.

"Trip McClure, I need to get some cigarettes from my car. You just come along with me."

"I have cigarettes."

"I don't want your awful cigarettes. I want my own."

"Amelia, we smoke the same kind."

"No, we don't." She marched off as if to war.

Trip zigzagged after her until she caught him at her Cadillac. She pulled him against her, then kissed him full on the mouth. Her tongue darted in and out. She purred at him, gurgling through their kisses. His hands traced the edges of her panties. "Why Trip McClure," she said. He lifted her skirt and she unzipped his pants. Amelia opened the door of the Cadillac and climbed in the back seat. Trip climbed on top of her.

"There you are," said a voice. "Here's your gumbo. Better eat it before it gets cold." Jude opened the door and shoved the Dixie cup at him.

* * *

Jude poured Trip into the shotgun side of Trip's pickup. Trip fell asleep. He woke up when he felt his head bouncing from side to side like a teeter-totter. It was Jude push-pulling on his shoulder.

"Whoa. Whoa. Hey, stop."

"Wake up, asshole."

"I'm awake." Trip felt for his tongue, which felt like it had swollen to the size of a football.

"You are some kind of asshole," Jude Winter said.

"What?" Trip's head pounded like a jackhammer.

"Parker is the best thing ever happened to you, and you were an inch from fucking it up. Literally."

Trip, more or less conscious, tried to focus on the centerline of the highway. "What are you talking about?"

"I'm talking about the blonde bitch in the back seat of that Cadillac," Jude said.

"Oh, her."

"Yes, her. Are there any other hers I should know about?" Jude looked at him sideways. "What exactly were you thinking?"

Trip looked out his side window. He rolled it down and stuck his head out to get some fresh air.

What was I thinking.

Trip lit a cigarette. Jude snatched it out of his mouth and threw it out the window.

"God damn it," Trip said.

"God damn you," Jude said. "Why?"

"It seemed like a good idea at the time."

"It seemed like a good idea? You asshole. Do you know what you almost did?"

"She smelled good."

"She smelled good? You'd throw away Parker because that floozy smelled good?"

"Amelia wouldn't tell Parker. She's married, too."

"For Christ sake, Trip. Is not getting caught a good enough reason to cheat on Parker?"

Trip thought for a minute. "No, but it's the reason why nothing bad would have happened." Trip looked back out the window. "Stop right here."

Jude stopped the truck in front of Amelia's latest for sale sign. "What's that all about?"

"Little George has a little money problem with the barge business."

"And?"

"And I think I'll get out right here."

"What for?"

"I need to do some work," Trip said of the phoenix-like sign.

I'm going to cut it down as many times as it goes up.

"I don't know full and all what's going on with . . ."

"You don't sound like a Yankee when you talk like that."

"Trip, I am here to support your efforts no matter how misguided or unsuccessful they may be."

That's more like it.

"You're a fool. A desperate fool."

"I've got a duck club to run." Trip opened the door. "And it all starts tomorrow."

Jude planted his foot on Trip's butt and booted him into the ditch. There was a splash, then a curse. Jude climbed back in Trip's truck and drove off.

* * *

Trip drove up the driveway to the Club House. The gravel crunched under the truck's tires. He stopped about a hundred yards from the Club House and climbed out, Cash at his heels.

Trip lit his second cigarette of the day. His head pounded and his ears rang. "I'm a fool. Thank God for Jude." Trip looked straight up. There were woods on either side of the driveway. Orion was setting. "It's clear, Cash. Just like the forecast. We'll be in the woods today."

Today was opening day of duck season, Trip's favorite day of the year, bar none. He waited for it all year. The first day. The day when the ducks dropped into the timber like falling leaves. Ducks not yet wary. Ducks that came to the call. Colored-out drake mallards.

Today, though, would be a different opening day. This was the first day of the big duck season with the sports. This was the real deal. Except for his three pals, the other hunters were all strangers. Strangers at Belle Oak. On opening day. Strangers who would pay enough to save Belle Oak from Little George, J.D., and McClure Tug and Tow. Not that it was that simple anymore. He still had to get by Theo Boxwood and the rice, the gummed-up drug deal, and maybe Jake.

He climbed back in the pickup and parked in front of the Club House. There were lights in every window. The guides—Big John, Church, Cad, and Jake—were outside with their dogs and gear.

"Just about ready, Mr. Trip," Jake said.

"It's time to go. Right now. Does everybody know where they're going and who they're going with?"

"It's all on the board inside," Jake said.

Trip looked at the guides in the flat white of the yard light. Chest-waders on all of them. Camo hats and jackets. Jake had a tiny light clipped to the bill of his hat, the latest thing from Mack's.

That's stupid. He looks like a coal miner.

"All right, then, let's get going. Be careful."

"Aren't you going to introduce yourself to the hunters?" Jake said.

There were about sixteen hunters at five hundred a gun. Eight thousand a day. He didn't want them at Belle Oak, but he wanted their money. He thought maybe he should introduce himself, but he didn't want to.

"Go get the sports, Jake. Big John, are all the boats up at the ramp?"

"Yes sir."

Trip turned to his truck. "Follow me, Jude," he said. "I would appreciate it if you would use your boots for walking."

They all met up on top of the levee. Below them, five johnboats, painted mud green all with twenty-five horse Johnsons, floated in the ditch that led to the Belle Oak timber, then to the break in the levee that Trip opened up a month earlier.

There was a sliver of moonlight but no sun. Trip thought he recognized some of the hunters—the ones who had lusted after an invite to the famed Belle Oak flooded timber for years but never got one. Their checkbooks bought them one today. He thought the rest of them were from out of state.

"Boys," he said, "there's only three rules at the Belle Oak Duck Club. One, treat others the way you want to be treated. Two, remember your gun safety. Three, don't guide the guides.

"Cad, you take the Otter Hole. Jake, Wood Duck Hole. Church, Archie's Hole. Big John, Trip Over Hole. I'll be at Mama's Blind. There's tape to each hole. Don't ram around in the woods. Get in and be quiet. Everybody out by ten, limits or not."

Trip nodded to his Vanderbilt pals and slid down the levee to the dock. Cash beat him into the boat. Trip yanked on the starter cord. The outboard kicked, then stalled. He choked it and the motor fired again. Once it caught, he pushed in the choke. The motor idled, more or less. His three pals on board, Trip cast off, putted down the ditch, then opened up the throttle. The four boats behind him followed suit, all of them heading to the famed Belle Oak timber—eight thousand dollars' worth of saviors, or so he hoped.

By the time they made it to the woods, there was a hint of daylight. Trip felt Cash's hot breath on him and smelled the gas and oil from the Johnson. One by one, the boats turned out of the ditch into the flooded woods and made for their holes. Trip stayed in the ditch and ran past the Crooked Tree all the way to the levee at Mama's Blind.

Trip dropped his three pals in a semicircle on the east side of the hole. He put them in a semicircle so they wouldn't shoot each other, and on the east side so the sun would be in the ducks' eyes. Cash sat on a fallen log next to him. Trip threw out seven decoys in the hole, tied off the boat fifty yards away, and waded back, careful not to fall in, shuffling through the knee-deep water, shuffling to feel the holes with his boots and the sunken logs with his shins. He leaned against a big red oak next to Cash. Jude leaned on a tree next to him, then Bobby and Everett.

Daylight came up in the woods, a soft, thin light that outlined the trees and cast shadows on the brown water.

The sun was just over the horizon, an orange sky through the trees. A chickadee lit on the barrel of Trip's shotgun, looked him squarely in the eye, hopped toward him on twig legs, then was gone. On his left a woodpecker pounded a dead hickory. A wood duck flew through the hole, screeching.

The sun rose above the trees. "Stay in the shadows, boys. Don't let 'em see your face."

Trip knew they should all have masks on. Their faces had a shine like the man in the moon, which spooked the ducks mightily. He let it go today. It was opening day, and the ducks shouldn't be too wary.

It's the best day of the year. Even if there's strangers close by.

The ducks started to fly just after eight. Trip heard the wingbeats as they flew out from Hollowell. Ones and twos. Soft quacks, like cotton.

He kicked at the water, splashing like a duck landing then swimming. He called at a hen mallard. She circled the hole, tighter and tighter. "Don't shoot this one." She dropped her feet and landed. She sat there for a minute then swam in a slow lazy circle. Cash quivered. It was all he could do to sit on his log. It was all his pals could do not to shoot her on the water.

"Trip, you about done showing off?" Bobby said.

I'm not showing off.

This was the one thing that held Trip to the earth and hooked him to his life. He loved it more than anything. It made a fool out of him, and he almost knew it.

There were shots off in the distance, first from the Government Addition, then from where Jake was supposed to be. Jake was a killer. He always managed to get underneath the ducks.

The hen mallard sat up straight and flew off.

Trip stopped the next bunch, swung them around and around. Two hens and five drakes. Five big greenheads. With the sun full up, the drakes' heads shimmered in the light, green to blue to purple, smooth and satiny. He got them to dip below the tree line. He landed a hen and a drake. The other five cupped their wings. "Take 'em." The guns, twelve gauges all, boomed.

Four ducks fell. "Cash, fetch." The dog sprung from his hind legs, parted the water, and swam. He opened his jaws and clenched the first duck. Three more retrieves, the last a cripple swimming away through the woods. When Cash brought it back, Trip wrung its neck.

They killed their last duck at 9:30. Trip retrieved the boat, and they glided through the woods that had been dry just a month ago. When they got to the ditch, Trip opened up the Johnson and they planed back to the levee.

Jake and Church had been back for ten minutes. Cad and Big John showed up a few minutes after Trip. They all had limits. They all had big grins. Trip sent Jake and the ducks to the duck picker.

And so it went, Saturday through Wednesday. Clear, cold late November mornings, November mornings with weak light and ducks in the timber. Trip had yet to spend a night in the Club House or host a dinner, but Jake had risen to the occasion.

On Wednesday at noon and forty thousand dollars later, Trip shut down Belle Oak for Thanksgiving. He met Parker in the Club House.

"Baby," she said, apron around her waist, orange rubber gloves that stretched to her elbows, "I am absolutely not going into those bathrooms to scrub any more pee from the floor."

Trip looked down at his feet.

"You boys have got to learn to aim or sit down."

Trip still didn't say anything.

"You take a wad of that duck money and hire some help. And I'm done cooking, too. I don't cook for you except on Sundays, and I'll be damned if I'll cook for your hunters." Parker had her hands on her hips, not a good sign.

"We're just getting started."

"You're just getting started." Parker peeled off the gloves. "I'm just getting done. The only one of those damn hunters worth anything is Jude. And he's a Yankee."

"Baby, I need your help."

"Trip McClure, I will book your hunts and that's it. I want this to work, and I want to help. But you hire the rest out because I'm done with it. And you best watch out for that Jake Lawless. He is altogether too uppity with the sports. He's white trash and he'll do you harm if you let him go too far."

"Yes, ma'am."

"Don't you 'yes ma'am' me. Belle Oak is your duck club. Don't you let him have the sports to himself. He will harm you." She threw the gloves at him and marched out.

They look like ducks' feet.

* * *

Trip and Cash turned right on the main road away from the yellow house. He passed Pig Shelton's flooded timber. It wasn't bad, but it wasn't Belle Oak, not by a long shot. Two miles further, he pulled into a gravel driveway and drove past a matchbox of a house that once had been white but now showed no trace of paint. The truck bounced through the potholes of the formerly graveled driveway to a shed, a shed the size of a one-car garage with a fresh coat of white paint.

Trip was here to pick up the ducks for tomorrow's Thanksgiving dinner. He hadn't booked any hunters for Thanksgiving so he could spend the holiday with his family, but that wasn't the real reason. He didn't want his family to see Belle Oak turned into a hunting club.

Trip left Cash in the car and walked into the shed. The smell almost made him throw up, not to mention what he saw. There were dead ducks everywhere. Dead ducks piled in plastic tubs. It wasn't the dead ducks that smelled, it was what was left of the butchered ducks, the blood and the guts, the heads, wings, tails, and feet, were piled in overflowing trash cans. The smell nearly knocked him over.

A man with white hair chopped the limbs off a drake mallard with a hatchet. He didn't look up when Trip came in.

"Afternoon, Lucky," Trip said.

"Afternoon, Mr. Trip." The hatchet crashed on a stained, heavy wood table and severed a leg. Lucky, the duck picker, cleaned ducks for $2.50 each. He cleaned, wrapped, and froze them. He made thousands during duck season, more now that Trip had hunters.

"What you need?"

"I came to pick up some ducks for Thanksgiving dinner."

Lucky Lucious lay the hatchet on the wood table. He wiped his hands on the front of his black rubber apron. "Well now, Mr. Trip, you don't have no ducks to pick up."

"I've got at least a hundred ducks here."

Trip lit a cigarette to cover up the stench.

"Mr. Trip, you know I don't allow no smokin' in here."

Trip sucked on the cigarette.

"I can't stand the smell of cigarettes," Lucky said. "And it spoils the meat."

"I know it." Trip dropped the cigarette on the floor and stomped it out.

"And I can't have no cigarette remains on my floor."

Lucky took the mallard to the plucker, a whirling machine that stripped the carcass of feathers. When the feathers were all stripped, he chopped off the tail, reached into the carcass, and ripped out the guts. The duck picker sprayed out the insides with a hose hooked up to a rusty washtub. He dropped the duck into a tub of bloody brine.

"I'm here for my Thanksgiving ducks."

Lucky looked at him sideways. "And I told you, you ain't got no ducks here."

"Lucky, we killed over two hundred ducks in the past week, and there must be at least a hundred here."

"I know it 'cause I cleaned 'em all. And I would like my money."

"I gave Jake the picker money."

"You may have, but he sure didn't give it to me."

God damn it.

Trip crushed his cigarette on the floor and lit another cigarette.

"Let's don't start that again while we still got to figure out who's goin' to take that one off the floor."

Trip looked at his burning cigarette. "I need some ducks for Thanksgiving dinner."

The picker reached into the bin and took a drake wood duck in his hand. Green, red, blue, purple, orange, and yellow.

It looks like a clown.

"How about you give me a dozen ducks, and I'll replace them?"

"You know I can't do that, Mr. Trip."

Trip knew it all right. Lucky Lucious took great pride in matching the right duck with the right hunter, not that anyone would ever know. When he took over from his uncle Tobias, as tubby as Lucky was skinny, he cleaned up

Toby's casual approach to duck picking. Lucky's attention to detail among the carnage was legendary.

"If you haven't been paid, I'll pay you now and pick up my ducks."

"I already told you, you ain't got no ducks here."

Lucky looked him in the eye, then at Trip's half-smoked cigarette.

Trip crushed the half-smoked cigarette under his foot. He picked up both butts and threw them in the bin with the guts.

"How much do I owe?"

Lucky opened a drawer on the table and removed a bloodstained ledger.

Trip had seen this at least a hundred times. Lucky turned to the McClure's page. "Your balance is one-hundred-ninety-seven dollars and fifty cents."

Trip handed Lucky eleven twenty-dollar bills. The duck picker stuffed them in a stained, zippered leather pouch, not a thought of making change.

"About my ducks." Trip thought he was at last at the bottom of the duck mystery. The old man just wanted his money.

"You ain't got no ducks here, Mr. Trip. I believe I told you that at least four times now."

"Then where the hell are they?"

"There is no need to curse, Mr. Trip. Your man Jake, he drops 'em off and picks 'em up every day. Put 'em on your account. Surely you know that."

Damn that Jake.

The old man raised the hatchet over his head, crashed down on the wood duck's neck. He slid the severed head off the edge of the table with the blade of his hatchet. It fell into the bin.

CHAPTER FOURTEEN

The McClure clan straggled into Belle Oak that night. Mama, Little George and his family, J.D. and his family. Trip made sure he was in bed before they arrived. He slept in on Thanksgiving Day until five a.m. He kissed Parker on the forehead. "Go get 'em baby," she said and turned over.

Trip found Tully in the kitchen in the middle of the ritual McClure Thanksgiving Day breakfast. Fried eggs, grits, sausage, toast, and coffee, not a fruit or vegetable to be found.

This year, though, one thing was different.

"There's no ducks in the refrigerator, Mr. Trip," Tully said.

"That's right."

"Where are they, Mr. Trip?"

"They're in the timber."

"Sir?"

"We're going to shoot 'em this morning," Trip said.

'How come they're not at Lucky's?"

"That's a long story."

"Must have something to do with Jake. You best keep an eye on him."

Don't I know it.

"I'm leaving as soon as breakfast's done. So, I guess you're on your own."

"I know it." Trip lit a cigarette.

"Miss Parker don't allow smoking in here."

"Miss Parker's not in here."

"She's got a nose like a blue tick. You know that."

"I know it, but she's not here." Trip squashed out the cigarette in the kitchen sink, an old-fashioned porcelain sink with rust-colored veins running through hairline cracks in the porcelain.

"Who's going to clean the ducks?"

"I am." Trip poured himself a cup of coffee.

The old cook smiled at him. He cracked two eggs on the edge of the cast iron skillet and dropped them into the grease.

* * *

Celia insisted on hunting with Trip, just the two of them plus Cash. Little George, J.D., and their sons went off on their own.

She wouldn't let Trip help her in the boat. She didn't need his help, but he knew that she'd be offended if he hadn't offered.

He saw her outline in the predawn light, waders with a Barbour jacket and a felt hat. He could smell the waxed cotton of her Barbour. He could see just enough to see the soft, oily sheen of the coat, but it was the smell, the wax on cotton, that reminded him of his mother.

The bow of the johnboat cut a white "V" in the ditch. Trip ran full out.

She'll get after me if I baby my way in.

He took the ditch all the way to the levee that marked the edge of Bayou Meto. He cut the motor back, pushed up the sleeve of his Barbour.

Mama would never let me wear a parka.

Trip stuck his hand in the water and unhooked the lever that locked the motor in place. They coasted along the levee to Mama's Blind.

His mother had hunted here with Big George every Thanksgiving morning for as long as Trip could remember. It was McClure property on this side of the levee, but anyone who came in from the west, the public hunting grounds of Bayou Meto, would consider it fair game. But it was so far back in the woods and so well hidden, no one had ever hunted it but McClures. They could sit in lawn chairs, shoot ducks, and stay high and dry, but Mama always stood in the water.

Celia had insisted on an old-time Arkansas hunt. No decoys. "Trip, honey, if you can't call 'em in without decoys then I don't want them in the hole." He lit a cigarette. "I think I'll have one, too." She waded over to him before he could take her one. "Land the first bunch. We'll shoot the second bunch."

"Mama, we've been hunting pretty hard around here. I don't know how many chances we're going to get."

"Nonsense. It's going to be clear today and nobody's hunted here. Have they?"

"No, Mama," Trip lied.

"You call them down. Splash a little if you need to. You call so sweetly, you'll bring 'em right in."

"Thank you, Mama, but today we're meat hunters."

"Whatever for?"

"We don't have ducks for Thanksgiving dinner unless we kill them this morning."

"Lucky has ducks."

"He does, Mama. I'll explain it later, but we have to kill our Thanksgiving dinner."

"All right, but you land the first bunch. Then we'll kill them."

"Yes, ma'am."

The first bunch showed up half an hour later. Trip locked up a hen mallard on her first pass. He called to her softly, sang to her with the single reed cocobolo turned by Cad. A rich vibrato descending the scale. She craned her neck, peering down into the hole. Celia kicked at the water. Trip sang through the call. Another hen joined her, then a drake. They circled and circled. They were at the treetops, but they wouldn't come down. Trip stopped calling. The birds circled once, then lifted, still circling the hole. He chopped at them, then he whined through the call. Now there were at least a dozen above them. He pleaded with them. The ducks circled the hole. Once, twice, three times. They swirled and swirled. A colored-out drake, green, purple, blue in the early sunlight, hooked its wings and fluttered to the water. Then a hen. Then another. The rest of them sailed around the hole at the tree-tops. They dropped below the treetops and drifted down to the water. Trip watched his mother watch the ducks. They swam, gabbled, preened.

"Trip honey, you call so sweetly."

The ducks swam for half an hour. When the next bunch flew over, they saw the ducks swimming in the hole and dropped right in. Celia killed two drakes with her side-by-side. Trip shot one. Cash fetched them one at a time.

"We're partway there, Mama."

"We'd be halfway there if you'd shot better."

"Yes, ma'am."

"How's the duck club business?"

"Making money."

"Trip, honey, that's good because I need some of that money."

Trip's stomach turned over.

"There's a few bills that I need to get paid," she said.

"Mama, this money is to save the farm."

"So is this, honey."

"How much do you need?"

"Ten thousand."

Just when things were starting to look up.

"I need that money, Trip."

"So do I, Mama."

"You'll get it back," she said.

"What's it for Mama? I'll talk to them, settle it out."

"You can't, Trip. I need the money."

Cash looked up. Ducks circled at the treetops. Trip put the call to his lips. The ducks dropped down. He thought better of it and let the call fall on the lanyard hanging around his neck. He pulled up on the trailing duck, swung the gun through it and shot. He kept swinging through the second, shot again. Both ducks splashed into the hole, stone dead.

Trip called down another three groups, enough to get them both a limit. He didn't say another word to his mother. At the dock, Little George and company recounted the morning's adventures, including the adventures of his son, George the Fourth—known as "Four By" because of his girth—who had fallen in and filled up his waders, and Little George's dog, Duke, a hippo of a Lab who would fetch anything, anytime, anywhere, including Four By.

"Seems like the proprietor of a duck club ought to have ducks on hand," Little George said.

Trip cast a wicked eye at Little George standing on the dock, like the king he thought he was. Duke had his eye on Trip's ducks. Trip tossed one at Little George who ducked and grinned at him. When Little George ducked, Trip said, "Duke, fetch." The big dog leapt over Little George, but he caught him with his hind legs and tipped him butt first into the ditch. Duke landed on top of him. The dog retrieved the duck. He presented it to Little George, sitting in the ditch.

* * *

Trip and the always beautiful and the almost always good sport Parker cleaned the Thanksgiving dinner ducks. Trip soaked them in brine for an hour, then stuffed them with sliced apples, canned peaches, cinnamon, clove, and ginger. He poured the syrup from the peaches over them and cooked them at three twenty-five for an hour and twenty minutes in foil tents, one duck per person.

Trip served the ducks with a sauce made of horseradish, cream, dill, and a dollop of mayonnaise paired with rice, yams, okra with peppers, cranberry sauce, a green salad, and Beaujolais Nouveau.

After the coffee and sweet potato pie, the women and children left the table, and the heirs to the disappearing McClure fortune stayed at the table with Maker's Mark and cigars, the first Thanksgiving without Big George, who had started them down this road.

Trip had no more illusions about the cliché of their Thanksgiving dinner than he'd had about their fried chicken dinner. He just liked what they had to eat and drink. Neither did he have any delusions about the reason the three of them were still in the dining room. He knew full well that when it came to money, Little George was as unrelenting as the compounding of interest.

Cash had taken his customary position, curled in a ball not next to, but on top of Trip's feet. The dog warmed his feet, chilled from the ever-present foot-level draft in the dining room, the downside of floor-to-ceiling windows on three sides leaking November cold. Trip's feet were falling asleep, but it was worth it.

Little George swirled his whiskey. "Trip, thank you for the fine meal and the fine hunt."

"My pleasure." Trip noted that his brother hadn't said a word about falling in the ditch, but this was in keeping with Little George's perennial unwillingness to acknowledge defeat.

"Your hunters haven't shot out the woods yet," Little George said.

"There haven't been all that many hunters," Trip said, lying. He raised his glass.

Little George looked at him, his nose hooked over the lip of the rocks glass. "That's not what I hear."

Trip swallowed his whiskey and felt the sweet burn as it went down.

"We may as well get to it," Little George said.

Trip didn't say anything.

"I'll cut right to it. The barge company needs some money," Little George said.

Trip felt the wad of cash in his right front pants pocket. Ever since his trip to New Orleans, he had taken to carrying all the cash he had in his pocket. As soon as he had a thousand dollars, he would go to the bank and turn it in for hundred-dollar bills. It felt like the right thing to do, and it soothed him to have money in his pocket.

He inhaled his cigar and set the cigar down across his glass without tapping off the ash.

Little George stared at Trip's cigar. "Are you going to tip that ash, or am I going to have to?"

"Little George, you just can't stand it if you're not in charge." The ash had grown another half an inch. "And you are not in charge of my cigar."

"All you care about is that damn duck woods," Little George said.

J.D. stared at the ash. "We need to make a payment."

"I'm not the one who sunk the barge business."

"Neither am I. The one who sunk it killed himself," Little George said.

"Hush about that," Trip said. The cigars had clouded up the room with a hazy smog. Trip's eyes began to water but he refused to squash out his cigar.

"It doesn't matter how we got here. It matters what we do," J.D. said.

"It matters as long as it's what you want." Trip stuck the cigar back in his mouth. Little George and J.D. stared at the ash, which still refused to fall off the end of Trip's cigar.

"Will you get rid of that damn ash?" Little George said.

"Not as long as it bothers you."

* * *

Trip and Cash stepped into the quiet of the night. Clouds covered half the sky like a blanket pulled halfway over a bed. The other half sparkled at him. The leading edge of the clouds rolled over star after star, like the blanket being pulled up higher and higher. There was only the slightest breath of wind, but something was afoot. "Cash, maybe it will move more ducks down."

The two of them set off down the driveway. The gravel crunched under Trip's feet. Just past the shop, they climbed up on the levee. Trip felt the wet from the flooded rice fields on either side of him. He smelled the rotting stubble. He heard Cash splashing off to his left. There were no other sounds. Trip walked the levees and thought about Big George. He didn't think of him as his father. He thought of his Big George. It was his grandfather Archie who had taught him what he cared about: dogs, duck hunting, shooting, and calling. J.D. taught him how to throw a curve ball. Tully had taught him to fish for crappie. Neither Big George nor Celia got after him. They were worn out after the other two. Big George had been present in his life, but he couldn't quite say how.

Then it wasn't quiet anymore. His ears rang. The ringing was always worse when it was quiet. He took a joint from his pack of cigarettes and lit it.

He walked the levees, north and south, east and west. He found himself at Hangman's Blind, where his great-grandfather had let the cypress grow next to the levee. He saw the outline of Hangman's Blind, the blind where Big George—no not Big George, his father—where his father had killed himself. No, taken his life. It wasn't a euphemism. He had taken his life. That's what he had done. There had been an empty fifth of Maker's Mark. But the cap had been screwed on and set on the shelf in the blind. Big George had taken his own life thoughtfully. The pearl handle on the Colt had been rubbed down to the steel, rubbed down where his thumb rested on the grip. How long, how many hours had it taken?

Trip heard a splash, then wingbeats, hundreds of wingbeats, as Cash flushed roosting ducks. "God damn it, Cash," he said. "Get back here. That's not good for business." Trip heard the ducks swirl over his head, wings lifting them to another square in the tic-tac-toe levees.

He hadn't been here since his father had died. He opened the door, stepped in with one foot, then stepped out and shut the door.

"Come in here," said a voice.

Trip jumped.

"Come in here, Trip."

It was Celia.

"Mama, what in God's name are you doing in there?"

"Come on in here."

"I don't think I want to."

"You did a minute ago."

"I changed my mind."

"Come in here."

Trip stepped in.

"Don't sit on me. I'm right here," Celia said. "Sit over there."

Trip sat on the bench and leaned against the wall.

"Here," she said, passing him what he knew would be a flask of whiskey.

Trip took a pull from the flask and passed it back to her. "You don't have the Colt, do you?"

"No, baby. I surely don't."

Trip heard her drink from the flask. "Were you looking for me?"

"No, Mama."

Cash pawed at the door. Trip let him in. He shook off on Celia.

"Damn it, Cash." She drank from the flask again. "Can you feel him in here?"

"No. Can you?"

"No. I was hoping you could."

Cash jumped up between them. He looked through the opening in the blind.

"What's he looking at?" Celia said.

"There's ducks out in the stubble."

"You think he can see them? I can't even see you."

"He smells them."

"You think he can smell Big George?"

"He can smell the blood."

"Why are you all the way out here?"

"I just ended up here."

"I came on purpose. To see if I could feel him. But I can't." She drank more of the whiskey.

"Do you miss him, Mama?"

"When I'm not mad at him."

Trip felt Cash slide toward his mother, knew that she was scratching him behind his ear.

"Trip?"

"Yes, Mama."

"Do you have the money on you?"

"Yes, Mama." He reached into the pocket of his jeans. Who was it that he didn't trust? Little George, J.D., Jake, Mama, Jude, Parker? All of them?

He unfolded the money and fanned it out like a peacock. He peeled off ten bills and handed them to his mother. "Is this for the barge company?"

"In a way." Celia passed him the flask.

* * *

Trip and Cash walked back to the yellow house. Parker was in bed, but she was wide-awake. "Baby, where have you been?"

"On the levees."

"Did you find Mama in the blind?"

"How did you know?"

"How much did you give her?"

"Not too much," Trip said, lying again. He stripped out of his shirt, then his jeans.

"You brush your teeth before you come to bed. The cigarettes are bad enough, but I can't abide a cigar."

"Yes, ma'am."

"We don't have too much to give her, do we?"

"No, we don't." Trip didn't know if this was a lie or not. He thought it depended on how you looked at it. Trip wondered if Parker knew exactly how much was "not much." However much "not much" was, he had less than he started with. Whatever he was doing, he was getting in deeper and deeper, with less and less to show for it. No one here knew what he was up to with the New Orleans gangsters except Cash, and Cash wasn't telling, at least not yet. And there was Jake and the missing ducks, not to mention the missing money, but Jake was the least of it.

"Come to bed, baby." Parker threw back the comforter. "Lay right next to me. I miss you." Trip lay down next to her. "You are chilled. Come a little closer and I'll warm you right up." Trip closed his eyes and felt the day drift out of him. Parker rubbed his chest.

"Why, Mr. McClure, if you don't have the nicest muscles I have ever touched." Her hand slipped down to his belly, then lower. "Baby, what's wrong?"

"Tired," he said.

"You've never been tired like this before."

"I never had a duck club before."

"We aren't ever going to make any McClures this way."

"We will, baby. Just not tonight." Trip put his hand on hers.

* * *

Little George tracked down Trip and Cash at ten o'clock the next morning. Trip had gone out of his way to hide from his family and had taken refuge in the decoy shed. Little George found him at the workbench painting decoys.

The cold came in ahead of Little George. The temperature hadn't made it past forty. The cold always reminded him of Jude who always said forty wasn't cold in Michigan. Trip always said he wasn't a Yankee, and he wasn't in Michigan.

I wish I was in the cold with Jude instead of Little George.

"You have the money?" Little George said.

"Shut the door."

"I'm not staying."

"I am," Trip said.

Trip set down the paintbrush the size of a pencil and swung his right forearm to the door. "Cash, door." Cash got up off the floor and pushed the door closed with his nose. "Thank you." The dog lay back down on the floor.

"Little George. I have got to get these decoys ready for the rice fields."

"The woods aren't shot up yet."

"They will be. That and the clouds."

"You have some pile of decoys in here."

Trip had two dozen bags full of decoys, mostly mallards, but some pintail, gadwall, widgeon, and teal. Not to mention the coots. They were in olive mesh bags stacked floor to ceiling.

"I'm here for the money."

Trip dipped his brush in the sky blue and painted the speculum on a hen mallard.

"I gave it to Mama last night."

"Mama left already."

"Then you best track her down."

Trip set the hen mallard down and picked up a drake.

Little George yanked open the door and took off. The Yankee cold blew back in.

Trip looked down at Cash who looked back up at him. He knew full well what Trip wanted but he didn't get up.

"I'll get it." Trip set the brush down and kicked the door shut.

* * *

A would-be hunter showed up at the Club House the Tuesday after Thanksgiving at about 10:30 in the morning.

"Trip McClure?"

"I am."

"I'm here for my duck hunt."

"It's too late."

"No one told me."

"I'm telling you," Trip said.

"I booked this hunt for today, and I want to go now. I just paid the lady cash, and she sent me over here."

He didn't look like much of a hunter. He looked like he was about fifty—the wrong side of fifty. He was round, bald, and had a nose like an eggplant. What made him stand out, though, were his hands. He had big hands, hands like baseball mitts.

I know him from somewhere.

"It's too late to shoot anything."

"I'm here for a duck hunt. The lady said Tuesday morning, and it's Tuesday morning."

"Duck hunting starts about five."

"In the morning?"

"Yes."

"Five only comes once a day."

This guy was well on his way to annoying Trip. "You have a name?"

"Bruno. Louis Bruno."

Bruno's hand swallowed Trip's when they shook hands.

"Lou, I'm Trip."

"We already met. And it's Louis, not Lou."

"Louis, I can't promise you anything, but get your gear and let's go." Trip couldn't quite place him, and he didn't feel good about it.

"This is my gear."

Trip lit a cigarette.

I remember who he is.

"What are we waiting for?" Bruno said.

Louis Bruno had on a blue striped shirt, tan slacks, and loafers.

"You can't go like that."

"Why not?

"The ducks will see you."

"I don't care if they see me."

I give up.

"Come with me." He took Bruno into the wader room, found him waders, a coat, hat, and a shotgun.

"I've got a gun." Bruno fished a nine-millimeter Smith & Wesson from his pocket. The gun disappeared in his hand and made it look like a toy.

"What's that for?"

"That's how I'm going to kill my duck."

An hour later the two of them plus Cash sat in the fog at Mama's Blind. He didn't think any self-respecting duck would fly in the timber in this fog. They should have been hunting the rice, but he was damned if he'd shoot up a rice field for this clown. There was still shooting on the Bayou Meto side of the levee, but it was off and on, like the tail end of popcorn in a microwave. Trip threw out his lucky seven decoys.

Louis did not camouflage well. He refused to wear a hat, and he insisted on looking straight up whenever he heard a sound, any sound. They sat in the blind because Bruno refused to get into the water.

This is going to be some hunt.

"Where's all the ducks?" Bruno said.

"It's too late."

"What do you mean, too late?"

"The ducks have come and gone."

"I don't even get up until now."

"That's why you don't kill ducks."

They sat. And sat. And sat. Bruno fell asleep. Every now and then he snored. The fog collected on his head.

"This is some kind of fucked up duck hunt," Trip said to Cash.

Then it happened. Trip couldn't believe his eyes. Three ducks circled the hole just above the trees. "Here we go, Cash," Trip called softly.

"What's that awful sound?"

"Quiet," Trip said.

"I was sleeping."

Trip whispered, "This is what you came for." One of the ducks, a drake, made a tighter circle and peered down at them.

"Will you look at that."

"Shut up, Louis. And don't look up."

"Don't tell me to shut up," Bruno said, not whispering.

"If he sees your face, he'll spook."

"How can I shoot him if I can't look at him?"

"Keep your head down and peek every now and then."

"What's that thing you're blowing?"

"It's a duck call."

"What are those things on the string?"

"Those are duck bands, and it's not a string, it's a lanyard."

"What are duck bands?"

"They're on the leg of a banded duck." Trip blew the call again, softly now.

"Are they rare?"

"Very." Trip called ever so sweetly.

"I want one."

"It could take you a hundred hunts to get one."

"What if I just buy one of yours."

The duck dropped into the canopy. Trip purred at him. "Get ready, Louis."

The duck gave it up, cupped his wings and fluttered into the decoys.

The shotgun that replaced the pistol boomed. It rang Trip's ears. "God damn it, Louis." Trip covered his ears and ducked.

"It's getting away. It's getting away."

Trip sat up and killed the duck as it flew out of the timber. "Fetch, Cash." The dog leapt in.

"That was my duck," Bruno said. "You killed my duck."

"I just finished it," Trip said, lying one more time. "You hit it hard. I just finished it off for you."

"Yeah, I guess that's right. I did hit it, didn't I?" Bruno beamed and showed a mouthful of yellow teeth. "That noise you made. That tricked them."

Trip ignored the woeful hunter. He looked in the hole and surveyed the damage. His new best friend had missed the mallard, but he'd shot up the decoys. He'd managed to hit all seven, which were in various stages of sinking.

"Hey, what's wrong with those plastic ducks?"

"They're sinking."

"How come?"

"You shot them."

"That's how you hunt."

"Not exactly."

"Here's that dog. He's got my duck."

"He's a retriever."

"Isn't that something." Louis took hold of the duck. Cash growled at him. "He won't give me my duck."

"Cash, give." The dog opened his jaws. Trip handed the duck to Bruno. He squeezed the dead duck around the neck. Trip thought it a shame that a bird so beautiful would be in the big hands of a man like Louis Bruno.

"I'm going to eat this duck and then stuff it."

"You didn't come to hunt, did you?"

"Sure I did," Bruno said.

Trip scratched Cash behind his left ear. "From New Orleans."

"I'm from Metairie. We met at the Paison."

"Did you come for the money?"

"I came for the weed."

"Let's go," Trip said.

"Where's the weed?"

"Who sent you?"

"My cousin Carlo, the guy who gave you the twenty large. I'm like that dog. I'm here to fetch weed."

"I'll give you your money back." Trip didn't have all of it, but he thought his prospects were good.

"Carlo doesn't want his money back. He wants the weed."

"It's not quite ready."

"Why not?"

"It's still drying."

"You're lying."

"It'll be ready soon."

"I'm supposed to bring it back with me."

"I'll have it for you."

"When?"

"Soon."

"How soon?"

"Soon."

"I'll just take this dog with me. When you bring the weed, you get him back."

"No."

Louis Bruno was done playing the fool. "You want to keep this dog? I can see that. All right then." Bruno reached in the pocket of his borrowed duck coat and pulled out a stiletto. "You bring me the weed." Bruno patted Cash and scratched him behind the ears. Then he sliced Cash's left ear. "Keep the dog."

Trip held Cash while the cut bled out.

"If you ever touch my dog again, I'll kill you."

CHAPTER FIFTEEN

While the fog dripped on Trip and Louis Bruno, Celia and her Benz motored toward Little Rock. She fell asleep just past Coy. The Benz ran off the road, just as it had done on New Year's Eve with Big George. The crunch of the gravel woke her up. She skidded to a stop on the shoulder. She got out of the car and put on her ankle-length mink coat. She admired herself in the rearview mirror, got back in, and drove the rest of the way with the windows open. The fog blew on her face. Her mascara ran like it had in the blind the night before, but the cold, wet air kept her awake. "I'll touch it up when I get there," she said out loud.

At England, she turned north. The road followed the Arkansas River, more or less. The oxbows and cane breaks, sloughs and bayous kept the road a good distance from the river, but Celia could feel it just the same. "I wonder if any McClure tugs are up this way," she said. "I wonder how long there will be McClure tugs."

At Scott, Celia turned toward the river. She wheeled into the parking lot of Cothan's and bounced through the potholes until the Benz came to a stop as close to the door as she could possibly get. She looked in the rearview mirror. "I'm a fright." She fixed her face as best she could. She took the flask out of her purse, put it back in, took it back out and drank from it.

Cothan's was built over Old River Lake, an oxbow of the Arkansas River. Cothan's started out at ground level where the patrons entered, but then ran out on pilings over a bank that dropped to the bayou, each set of pilings taller and taller. The end of the building stood on thirty-foot pilings in three feet of water. The pilings gave the building the look of a millipede stretching its legs.

Celia always marveled at the sign above the door, "Where the Elite Meet." Why this place had the favor of prominent Little Rockians was beyond her. The plank floor was warped front to back and side to side and had a better than even chance to trip the unwary. The tables and chairs looked like they had come from as many garage sales as there were place settings. Still, the windows let in light, and even in the fog there was a good view of the water.

Cullen Dubose looked up at her from a platter of frog legs and hush puppies. "You're late, Mrs. McClure," he said, with a mouthful of frog.

"You started without me."

"Want one?" He passed her the platter.

"How can you eat those?"

"They were just gigged last night. Fresh and fried. Must be from Louisiana."

"They'll make me ill."

"Drink too much again, did you?"

"No."

He looks like a greasy fox.

"You bring it?"

"I did."

"Must of took a lot of foxes to make a coat like that. Foxes like frog legs."

"It's mink."

"Better yet. You sure you don't want one?"

"Quite."

"Suit yourself." The greasy man splashed Frank's Hot Sauce on the frog legs. "This place is famous for the hubcap burger. Huge thing," he said. "But there's nothing I like better than fresh, fried frog legs with hush puppies, hot sauce, and ketchup."

"That's very interesting."

"That and ten thousand dollars."

"This is the last of it." Celia handed him an envelope. She thought she might be ill, but she didn't know if it was from the Maker's Mark, the frog legs, or handing this greasy fox of a man ten thousand dollars. "I am leaving now."

"Stay a minute. You sure you don't want one? No? How about a drink. You look like you could use one. Hands shaking like that."

"I'm cold."

"You been crying?"

"Most certainly not." Celia dabbed at the corners of her eyes with a napkin. "I won't see you again."

Dubose dipped a hush puppy in a pool of ketchup. He popped it in his mouth and shoved it into his cheek like a jawbreaker.

"I said, I won't see you again."

Dubose chewed on the hush puppy. "Excuse me, but I don't like to talk with my mouth full. You never know what might happen." He pawed through the platter and picked out the smallest frog leg. "These ones are the most tender." He chewed the meat off the bone and smiled at Celia with another mouthful of frog.

CHAPTER SIXTEEN

Trip took Cash straight to the vet who stitched up his ear, which was healing nicely. There hadn't been a word between Trip and Bruno on the way back. Bruno left without paying. Trip didn't want to ever see him again, but he knew he wasn't going to be that lucky, especially since he didn't have any weed.

Now, three days later, Trip sat on the stool in front of the workbench in the decoy shed. Cash napped on the cast-off couch from the yellow house.

He dipped his paintbrush in the sky-blue paint and touched up the speculum on a hen. He'd need all the decoys he had to hunt the rice. He had another four dozen to go.

There was a drake pintail on the corner of the workbench. It had a long, pointed tail that gave it its name. This particular pintail had a sealed, plain white envelope speared through its tail. It had been there for the last two days, but Trip was damned if he was going to open it.

He hadn't figured out what to do about Louis Bruno and company, but it was pretty clear that they had a hold of him and weren't about to let go. It looked like all sales were final, not that Trip had the twenty thousand less the vig. He needed money on all fronts, and he was flat out of it. "Cash," he said, "I feel like a robin with five chicks and one worm." He dipped the brush in the paint again and finished up with the blue paint. "If I can keep all the plates spinning until the end of duck season, we just might come out on the other side."

He put the lid on the paint and cleaned his brush. He reached for the envelope, thought better of it, and stood up. "Let's go, Cash."

* * *

Trip and Cash cruised the streets of Stuttgart. He was looking for Jake, who was never easy to find because he hardly ever slept in his own bed. Trip, though, had experience. This wasn't the first time he needed to roust Jake from a sleepover.

After a fair amount of driving around, Trip found Jake's truck on Magnolia, parked in front of a small, white ranch house with a red door and peeling red trim. Trip thought the owner must be a Razorback fan. He knocked on the front door, then stood off to the side. This wouldn't be the first time Jake ran out the door. No answer. Trip knocked again. Still no answer. He knocked a third time.

"Keith don't live here no more," said a woman from the other side of the door.

"I'm not here about Keith," Trip said.

The door opened a crack and two eyes, one on top of the other, looked out at him. He cocked his head to the side and looked back at the vertical pair of eyes.

"What's wrong with your head?"

"Nothing," Trip said.

"Then why are you looking at me sideways?"

"I'm here for Jake."

"There's no Jake here. And there's no money for Keith's bills."

"Jake's truck is right there." Trip pointed at the black truck with the dent.

"Would you please straighten up your head, please?" She opened the door a little further and straightened out her head.

Trip untilted his head.

"That's better. Now maybe I can concentrate."

Let's hope so.

The woman looked like she was about forty. She had a turned-up nose, puffy eyes, and shoulder length blonde hair that needed brushing. She hid most of herself behind the door, but Trip could see the edges of a white bra and pink panties.

Jake is at it again.

He smiled.

"What's so funny?" the half-hidden woman asked.

"Nothing ma'am. I'm just looking for Jake."

"You're not about bills? Or Keith?"

"No ma'am."

"What's Jake done?"

"Nothing. Nothing at all."

"Then why do you want him?"

"I need to talk to him."

"Well, I'm like to freeze, standing here in my underwear. And don't tell me you haven't looked. I seen your eyes."

Trip smiled at her.

She looked back into the house. "Jake, honey. There's some guy here to see you." She turned around and walked away. Trip admired her pink bottom. She's just about seen the last of her days as a looker, Trip thought. That wouldn't matter to Jake because he never stayed for nine innings.

Jake came to the door in blue jeans, no shirt and barefoot.

"Hey, man."

"Jake."

"What's up?"

"We need to talk."

"You got a cigarette?"

Trip passed him the pack and a lighter. "You're going to run out of houses to park in front of."

"You tracked me down to tell me that?" Jake lit his cigarette.

"It only takes the wrong one to be the last one." Trip wanted to call Jake on his hijacked ducks, but he had more important business with him.

"Unless I misremembered, I'm not working for you today."

"I want to buy back the weed you sold for me."

"Buy it back?"

"Yes."

"Why's that?"

"I just want to buy it back."

Jake took a long drag on the cigarette and blew the smoke out through his nose. This is high drama, Trip thought.

"I sold it and gave you the money. Minus expenses."

"I want it back."

"How much?"

Now we're getting somewhere, Trip thought. "I thought you said you didn't have it."

"I don't, but maybe I can get it."

"Jake, honey, come on in here," pink and white said.

"I got to go."

"You could invite me in," Trip said.

"How much?"

"Get me a price."

Pink and white appeared behind Jake and turned him toward her by one of his belt loops. He flicked the cigarette over Trip's ear and shut the door with his big toe.

* * *

There were three days to go in the first split. Then, the season would close for ten days and open back up on December 17th.

The woods were shot up, so Trip only took his hunters into the timber on the odd day. The rest of the time he hunted the flooded rice, the catfish ponds, the little reservoir, the big reservoir, and the sloughs. They hid in pit blinds, stake blinds, coffin blinds, in the weeds, in camouflaged boats. They put out a hundred decoys or maybe a dozen. Trip and the guides called them in and the sports killed them.

Trip hadn't heard from Little George, Theo, Louis, or Jake. He hadn't seen Jake since that day with pink and white. Church and Big John were enough right now. Cad kept turning calls in Clarendon.

Jake will show up when he runs out of money.

Trip, Cash, and his three hunters hid in Archie's Pit, the first pit blind built by Trip's grandfather and the first pit blind ever built in the middle of a rice field. Archie had dug the blind by hand, poured concrete walls and a concrete floor in the middle of field number three. He'd built a steel roll-top that slid east to west.

Archie was the laughingstock of the Grand Prairie for ruining a perfectly good piece of rice ground, but the ducks wanted to land in the middle of the field, away from the levees where the hunters hid. Sitting in a blind in the middle of a field didn't seem like a big idea to Trip, but it was in Archie's time. Most farmers still wouldn't give up good rice for a duck blind.

The blind was half buried in the Arkansas clay. The walls rose just high enough to keep the water out when they flooded the rice during the growing season. Weeds had grown up over the dirt, which sloped up to the concrete wall. The steel roof had been camouflaged with rice stalks, and a hole in the middle of the roof where they could watch for ducks.

Trip was with three sports from Louisville. In the fog. They weren't bad guys. It was just that Trip didn't want to share Belle Oak with strangers.

I have to share it to keep it.

So here they sat. In the fog. The air wet and still. Trip smelled the rotting rice stubble, gun oil, wet dog, and tobacco.

Good smells.

Hunting the rice in fog almost always worked. The hunters couldn't see the ducks, but the ducks couldn't see the hunters. They had to fly low to the ground, and they were easy to decoy into the shadowy spreads. If you called softly, they'd come right in.

"I can't see a thing," said the sport with the mustache.

"Neither can I," said the one on the end with a shiny round face.

"There's nothing to see anyway," said the third, the one who looked like he'd been swallowed up by his waders. "There's no birds flying."

Trip quacked softly, waited, quacked again. Still nothing. Then a noise—not a quack but the low thrum of a drake.

"Hear that?" said the one swallowed up by his waders.

"I sure did," said the mustache.

"Shut up," said the round-faced man.

Trip quacked again. Softer still. The duck quacked again, overhead this time, then nothing.

"Where'd he go?" said the one in the waders.

"Here he comes," Trip said. "Let him land."

"Let's shoot this one," said the mustache.

"There's more on the way," Trip said. The drake stuck out his orange legs and splashed into the decoys.

Quacking and clucking overhead. Invisible ducks all around them. The lone drake on the water preened, not a bit worried about the plastic ducks around him. Trip clucked at the ducks. There was quacking all around them, but they couldn't see the ducks. Cash's leg shook.

Suddenly, from the other end of the blind, a noise that could only be described as the dying sounds of a mule. It was worse than that because it echoed off the steel roof. Again and again. The drake exploded into the sky.

"What the hell was that?" said the one in waders.

"I am calling them in," said the round-faced hunter.

"The hell you are," said the mustache.

Trip, his call just off his lips, stared into the fog. "A duck call in the wrong hands is the greatest conservation tool ever invented."

The hunter in the oversized waders yanked the call from the round-faced hunter and threw it into the flooded rice. A hen mallard heard the splash and splashed down herself.

They had limits by ten. Trip led them out through the flooded rice. The round-faced hunter fell in and filled up his waders.

* * *

When the first split was over, Trip told Church and Big John to pick up the decoys and pile them back in the decoy shed. Church protested, it being the custom on the Grand Prairie to let a decoy, once set, sit for the entire season, whether or not it sank from being shot, frozen into the ice, or simply tipped over.

Trip needed the money, and he wasn't going to take any chances with decoy-shy ducks. "In they come," he said. Trip couldn't see how Big John could hear him over Skynyrd, but the big man set to picking up decoys. Church heard him and complained again.

Trip sat at the workbench patching holes in leaky decoys with superglue, a fair amount of which was stuck on his fingers. The pintail with the envelope poked through its tail still on the corner of the workbench.

Church came in with a bag of decoys. "Mr. Trip, I just do not see the sense in bringing in these decoys."

"I know you don't."

Church went out and came back in with another bag of decoys. He stopped at the workbench. "Mr. Trip, this envelope through the tail has got me. What does it say inside?"

"I don't know."

"Haven't you read it?"

"No."

"Why not?" He flung the decoy bag over to the wall.

"Careful, Church."

"Don't you want to know?"

"No." He set the glue down and looked at the skewered envelope. He did want to know what was in it, but he was damned if he'd read it. Not the way it was delivered.

"What if it's something good?"

"The news will find me soon enough." He drummed his fingers on the workbench.

"What if it's something bad?"

"If it's bad, it will find me sooner." He stopped drumming, then started again.

What if it is bad?

"Respectfully, Mr. Trip, what with all that I believe to be happening around here, you might be wise to open that envelope before a fire starts that no one can put out. And I notice from your finger tapping that you are giving that possibility some consideration."

Trip stopped the drumming. He started up again, then he stopped. He touched his fingers together. They stuck.

* * *

On a crystal-clear day, a week after the end of the first split, Trip walked up to the courthouse steps and posted bail. He took his receipt and walked down to the basement. Jake was sitting in a cell looking down at his feet.

"What was it this time?"

"Nothing much."

"It must be something much to cost me five thousand dollars."

"That's not even a day's worth of hunters at the duck club."

"What did you do?"

"I ran my truck a little hard."

"That's it?"

"Yes, sir."

"Where'd you run it?"

"Into Lorna's living room."

"You mean pink and white?" Trip said. "Into her living room?"

Jake looked up and smiled his puppy dog smile. He had a black eye.

"Got the whole cab through the picture window."

"Why'd you do that?"

"We weren't getting along all that well, so I left for a few days. To find your weed."

Trip looked at him sideways.

"While I was looking for the guy I sold the weed to, I ran into Carla at the Gator. We were havin' a few and Lorna walks in. You can guess what happened next."

Trip nodded.

"Just as those two girls are starting to fight, in pops the guy I need to see about the weed."

"Jake, we're in a courthouse."

"Oh, yeah." Jake started to whisper but it was louder than he had been talking. Trip stepped up next to him.

"Quiet, Jake."

"I am already whispering. Thanks for getting me out, Mr. Trip. I can work it off guiding."

If this keeps up, it'll take him three duck seasons to work it off.

"What about the weed?"

"Lorna gets mad at me 'cause I am not paying attention to the lickin' she is giving Carla. She knows I love a good catfight. She's really pissed off at me and throws a beer in my face. Then she hits me in the eye with the glass."

"That explains the black eye."

"What's that?"

"Nothing."

"Lorna runs out the door. I meant to go after her, but I have some business to transact. I get a price for the weed. Then I go after her. She has a little Red Rodeo that gets going pretty good. She won't let me in and damned if that red door won't kick in. So I get in my truck and enter through the living room. That's why I'm here. That and the wrecked furniture at the Gator."

"You got in through the living room?"

"I got the cab all the way inside."

"That's what you said."

"Right through the picture window."

Trip couldn't believe what he was hearing, but then this was Jake. "What about the weed?"

Jake stood, put his hands in his pockets. "The price has gone up considerable since I sold it for you."

"How much?"

"Well, Mr. Trip, it must be pretty good weed." Jake rubbed his black eye.

"How much?"

"Eleven."

"Hundred?" Trip said, relieved.

"Thousand."

Trip fished Jake's get-out-of-jail free card from his pocket and ripped it down the middle. The two pieces of paper drifted to the floor.

* * *

Trip and Jude squared off in opposite corners of the decoy shed. The rain tapped on the roof like so many woodpeckers, which meant that Jude must have really wanted to see him.

"This is a popular place," Trip said. "I should sell memberships."

"At the rate you're going, you won't have anything left to sell."

After the first split, Trip had started to the decoy shed right after breakfast. Everyone knew where he was, but they mostly stayed out of his way. Except this morning.

Jude had come in and walked over to the workbench. He shook the rain off his hat, a Detroit Tigers hat—the away hat—midnight blue with an Old English orange "D." Water ran off his shoulders, down his parka, and puddled around him on the plank floor, outlining him in a wet ring.

He pulled the envelope off the pintail, opened it up, and read the letter.

Trip lit a cigarette. The smoke sank to the floor.

A raindrop ran down Jude's ear. It hung on his earlobe like an earring, then fell to the floor. There was an awkwardness between them, but the truth was, he was glad Jude had come back. Trip looked down at his feet. He scuffed the floor with his boot.

"So, Trip," Jude said.

Trip looked up at his friend.

"What's the plan after you lose Belle Oak?"

"I'm not losing Belle Oak."

Jude skewered the letter on the decoy and tossed it at him. "What about this?"

"What about it?" Trip dropped the decoy on the pile behind him.

"Did you read it?"

"No."

"Trip, you're a fool putting on a show, and everybody knows it's a show."

"I'm not putting on a show."

I might be a fool.

"Pretending it's all right when it's not."

Trip looked down at his boots again.

"If you're not pretending, then you're a bigger fool than I thought."

Trip looked over at Jude. "I'm just trying to make money with a duck club. So I can keep the farm."

"You're sure going about it in a half-assed way."

Trip replied with his classic reply, which was not to reply.

"Whatever is going on, you need some help."

"I can manage."

"You couldn't manage a train wreck."

Trip crushed out his cigarette under his boot and lit another one.

"Every time you get worked up, you light a cigarette. Did you know that?"

Right now, that's most of the time.

"Those things are going to kill you."

"At the rate I'm going, I expect something else will get me first." Trip took a drag on the cigarette.

I'd rather be smoking a joint.

"Did you read the letter?"

Trip shook his head.

"You're acting like an ostrich, except that you've got your head up your ass."

The only time he was ever this pissed off was when he kicked me out of my truck.

"It's from Planter's Bank. To George H. McClure, Jr., President, McClure Tug and Tow."

Trip dropped the second cigarette into a coffee can.

"Do you know what it says?"

"I can guess," Trip said.

"It says that the company defaulted on its loan, and the bank is executing on its collateral. You know what that means?"

Trip nodded.

"There's more." Jude wiped off his face again. "It says that the bank foreclosed on the farm. There's been a sheriff's sale, which means the bank has bid in its loan. That's why Little George put the farm up for sale." Jude reread the letter. "This letter is dated August 15th."

"He had the letter before the dove hunt," Trip said. "He never told me the bank was foreclosing on the farm."

"There's a six-month redemption period in Arkansas. If you don't pay off the bank by February 15th, you lose the farm." Jude folded it into a paper airplane. He flew the paper airplane of foreclosure over Trip. It sailed gently in the wet air.

* * *

The second split started up the third week of December and ran through New Year's Day, except Christmas. Even diehard duck hunters had to rest their shotguns for one day.

The great migration hadn't really come on yet, but there were ducks around. Not a lot, but more than enough to shoot at.

Jake showed up the first day of the second split. It was clear and cold. He didn't say anything about the busted bail, and Trip didn't say anything about the extortion rate price for the marijuana or the missing ducks.

I've got to figure out how to get the weed for DeMarco without Jake. Church can take the ducks to Lucky.

He sent Jake, Big John, and Church into the timber. By the fourth day, the Belle Oak woods were shot up, so he switched to the rice fields and the catfish ponds, which held up for another three days.

Then he had Big John pull the boats over the levee at Mama's Blind, and they ferried the hunters into the Bayou Meto WMA. This was strictly illegal. Hunters had to register at an access point. Guides and guided hunts were prohibited, but Trip had a business to run, and he didn't think Game and Fish was smart enough or enterprising enough to find them. He figured that if they heard the shooting, they'd assume it came from the Belle Oak side of the levee.

Trip had hunted in Bayou Meto his whole life. He knew the holes, the holes that had names that only the old boys knew. Holes that few could get to and fewer still could find. Heaven's Gate, Mr. Jim's, Indian Mound, and the Beaverkill. The ducks dropped into the Heaven's Gate, Mr. Jim's, and Indian Mound, but they swarmed into the Beaverkill.

Trip ran tape lines, orange, fluorescent tape through the old ditch that ran to Bayou Meto, and then a tape line to every hole, except the Beaverkill.

After the guides took the sports to their holes, Trip took out his compass and ran the heading to the Beaverkill.

Cad might be able to find his way without tape, but he was the only one.

About halfway to the hole, he passed Snake Island, a tiny hummock not much bigger than a living room. Snake Island was a high spot that never flooded, favored by snakes on warm winter days. They slithered there by the hundreds on a sunny day and took in the heat from the sun that gave them life. Trip shuddered every time he passed by.

* * *

The Beaverkill was the first hole his grandfather had taken him to, and Trip never shared it with anyone. He was eight when his grandfather took him on the levees for the first time. He had to wait until he was ten to go into the timber.

They'd gone into the woods on the first day of the second split. It was a cold, clear December morning, skim ice in the woods. Archie knew the way in without the tape.

He'd dropped Trip off on a fallen white oak. Trip sat there in his first pair of waders and his first shotgun, a twenty-gauge 870 pump. Lucy, his grandfather's dog, sat next to him. His grandfather stood in the water against a tree.

The ducks swirled over the hole. His grandfather called them down and landed them in the hole. They shot ducks until Trip fell off the log and filled up his waders.

"Damn it all, Trip." He lit a cigarette and watched his grandson. Trip splashed around and finally climbed back on the log. He was soaked from head to foot, but he kept his gun dry.

Archie finished his cigarette. "I guess we better go."

Trip shook his head "no." They finished the hunt, and Trip was hooked on flooded timber.

* * *

Trip and Cash drifted into the Beaverkill. He sat Cash on the log he'd fallen off when he was ten. Trip stood in the shadow of the white oak, just like his grandfather. Trip looked up through the trees. He called them in, and shot them. Cash retrieved them. Trip fingered the bands on his lanyard. When the ducks quit flying, Trip motored back to the ditch and waited for the guides at Mama's Blind.

CHAPTER SEVENTEEN

While Trip poached in Bayou Meto, Celia and Parker went Christmas shopping in Memphis. Celia much preferred giving cash, but in these days of foreclosure and Cullen Dubose, check writing was definitely out.

I'm going to buy geegaws this year.

The two of them met downtown on a sunny day turned gray. They shopped in what was left of downtown Memphis, then drove over to the Peabody for a late lunch and drinks.

From the outside, the Peabody Hotel had very little going for it. It was a square, ten-story brick building that covered the better part of a city block and was pocked with little square windows.

Inside was a different story altogether. The Peabody had a massive lobby with thirty-foot ceilings, marble columns, oak paneling, a mezzanine with iron railings, and in the center, a marble fountain the size of a swimming pool.

Celia and Parker walked past the fountain to the Capriccio Grill in the corner. They had a most elegant lunch beneath the Tuscan murals. The Peabody was the only charge account Celia had left. The Peabody billed by the tenth of each month, which she promptly did not pay. This had been going on for the past year.

I wonder how long it's going to last.

After lunch, they moved to a bar in another corner of the lobby. Celia admired Parker's thin dark eyebrows and her black shiny hair framing the creamiest skin she had ever seen.

She's a beauty, but out of place at Belle Oak.

Celia thought it would take a baby or two to keep Parker at Belle Oak, but after nine years of marriage, there were no babies, and Parker was still at Belle Oak.

She nodded at Oswald, the bartender. He was a relic of the Peabody, a tubby man with a fringe of hair, once blond, now white. He not only knew Celia by name but knew just what she wanted. He brought it right over.

Celia had switched to her winter drink, a Maker's Mark Manhattan with a splash of bitters, a teaspoon of Maraschino cherry juice, and two cherries. She was on her third when the trouble started.

"Celia."

"Yes, dear."

"It's about the money."

"What money, dear?"

Parker wore a belted, white cashmere coat over a wine turtleneck and blue jeans tucked into knee-high black boots. Celia thought she looked like Snow White, but she was afraid this was headed in a very un-Snow White direction. She wrapped her fur around her shoulders.

"The money Trip gave you."

Just as Celia was about to say "what money" again, she was saved.

Without warning, the lobby stirred with the tinny, prerecorded strains of a march, not just any march, but a John Philip Sousa march.

"What on earth is that?" Parker said.

Thank God.

Celia gulped her Manhattan. She waved her hand at Oswald. "Build me another." To Parker, "That, my dear, is the 'King Cotton March'."

Before Parker could say another word, a man in a bright red waistcoat appeared. He carried some kind of scepter, as if he were leading some kind of invisible band. With pomp and circumstance not warranted by the circumstance, he marched to the white marble fountain. A crowd crowded around him.

"What is going on?"

The man dressed like a drum major blew his whistle. Half a dozen mallards jumped out of the fountain. He blew it again and they followed him to the elevator.

"Oh my God. What's going on?"

"Those are the Peabody ducks," Celia said. "They live in a penthouse on the roof. Every day at 11 in the morning, Jason marches them to the fountain and every day at 5 p.m. he marches them out."

"What in god's name for?"

"They've been doing it for fifty years. One night some of the boys, including Archie McClure, got back from an Arkansas duck hunt a bit late and a bit drunk. They came in here for a nightcap and dumped their call ducks in the fountain. And left them."

"Call ducks?"

"Used to be you could use real ducks as decoys. They'd call and decoy the wild ducks and the boys would shoot them."

"Traitors."

"I'm not sure the duck brain can think that through."

"That's awful."

"The first ones here were English call ducks. They turned out to be a big hit, and pretty soon the Peabody switched to mallards. Ducks have lived at the Peabody and swam in that fountain ever since."

Oswald appeared with Celia's fourth Manhattan. The two women watched the ducks waddle out.

"No matter where I go, I can't seem to get away from ducks," Parker said.

"That's about right." Celia sipped her Manhattan. King Cotton faded away.

"What about the money?"

"What money is that, dear?" Celia said again.

"Trip gave you ten thousand dollars. After Thanksgiving. In the blind."

The third Manhattan emboldened Celia. "I'm sure he didn't."

"He told me he did."

"He didn't give me any money." Celia fished out a cherry by the stem and licked the whiskey off it.

This isn't very ladylike.

"He told me he did," Parker said again. She held on to the edge of the table with both hands.

"Lord knows, dear. I could surely use ten thousand dollars. What with Big George being gone." Celia cocked her head slightly, pursed her lips and sucked the cherry into her mouth. She bit off the stem, dropped it in the ashtray, and chewed the cherry.

CHAPTER EIGHTEEN

Trip and Cash were set up at Mama's Blind. Just the two of them, three decoys, thirty thousand acres of timber behind them, and Belle Oak's flooded timber in front of them. No ducks. No shooting. But then again, it was cloudy and warm.

Not that he cared much about the duckless state of affairs. He had his own affairs to worry about, and he was out here trying to figure it out. He lit another cigarette and watched the smoke rise straight up. He jangled the duck bands strung on his lanyard.

I love these bands.

Trip worried about his future. Cash watched for ducks, ever vigilant.

After who knew how long, Trip heard an outboard. One of Belle Oak's johnboats poked out of the woods. Trip saw the outboard pop up when the shaft bounced on a sunken log. There were two men in the boat. No dog.

The boat nosed into the far side of Mama's Blind, Jake in the stern. The omnipresent cigarette hung out of his mouth like a bass plug from a hooked largemouth. Whoever sat in the bow had his back to Trip. Jake cut the engine and the johnboat coasted across the hole to the blind. The man in the bow became a hooded roundish shape in a parka and waders.

The johnboat drifted up to the blind.

"Good morning, Mr. Trip," Jake said.

Trip nodded at him.

The hooded man turned to him. A big, fat cigar stuck out of the side of his mouth. "Good day, Mr. McClure," Louis Bruno said.

Trip had known that his dealings with the New Orleans gangsters were far from over, but he hadn't expected Bruno to show up at Mama's Blind unannounced.

"Thanks for the taxi, son," Bruno said.

"Glad to do it, Mr. Louis," Jake said.

Those two make a fine pair.

"We were just leaving," Trip said.

"I'm here for my duck hunt," Louis Bruno said.

"You don't have a hunt booked," Trip said.

"I do now."

"We were just leaving," Trip said again. He took the lanyard from his neck, wrapped it around his calls, and slipped them in the pocket of his coat.

Bruno reached for his shotgun case.

He's upped his game.

The would-be hunter stood and stepped toward the blind. One boot on the blind, one on the boat. The bow of the boat began to slide away. The gangster, a foot in each camp, started to split in two.

This both amused and dismayed Trip, who faced the imminent prospect of rescuing a kersplashing Louis Bruno.

The bow drifted a bit more. Bruno flailed his arms. His legs split further than Trip thought possible. Bruno lost his perch on the boat and fell into the stained water.

Trip grabbed the big fingers on Bruno's big hand and yanked as hard as he could. Bruno crashed through the brushed wall of Mama's Blind and crumpled to the ground. Jake had seen enough. He started the outboard. "I'll just get back to that power unit, Mr. Trip."

Trip looked at Jake, then down at the crumpled, camouflaged gangster.

Bruno lay in a heap.

I hope he's dead.

Smoke drifted up from the fallen gangster.

He's caught himself on fire.

Trip improvised in a way that would have made Church proud. He dunked his thermos in the muddy water and poured it on Bruno. The soggy gangster sputtered and started wiggling. After four refills, the fire was out, but Trip's worst fear had been realized.

He's not dead.

Slowly, Louis Bruno untangled himself from the branches. He found his now drowned cigar and stuck it in his mouth. He stood, unzipped the right pocket of his parka, and reached in. Trip pointed the Parker at him and clicked off the safety.

The click swiveled the gangster's head. "What are you doing?"

"I'm protecting myself. And my dog."

"From what?"

"From you. Take your hand out of your pocket. Without a gun."

"Jesus, Mary, Joseph. First you try to split me in half. Then you try to burn me up. Then you try to drown me. And now you're going to shoot me."

"You are most unwelcome here."

"I can see that," Louis Bruno said, hand still in his pocket.

"If you ever touch my dog again, I'll kill you."

"I believe you would." Bruno cut a sorry figure. He was soaked from head to foot. What was left of his hair hung over his ears. A drop of water hung at the tip of his eggplant nose.

"Don't worry, Mr. McClure, my gun is in the other pocket. Put that safety back on and we'll have a little talk."

"We don't have anything to talk about."

"Oh, but we do." Without waiting for the comforting click of Trip's safety, Bruno took his hand out of his pocket. He had a Ziploc bag with five cigars, a gold lighter, and a small knife. "That wasn't so bad, was it?" He kicked the branches away and sat in one of the chairs inside what was left of Mama's Blind. He spit the ruined cigar into the water then took a fresh one from his plastic bag. He cut the end off with his knife and lit the cigar with his gold lighter.

"Put that knife back in the bag. Put the bag in your pocket and zip it up."

"Glad to do it."

Bruno smoked quietly for five minutes. Trip smoked a cigarette. He knew that "vengeance is mine saith the Lord," but he was going to make Louis Bruno pay for Cash's sliced ear.

At last, Bruno broke the silence. "I expect you're wondering why I'm here."

"No," Trip said, who was wondering mightily.

"I'm here for a duck hunt."

"You picked another bad day."

"Call them in."

Trip didn't say anything.

"I'm told you call so sweetly."

Bruno puffed on his cigar. Trip watched the smoke drift in the blind then melt away. Still not a breath of wind.

The ducks aren't going to fly today.

"I'm here to talk a little business."

He put the safety back on and leaned his shotgun against the blind.

"The twenty large you owe us," Bruno said.

Trip looked at Bruno.

"I just love you rich white boys, or used-to-be rich white boys. Protestants, you're all Protestants. You get on the ropes and you act like I'm the problem. Well, I'm not the problem. Give me the weed or you're the problem."

"I don't have it."

"When will you have it?"

"Soon," Trip said.

I have no idea if I'll ever have it.

"We made a deal."

"Things changed," Trip said.

"Not at our end." Louis Bruno rolled the cigar from one side of his mouth to the other with his tongue.

"I'll give you your money back."

"We don't want the money. We want the weed."

"I'll get it for you."

"As a matter of fact, we don't want the weed either."

Trip reached for his shotgun.

"You're not going to shoot me. We both know that."

Trip gripped his shotgun, one hand on the forearm, the other on the stock.

"You just pretend you're going to shoot me, and when you're done pretending, I'll cut your dog's balls off and stuff them in your mouth." Louis Bruno rolled the cigar in his mouth, two turns.

"Here's what we want," Bruno said. "It's good for you. Very good." He took the cigar out of his mouth and studied it. "I know that looked a bit theatrical, but I always wanted to do it. Carlo wouldn't like it, but he's not here." He put the cigar back in his mouth. "You got a nice little setup here. Way out here in this swamp."

"It's flooded timber."

Bruno ignored him. "Here's what. We have a little recipe and we want you to cook. You cook it up. We'll forget all about the weed, and we'll get you some cash. So you can save your beloved farm."

Trip scratched Cash's ears so hard that the dog yelped.

"Got your attention?"

He's definitely got my attention.

"After our last little duck hunt out here in the swamp, I got to thinking. We could use one more recipe maker, and I thought you just might fit the bill."

All in all, Bruno had Trip's attention. "I'm listening."

Bruno spoke with the cigar stuck in the corner of his mouth. "Since you're a farmer, you've got easy access to the ingredients. You may even have them on hand."

"What do you want me to cook up?"

"It's a recreational drug." Bruno curled his lips around his cigar. He slid the cigar back to the middle of his mouth. It bobbed up and down as he spoke. "It's a recreational drug," the gangster said again. "That's all it is. Just for fun."

"What kind of fun?"

"Just good clean fun."

"What is it?"

"Crystal. Just a little crystal."

"Crystal methamphetamine?"

"We just call it crystal."

"You mean meth." Trip stood. "It's time for us to go."

"You accept?"

"I do not."

"Why not?"

"I'll go get the boat." Trip stepped into the water. "Cash, come." The dog jumped in and Trip started to wade through the flooded timber, shuffling through the water, careful about the sunken logs.

"I might put some cash in with it."

Trip turned, lost his balance and sunk to his knees. Water leaked in over his waders. Cash licked his face.

* * *

It was Christmas Eve morning, two days after Louis Bruno's proposition. Trip had given the guides the day off, but they all wanted to hunt, so he said he'd take them all, plus Jude, on a guided hunt. He'd call and Cash would retrieve.

It was five-thirty in the morning. Orion, low in the sky, hadn't quite set. It was clear and cold, a sheet of skim ice in the woods. Trip could see his breath.

They dragged the boats over the levee at Mama's Blind. They ran up the ditch to the triple tape, then they cut into the timber, past Snake Island, and made for the Beaverkill.

Trip had rested the Beaverkill for two weeks. It was a mile from the nearest hole and two miles from Mama's Blind. The Beaverkill was in the middle of nowhere, even by Bayou Meto standards. He knew the ducks would use it today.

He never hunted this hole with anyone, but he decided to share it today, this one time only.

Trip dropped them off one by one in a half circle around the hole. "Just like the sports," Church said. Trip sat Cash on the fallen tree, hid the boat and waded back.

The guides acted like sports. Jake pretended to fall. Church stared up at the first flight and spooked them. Big John slept standing up. Only Cad and Jude were attentive to the matters at hand.

Twenty minutes after that first spooked flight, the ducks began to fly like they meant it. Ones and twos. Then flocks of ten, twenty, thirty. They came to Trip's call. The guides, unlike the sports, picked their shots. Drakes only. Nary a miss. Sometimes they didn't shoot and waited for Trip to land them. He landed the fifth bunch, about twenty mallards, in the middle of the hole. They swam around the hole, in and out of the decoys, ignoring the hunters and the trembling Cash. Finally, they formed a procession, just like the Peabody ducks, and swam between Trip and Jude, out of the hole and into the timber.

"Don't that beat all," Church said.

"Sure does," Jake said.

"Seen that once before," Cad said. "Just once."

And so it went. The guides dragged it out, holding off reaching their limit, standing in the water, in the timber, of the floodwaters of Bayou Meto.

Trip looked down at his lanyard. Three calls, seventeen duck bands, and seven goose bands. He knew where and when he had killed each of them and what they were. The lanyard had frayed near the call. He took out his knife, looked at Jude to his left, Cad to his right, then stepped further into the shadow of the oak. He held the lanyard in his left hand and sliced the lanyard in two. He slid the bands off the severed lanyard and zipped them into his pocket. No one saw him do it. Then he dropped the calls into the water. They splashed softly.

"Damn it," he said. No one turned to him. "Damn it," he said, louder this time.

"What happened?" Jude said.

"God damn it," he said. "My lanyard broke." He reached into the water and picked up the floating calls.

"Did your jewelry fall in?" Cad said.

"All of it."

"You lost all your duck bands?" Church said.

"Every last one."

"That's a lifetime of duck hunting," Cad said.

"I'll help you find them." Church started to wade across the hole.

"Stay right there," Trip said. "All of you. Nobody move." He unloaded his Parker. Then he drove the shotgun barrel first as hard as he could into the mud. Then he backed up.

"Just what are you doing, Mr. Trip?" Church said.

"This hole is officially closed for the rest of duck season."

"What are you up to, Mr. Trip?" Church said.

Cad shook his head. "Man's whole life just fell into the water. He'll come back when the water drains out. Find them all. As long as nobody disturbs them."

"Be March by then," Jake said.

"You can't just let them go," Cad said.

"That Parker will surely be ruined," Church said. "Must have cost at least five thousand."

"It's just a shotgun," Big John said, who had heard everything, Lynyrd Skynyrd notwithstanding.

That should keep them all out of here for the rest of the season. Even if they could find their way.

Trip climbed into his boat, started the engine, and towed the other boats back to the hole. No one moved. He picked them up one by one. He steered clear of the spiked shotgun and coasted out of the Beaverkill.

* * *

Mercifully, Arkansas Game and Fish closed duck season on Christmas Day. This charitable act saved a multitude of Arkansas marriages since the male half of Arkansas County would rather be in a duck blind than anywhere else, even on Christmas Day.

For his part, Trip couldn't help but wake up at 4:30 in the morning. He laid there for an hour, then with one foot on the floor and the other about to be on the way to the coffeepot, his one true love grabbed him by the shoulder. She kissed him on the mouth, softly at first. Trip kissed her back, the first time he had meant it since the inaugural hunt of the Belle Oak Duck Club.

They started out Christmas morning on the right foot. When they had finished, Parker kissed him one last time, then she rolled on her side and fell back asleep.

Trip lay on his back, relieved that his plumbing was working again, but disappointed. He'd wanted to talk things over with Parker, but she was sound asleep. He could hardly blame her. It was 5 a.m. and Christmas Day. With no little ones storming the Christmas tree, Parker had no reason to do anything other than sleep. It was probably best that she had fallen back to sleep. Now she wouldn't be a co-conspirator. But then again, she would have put a stop to this foolishness. Jude would have, too, but they couldn't stop what they didn't know.

Trip dressed, made his way to the kitchen, and brewed the coffee. He poured in two fingers of Maker's Mark to celebrate the day. He stepped outside at first light. Christmas Day had started out clear and cold with the weak sun of the solstice. Not as weak as the Yankee sun, but weak just the same. He lit a cigarette, then he heard them, heard them before he saw them. Just ahead of the clouds, the snows—snow geese—thousands of them, flying in V's, high in the sky, in giant flocks. He heard their brittle cackling a mile high. Down from the Arctic Circle to ravage the winter wheat.

* * *

Parker woke up for good at 8 o'clock, which was early for her. Trip brought her fresh coffee sans Maker's Mark. He was on his third pour. He cooked her breakfast, an omelet with onions, red peppers, black olives, jalapeños, and jack cheese; grits with Velveeta; biscuits; grapefruit sectioned with a paring knife; tomato juice; and more coffee.

Parker, propped up by three pillows, sat up in bed and primly received the tray Trip laid on her lap.

"Why, thank you, Trip." She picked up a pencil-sized box wrapped in blue foil with a silver bow that lay on the side of the tray. "And what might this be?"

"I surely don't know," he said. "I found it under the tree."

Parker sipped her coffee and shook the box, which rattled slightly. "What could it be?"

"Only one way to find out, baby."

Parker turned the box over twice. She held it up to the light. Shook it again. It rattled again. Finally, she unwrapped it, so carefully that she could have wrapped it back up and no one would have been the wiser.

A long, thin, white box. She turned it over and over in her hands. Finally, she opened it.

Pearls. A string of pearls. Twenty-four inches. Big pearls, with a soft, ivory luster.

"My God, Trip, they're beautiful." She hung them around her neck. "They're beautiful." Then she put them back in the box. "There's two thousand dollars' worth of pearls here," she said. "We can't afford these. Not now. Mr. McClure, you must return them."

Trip took the pearls out of the box and held them in his hand. They coiled like a snake.

I'm three thousand into these pearls.

"You know I love pearls. They're my favorite, but we just can't afford them, not now."

Trip stood beside her, draped the pearls around her neck, clasped the two ends together, the snake now a necklace.

* * *

Trip got going on his Faustian bargain after breakfast. He told Parker he needed to do some scouting. She pooh-poohed him but gave in because she knew he needed only the poorest excuse to be outside. That and the fact that she so loved her pearls she would have granted him passage for just about anything.

He towed a trailer of lumber he'd bought behind the four-wheeler to the landing, Cash running beside him. Trip loaded the lumber into two johnboats and started down the ditch, towing the other johnboat.

At Mama's Blind, he pulled one of the boats over the levee. He loaded his shotgun and set it beside him, barrel pointing out the stern. He hauled the lumber to Snake Island, the only patch of high ground for miles and snake-free in the cold. His ears rang and he felt even more anxious than he usually did. He lit a joint, sucked in the smoke, held it, blew it out. Four tokes later, he felt much better. Then he hammered together the shabbiest lean-to he could manage.

It was open on one side, the side nearest to a scraggly nuttall. He brushed the blind. Then he made two more trips. One for the stainless-steel cauldron he used for crawfish boils. The second trip out, he hauled the propane cooker and the propane tanks, squat silver tanks, the size of watermelons. When he got back to Snake Island, he deadened their shine with mud. He thought he had time for one more trip, but by the time he made it back to the shop, it was time for Christmas dinner.

He smoked another joint at the shop. Then he went back to the house for two more fingers of Maker's Mark and Parker's rare prime rib with roasted baby potatoes and green beans. She had on her new Christmas pearls and couldn't keep her hands off them. After dinner, they bid adieu to Christmas Day the same way they'd welcomed it.

CHAPTER NINETEEN

While Parker fondled her pearls between her fingers, Celia ground her diamonds between her teeth. The Christmas Day cloud cover had reached Memphis after Stuttgart, and with it, gloom descended on her.

She'd fled to Little George's den, as far away as she could get from Little George and his family and still be in the house. She sat in the oversized red leather chair favored by Big George and looked out the window.

On this, the first Christmas since the passing of Big George, Little George insisted that she spend Christmas with his family. It seemed a good idea at the time, but now she was sure she'd made a terrible mistake. She'd worn her regal purple dress and the diamond necklace Big George had given her during better times. She drove herself to Little George's house, ten blocks from her own home but much newer.

She was alone and chewing on her diamond necklace in Little George's den because of her Christmas gift to Little George. Even though she didn't have any money, she wished she'd somehow bought him a present rather than give him what he'd asked for. It seemed so simple at the time.

He had asked her not to have a drink on Christmas Day. Not one drink. That's what he'd asked for. What could have been easier.

It'll be good for me. Maybe I'll quit altogether.

She'd left her flask at home, and Little George had made it easy on her— no cocktails before Christmas dinner and no wine served with their prime rib—all the McClures served prime rib on Christmas Day. Celia had done just fine until after dinner when her grandchildren opened the gifts she'd bought them.

At first she felt a touch of nerves, just a touch, but it had grown to a full-blown panic. She'd hung on as long as she could. When her hands started shaking, she excused herself and ran off to the den.

And here she sat, chewing on her diamonds, her hands gripping the arms of the chair. This was the best she could do. There was something soothing about chewing on her diamonds. They had no taste, none whatsoever, and they absolutely did not yield to her teeth. She enjoyed their hardness, felt their cut, the bevels in each stone. Celia was still chewing when Little George peered through the French doors, then came in.

"Mama, what are you doing?"

She mumbled through a mouthful of diamonds. "I'm just resting a bit."

"What do you have in your mouth?"

She spat out the necklace. "Nothing."

"Is it Big George?"

"I miss him. Truly, I do." She looked down at her hands. The leather arms on her chair had creases where her fingernails had dug into them.

"I'm sorry, Mama."

"I am, too, Little George." Celia surely did miss him, but at the moment she missed her Maker's Mark more than her dearly departed husband. Big George would have known what to do about Cullen Debose. That awful man. He wanted more money, and she had no idea where to get it. She didn't have any more money. Little George didn't have it. Trip didn't have any more to give her. Maybe she could sell her diamonds.

"Mama, I'm sorry," Little George said again.

"I know you are."

"Thank you so much for my Christmas gift." He sat on the couch that backed up to the paned windows.

"I didn't give you anything this year."

"You haven't had a drink."

"Oh, that." She twirled the necklace between her fingers. "How do you know I haven't?"

"Because you're about to shake yourself to death."

"I'm just a little blue."

"You're about to fall right off the edge." He walked over to the liquor cabinet and poured them both two fingers of the family brand in leaded crystal. "Here," he said. "Thank you for my gift."

Celia reached for the glass and did her best not to appear desperate. She failed. Then she swirled the brown liquid and watched it slide down the glass. She sniffed at it, pressed the glass to her lips and held it there. She set it on the end table.

"Thank you, Little George, but I don't think I will just now."

"Mama, you gave me my gift. This is my gift to you."

"This will be my gift to myself." It was all she could do to stop shaking. *I wish that damn whiskey wasn't right next to me.*

Little George threw his back in one gulp. "We do have some money problems."

"We do indeed." Celia stood and got as far as she could from the whiskey.

"The foreclosure sale is in February," Little George said.

"I know it."

"This wouldn't be happening if we had the money Big George borrowed."

"Well, we don't." Celia inched toward the whiskey.

"What happened to it?"

She inched closer.

"You know, don't you?" Little George poured himself two more fingers.

"If I did, what difference would it make?"

"What happened, Mama?"

"I don't know, Little George. I wish I did."

"What happened to the money Trip gave you? The money he was going to give to me?"

"What money?"

"Mama, what in the name of God is going on?"

Celia inched next to the whiskey.

Dear God, I want that.

"Mama, what is it?"

She lifted the glass.

It smells like heaven.

"We all have obligations." She simply couldn't keep going like this. She dipped her finger in the whiskey, stuck it in her mouth and sucked the whiskey off. The glass shook in her hand. She set it down and walked through the French doors.

CHAPTER TWENTY

The day after Christmas dawned late. Yesterday's cloud cover brought rain, pounding the Grand Prairie with a cold, driving rain from the southwest. A fresh set of hunters were due in for tomorrow's hunt. If it all went the way it was supposed to, Trip thought he just might have the money to hold off the Memphis bankers, but he still had to make the recipe.

Trip ran into town to Bricker's Farm and Fleet for the recipe. The hardwood floor, the varnish long gone, creaked under his feet. Bricker himself stood behind a long counter, alone in the store, save Trip.

"Ain't it a bit early for this stuff?" said Brick Bricker, a bent-over man in his sixties.

"I've got to get a jump on it while I can, Brick." Trip lit a cigarette.

"You got at least six weeks after duck season to get your fields ready."

"You never know."

"What I hear, you won't be farming this year."

"I'll be farming."

"Only if you got cash." Bricker's cigarette wagged like a dog's tail as he spoke.

"Cash when it's in the truck."

Bricker crushed his cigarette under his boot then grabbed a fifty-pound bag of ammonia and threw it over his shoulder. "Put that smoke out. You'll blow us all up."

Trip's next stop was Rexall Drug. He bought as much Sudafed as he thought he could get away with. Then down the street to Hovey's Pharmacy. Ollie Hovey raised a fluffy white eyebrow at him. "That's plenty of sinus."

"It's for the hunters," Trip said. "In and out of the water. It kicks up their sinuses."

"If they need that much, you best take them to the doctor."

Trip handed him cash, which quieted him right down.

Trip drove over to Pine Bluff and hit all three drug stores. It was still raining when he got back to the farm. He punched the orange button that opened the barn-sized overhead door to the shop, then drove the white pickup inside. He'd wanted to get the ingredients out to Snake Island that afternoon, but he couldn't afford to get them wet. He hid the Sudafed behind the chainsaw in the tool crib then locked it up. Outside the shop, he punched the orange button again. The door rolled down. This time, though, he ran a padlock through the eye on the door. He rammed the hardened steel into the lock. It snapped shut.

* * *

The wind blew from the northwest for the next three days. It was clear and cold, and the ducks flew into the timber. Business was good, but the ingredients stayed locked up in the shop. All four guides were around and there were hunters everywhere. Trip knew he had to get going. Bruno had given him a deadline and he was behind. Finally, on the fourth day, with the wind still blowing and the sky still clear, Trip decided he couldn't wait any longer. He said they'd hunt the rice and the sloughs, no matter that the woods were still full of ducks.

That morning, he got up at 2 a.m. and drove his truck out to the landing. He ferried his cargo to the levee at Mama's Blind, then over the top and into the johnboat on the other side. He made his way to the lean-to. He stacked the ammonia next to the cauldron, then he put the Sudafed in a black trash bag and buried it next to a hickory.

It took him a long time, too long, to get back to the landing. Jake was standing on the top of the levee. Trip shut his eyes, coasted into the dock. Jake scrambled down the levee and took the bow line.

"Morning, Mr. Trip."

"Morning, Jake."

"You're out early."

"That's right." Trip climbed out of the boat, started up the levee.

"What you doing out here this time of day?"

"Scouting."

"The ducks ain't even up yet." Jake ran up the levee behind Trip.

"I wanted to see if there's any roosting in the timber."

Trip stepped up into the truck and started the engine. Jake rapped on his window. Trip rolled it down, eye level with him. Jake's scar, lit up by the lights from the dashboard, had a white cast to it.

"Why'd you bring the truck? Get it stuck out here."

"What do you want, Jake?"

"Where you want us this morning?"

"I told you last night."

"The ducks ain't in the rice."

I may have some trouble with Jake.

Trip rolled up his window. Jake said something through the glass. Trip watched his lips move, drove away.

The ducks never made it to the fields that day. All of the sports got skunked, except for the Yankee who shot a spoonbill that no one wanted to eat.

This won't do.

Trip sent his hunters to the timber the next day. And the day after. The recipe stayed uncooked. The day after that, Louis Bruno showed up early in the morning. He climbed out of a beige Fleetwood and stood in front of the Club House.

"I'm here for a sample of the recipe."

"It's not done yet."

"You've had the better part of two weeks."

Trip lit a cigarette. "I can't get out there. What with the hunters."

"You have all the ingredients?" Bruno held out his hand for a cigarette.

"They're all out there."

"Then go start cooking." The gangster stuck the cigarette in his cheek, like a cigar, waited for a light, which Trip did not oblige.

"I told you I can't get out there."

Bruno began chewing on the cigarette like a cigar. He bit into the filter. "These are awful. I don't see the attraction."

"Most people smoke them."

"I'll be back Friday for a sample." Bruno spat the cigarette out of his mouth, picked the filter out of his teeth, and spat again. He got back in the Cadillac and drove off.

* * *

The next day, with hunters in the woods, Trip chanced it. He and Cash took the four-wheeler to the landing at 3 a.m. They ran the ditch to Mama's Blind, then on to Snake Island and the cooker. He fired it up and started cooking by flashlight. The smell nearly killed him. He wrapped a handkerchief around his nose and stood upwind.

Trip pored over the directions and cooked his strange brew.

Is this what it's supposed to look like?

There was no way he could know, and he was damned if he would try it. At last he shut down the burner and bottled up what he had, which wasn't much.

"Cash, this deal already has a tire in the ditch and we've just started."

* * *

By Thursday morning, Trip had a new plan—not exactly a new plan, but a variation on a theme. He pulled Jake out of the Club House, who was regaling the sports with tales of his hunting prowess. Jake shook his head but followed Trip outside.

In the cold and black of the predawn, Trip offered Jake a smoke.

"Why thank you, Mr. Trip. I do believe this is a first."

"The first of many."

"Sir?"

"Jake, I want you to buy me something today."

"I'd sure like to, Mr. Trip, but I've got hunters this morning. It should be good if it ain't all froze up." Jake stomped his feet on the porch. It wouldn't be frozen out there yet, but there might be some skim ice if the cold stayed on.

"Jake, take your hunters out this morning. After you get back, I want you to go into town and buy me some meth."

"Meth?"

"Don't pretend you don't know what it is." Trip reached into the front left pocket of his jeans and took out a roll of bills held together with a gold money clip.

Jake stopped his stomping and stood like a statue. "I surely didn't know."

"It's not for me."

"I don't know where to get any."

"If you know where to buy weed, you know where to buy meth. I need it before tomorrow's hunt." Trip handed him a hundred dollar bill.

"I don't know, Mr. Trip. I just don't know." Jake stared at the bill.

Trip peeled another hundred from his roll and handed it to Jake.

That morning's hunt went the way it was supposed to. The ducks had to eat, and the skim ice pushed them into the holes opened by Trip's guides. Jake winked at him when he came in, one shy of a limit.

Trip nodded to him. He trusted Jake even less than before, if that were possible, but he needed him, at least for now. He sat in his truck with Cash and watched him drive off.

"Cash," he said, "if we can get past tomorrow, we've got a chance. The second split closes on Sunday. Then we'll have a week with the woods to ourselves to cook. Then maybe, just maybe, we can cook up enough to buy some time for the farm. But a lot of things have to go right."

* * *

Trip sat in his truck in front of the Club House at 4:30 a.m. Clouds had loafed up from the south that night, high, thin clouds that covered the half-moon like a veil, spreading out the moonlight. "If they thicken up, it will rain," he said to Cash, who paid him no mind. Ten minutes later, Jake rolled up beside him. He bounced out of his truck, and by the way he strutted over to Trip, Trip knew he had scored. Jake rapped on his window. Trip rolled it down.

"Got some bad news, Mr. Trip."

"That so," said Trip, who had a pretty good idea of what came next.

"This meth stuff is one hellacious problem to find on short notice."

"Is it?"

"Yes, sir. It surely is."

"So we're outta luck?"

"No, sir," Jake smiled his own half-moon smile, full of teeth, brighter than the moon, Trip thought. "I got it, I surely did, but it was expensive."

"More than you thought?"

"Yes, sir."

"About how much more?"

Jake fished in his pocket, pulled out a Ziploc bag with a white powder that barely covered the bottom of the bag. "I got it all right, but it really cost."

"How much?"

"Two hundred more."

He's shameless.

He handed the thieving guide another two hundred.

* * *

Trip drove to the duck shed. He compared his meth to what Jake bought.

"Damn it, Cash, ours isn't even close." Jake's had a fine, white crystalline sheen. "Ours looks like brown sugar."

He studied the two, not that they required much study. He smelled them both, then he licked his forefinger and dabbed it in Jake's. He poked his finger with the tip of his tongue. He spat it out. Then he tried his own.

He poured about three quarters of Jake's in an empty baby food jar. The rest of it in another baby food jar.

I guess there's something good about Parker feeding her cats baby food.

He screwed both tops on. He put on his coat and carefully, ever so carefully, put both jars in his coat pocket. He picked up the jar he'd made and walked outside with it. He started off to his truck, stopped, and turned back to the duck shed. He threw it as hard as he could against the wall.

Bruno roared up the driveway at dark. His tires sprayed gravel on Trip and Cash.

Bruno struggled out of his boat-sized Fleetwood.

He needs a gangplank to get out of that thing.

Trip scowled at the gangster.

"I haven't been here long enough to piss you off," Bruno said.

"I'd appreciate a more sedate approach up my driveway."

"Let's see what you got." The porch light cast a waxy yellow on Bruno, who had on a black pinstripe suit and white shirt open at the collar.

"You struck my dog with a stone from the driveway."

Bruno reached into the breast pocket of his jacket, fumbled a bit, then took a cigar. He started to unwrap it, but just as he was about to rip the wrapper, he stopped. "I don't have the time to smoke this right now."

"Be careful about my dog." Trip decided he had time for a cigarette and lit up.

"Let's see what you've got," Louis Bruno said again.

Trip handed him Jake's bottle. Bruno pocketed it. Trip thought surely Louis would test it. Taste it. Smell it. At least look at it. The gangster boarded his car.

Trip rapped on the window. "What about the money?" he said.

"What money?"

"The money for the jar."

"The jar?"

"The jar I just gave you."

"I'm not paying for one jar."

"What's inside it then."

"What is inside it?"

Trip sucked one last suck on his cigarette. "Powder," he said.

"You don't want to say what it is, do you? You're above all this, aren't you? You and your farm. Your woods. And that dog."

Trip inhaled the cigarette, then blew the smoke out.

"Don't blow that smoke this way. I don't allow smoke in my car." Bruno unwrapped his cigar and stuck it in his mouth, unlit. "What is it?'

"What's what?"

"God damn it, what's in the jar? Say it. Say what's in the jar."

Trip bit his lower lip. He'd settle up with Bruno, but not tonight. "Meth."

"Meth? Is that it?" Bruno rolled the cigar in his mouth.

"Crystal methamphetamine."

"Very good."

"Where's my money?"

"What money?"

"The money for the jar, the meth."

"There's not a hundred dollars' worth here. If it is meth. We'll test it. Go make enough to make it worthwhile. I'll be back in a week." He started the car. The Fleetwood u-turned and sped off in the dark, spitting gravel.

Trip threw a golf ball-sized rock at the speeding Fleetwood. He heard a 'tunk'. Brake lights flashed on, then off. The car sped off again, leaving a wake of gravel in its path.

"Cash, I'm up to my eyeballs in this fool business, but the only way out is to cook up more of this damn recipe. If I could just figure out how to do it."

For the next two days, Trip got up early and cooked. He changed the recipe until it started to look like what he'd bought from Jake. It smelled powerfully bad at Snake Island, but he thought the wind would break it up. He brought his recipe back in baby food jars and hid them in the duck shack.

CHAPTER TWENTY-ONE

Trip and Cash ran up the ditch in the johnboat. In the half-light of dawn, the skim ice rose and fell in the wake of the boat. He'd sent the guides out earlier, and he could see the jagged ice where Big John, Church, and Cad had turned into the timber. There was skim ice where Jake was supposed to have gone.

Trip ran on through the ditch. There should have been ice here, but there were sheets of floating ice. He killed the engine and coasted, watching the ice rise and fall in the wake, like so many pieces of a jigsaw puzzle.

I've got a few more pieces to fit into mine.

"Cash, Jake didn't go where I told him to go, and I'm pretty sure he went right where I didn't want him to go. He is just about the most miserable son-of-a-bitch I ever met."

Trip shifted the Johnson back into gear and started out again, slower this time. He had a strong suspicion about Jake's whereabouts. He kept to the ditch, hoping he'd see open water off to the side, but the woods were full of skim ice and the ditch ahead was open. He heard shots ahead and turned off the engine. Then more shots.

"Damn it, Cash. He's at Mama's Blind. Damn it to hell. We can't get to Snake Island with him there." Trip turned the boat around and headed back to the farm. There were other ways in, but until the ice melted, he'd give himself away. Jake might not have too much in the way of brains, but he didn't miss a thing in the woods.

Trip ran back through the ditch at half throttle. There was no reason to hurry. He'd give Jake hell and figure out how to keep him and everybody else away from Mama's Blind and the meth cooker.

When he was in sight of the landing, he saw a familiar but unwelcome figure standing on the levee.

Trip slid the johnboat along the dock. He flinched at the silhouette outlined by the nine o'clock sun, a stick figure of a man with a flat-brimmed trooper's hat. Slowly, ever so slowly, Trip climbed up on the landing to the always imposing figure of Captain Arcenault. Trip had a sinking feeling in his stomach.

"Morning, Captain."

"Morning, Trip." Captain Arcenault's pencil-thin mustache, black as night, twitched above his upper lip. He was awash in his olive wools and his flat-brimmed campaign hat. "Everybody out this morning?"

"Yes, sir." Trip offered the Captain a cigarette.

"Obliged."

Trip lit the Captain's cigarette, then his own.

"Been shooting any?"

"A few."

"More than a few from what I hear."

"There's ducks in the woods," Trip said. "When it's clear."

"Your boys got all their licenses?"

"Yes, sir."

"I expect they do. Not that I came to check." Arcenault picked a fleck of tobacco from his mouth. "You just about ready to let this place go?"

"No, sir."

"Game and Fish will buy it. It ought to be part of Bayou Meto. You might as well sell it before you lose it."

"I'm not going to lose it."

At least I know why he's here.

"You change your mind, you let us know."

"I will." Trip settled down.

"That's not why I'm here." The Captain sucked on his cigarette. "I'm here about the smell."

"The smell?"

"Reports of a noxious smell at Hollowell. When the wind blows from the east."

"What kind of smell?"

"God awful smell," Captain Arcenault said. "Just like somebody's cooking up some crystal methamphetamine. You heard of it?"

"I've heard of it."

"You smell it?"

"No, sir, but I don't know if I'd know the smell even if I did smell it."

"You'd know it all right. It gives off a powerful smell of ammonia." He crushed out his cigarette under his boot. "You see any strangers in your woods?'

"No, sir."

"What about the guides?"

"Nobody said anything, but I can ask."

"How about you run me out there so's I can have a look see."

Damn it.

"I can do it." Trip's sinking feeling came back and sank all the way to his feet.

"We can jump into Bayou Meto from Mama's Blind," Arcenault said.

"We haven't been over the levee."

"You best not. No guides on my side."

"I know it."

"I know you know it." Arcenault stepped between Trip and the sun. Trip couldn't see his face.

He did that on purpose.

"There's some good holes on my side," the Captain said.

Trip nodded.

"The Beaverkill's always been a good hole. Hard to get to from my side," Arcenault said.

Trip stepped around Arcenault so the Captain had to look into the sun.

"Let's have at it." The Captain moved around him, toward the sun.

"Jake's hunting at Mama's Blind. Can we wait a bit?"

"I suppose we might." Captain Arcenault walked around Trip, back onto Trip's sunny side. "I thought only McClures hunted Mama's Blind."

"That's how it used to be." Trip stepped in front of him again.

The sun ran right along the landing, and their pas de deux, eyes-in-the-sun dance might have gone on until they fell in, but Jake and his hunters pulled into view.

Trip was relieved that the one-upmanship with the sun was over, but he wasn't looking forward to seeing Jake.

He's the original loose cannon.

Trip steadied Jake's boat while the hunters tumbled out onto the dock. Jake took one look at the flat brim on Captain Arcenault's hat and stayed in the boat. "Damn," he said. "Shit damn." This from an Arkansas boy who'd had more than one run-in with the law.

Jake jumped back in the johnboat, and started fussing with the engine which didn't need any fussing with.

"Jake, how might you be this fine morning?" Captain Arcenault said.

"Fine, Captain, just fine." Jake studied the starter rope on the outboard.

The sports straggled past the good Captain, oblivious to the manners and protocol when in the presence of a man of Captain Arcenault's stature.

Trip stood next to Arcenault and hoped like hell that Jake had not let them shoot over their limit.

"You boys got all your licenses?"

"I checked them all before we went out," Jake said.

"That's fine." Captain Arcenault made no effort to check them himself.

"Anybody over their limit, Jake?"

Jake started to fool with the choke. "No, sir. We're all legal."

"That's fine." The Captain made no effort to check the pile of ducks in the boat.

The easier the visit became, the more worried Trip became.

Jake feels the same way. Maybe for a different reason.

"Any of you boys smell anything funny out there?"

Jake looked at the Captain for the first time. "No, sir."

One of the hunters turned to the Captain. "Butch over there, he farted in his waders. They smelled pretty funny."

"You boys want me to check you?" Captain Arecenault said. "If I look hard enough, I'm sure I could find something to write up."

The sports all looked down at their feet, like schoolboys dressed down by their football coach.

"We didn't smell nothing, Captain," Jake said.

"Did you go over the levee?"

"No, sir. We can't guide on 'tother side."

Captain Arcenault cocked his head ever so slightly. "Since when did you worry about which side of the levee you hunted on? Or anything else that didn't suit you?"

"There's plenty of ducks on the Belle Oak side of the levee," Jake said.

"You see anybody over there?"

"No, sir," Jake said. His eye contact—straight on to the Captain—made Trip nervous.

"Any sign of anybody over there?"

That's a different question.

Trip had run orange tapes from Mama's Blind to the holes they'd been hunting. He could always say they were for his own use. That would probably satisfy the Captain. There was no tape to the Beaverkill or Snake Island, but if they got too far out there, they might run across Snake Island.

Jake piped right up. "No sir, no sign of anything on the other side of Mama's Blind."

"That's fine, Jake."

"Why don't you just take these boys and their ducks to the Club House then," Trip said.

"Yes, sir." Jake gathered up the ducks and hopped out of the boat. He scooted by Trip and the Captain quick as quick could be, a private wink at Trip as he passed by.

"Well then, Trip," Arcenault said, "how's about you and me take a little boat ride and have our own little look-see?" The Captain marched down to the johnboat as if marching off to war.

The Captain sat in the bow. Cash sat on the middle seat, nonplussed about the new seating arrangements, but always up for a boat ride and a duck hunt.

Not only is there no duck hunt, it may be the end of me when Arcenault sees that orange tape.

Trip, in no hurry to meet this part of his destiny, cast off the dock line. He turned the boat around slowly and nosed the bow toward the woods.

The johnboat ploughed through the ditch. Ploughed because Trip had throttled it back far enough so it wouldn't plane. He needed a plan, and he needed time to think of a plan.

It won't be the tapes that do me in, but if Arcenault finds the cooker, I'm cooked.

He could always say he didn't know anything about it. How would he know? He could say they hadn't been back there in a while. Yes, he could say that. That part was true.

They ran through the ditch on their way to Mama's Blind. A wood duck screeched by them. Arcenault looked straight ahead, Cash still on the middle seat. When they came to a straight part of the ditch, Trip held the tiller between his legs and turned back to the outboard. He grabbed the fuel line, the rubber hose that connected the gas can to the engine. At the fitting, where the host connected to the engine, Trip squeezed the clip that held the hose tight against the motor. He pulled the hose back half an inch, enough so it was still connected to the motor and looked like it was attached, enough so the fuel pump would suck in a little gas, but not enough to keep the motor running for very long.

Trip turned back around. Arcenault still faced forward. Trip didn't have to wait long. The engine coughed, kept going, coughed again, sputtered, then died.

The johnboat glided through the ditch. Trip heard the waves from their wake lap against the tree trunks. Then a chickadee—*chick a dee dee dee dee dee*—and the tap, tap, tapping of a woodpecker. It sounds like a big one, Trip thought, maybe a pileated.

Arcenault turned around but didn't say anything.

"We been having a little bad gas. Might be watered," Trip said.

"From your own tank?"

Trip yanked on the pull cord, once, twice, three times. Then it caught. It sputtered but kept running.

"There you go," the Captain said. He swiveled back to the bow.

Trip gave it some gas. The engine caught. The johnboat spurted ahead. Then, as he knew it would, the engine conked out. They glided again. Trip turned back to the engine and repeated the process. The boat jerked forward.

"Captain, I think we better turn around. Can you come back tomorrow? I'll have it sorted out by then."

"You have other motors."

Trip was ready this time. "If one's got bad gas, they all do." Trip turned the boat around. Safe for now. Safe enough until he could cut down those tapes.

"Let me take a look," Arcenault said.

Before Trip could think, let alone speak, the Captain climbed back to the stern. Trip went up to the bow. The Captain studied the motor.

"You know about motors?" Trip said.

"Not too much."

That's something.

Captain Arcenault made a show of checking the engine.

Stay away from the hose. I pray you stay away from the hose.

"Looks like we'll have to turn back," Captain Arcenault said.

"'Fraid so," Trip said.

"One more thing." The Captain lifted up the gas tank. "Plenty of gas." He set the tank back down. "How about this?" He took a hold of the ball of the hose, the bubble that when squeezed filled up the gas line. "Let's try this." He squeezed it with his right hand. Once, twice, three times. "Let's try it now." Captain Arcenault bent over the motor. He yanked the starter cord. The engine sputtered as before. Then he looked at the water sloshing in the bottom of the boat. "Look here."

Trip sank. He knew full well what Arcenault saw.

"Look here," Arcenault said again.

Trip didn't move.

"Come and look at this."

Trip eased his way back to the stern. Arcenault pointed at the water in the bottom of the boat.

"Gasoline," Arcenault said.

"Yes, sir. That's what it is all right."

There's still a chance.

"Let's see here." The Captain jiggled at the hose where it hooked to the motor. It came off in his hand. The Captain reattached the hose.

"Thank you, Captain."

"Not a problem. Not a problem at all. Glad to be of help. I don't know how you didn't see that. Someone with your experience."

Trip didn't say anything. They switched places. Trip started the engine.

The jig's up.

He could always tip the boat over, but that would only make matters worse. Then the Captain would surely figure out that something was up. He ran wide open up the ditch until they got to Mama's Blind.

"Run her right up to the levee," the Captain said.

"Yes, sir."

The johnboat coasted up to the levee. The Captain climbed up the bank. Trip stayed in the boat, worrying. The Captain stood on top of the levee. He took a deep breath and turned a quarter turn and took another deep breath, repeating until he made a full circle. "I don't smell a thing." He turned upwind and took one more deep breath. "Nothing." Then he turned, hands on hips and looked into Bayou Meto.

This is it, Trip thought. If he walks down the levee and finds the boat I hid on the Bayou Meto side, I'm cooked. If he sees the tapes out there, I'm cooked, and if we pull the boat over, I'm really cooked.

Captain Arcenault turned toward him and slid down the levee to the johnboat. Here it comes, Trip thought.

"Let's go," he said.

"What?"

"I can't smell a thing, and I can't see a thing."

"What?" Trip said again.

"Let's go."

I can't believe it.

"If we skedaddle, I can be home in time for lunch with the missus. I coulda swore there'd be something out here." The Captain lit a cigarette. The smoke blew toward Belle Oak.

* * *

"Don't you dare step in my kitchen with those muddy boots," Parker said.

Trip had already taken his boots off. He stood beside them, out of Parker's sight. He hadn't made it past the foyer with his boots on in five years.

"And you make sure you wipe off Cash's feet."

Parker said it every time he came in, even on the driest day of the year. It was part of their marital ritual. Actually, he quite enjoyed it, the everydayness of it.

Cash loved Parker, but some days he just couldn't wait to have his feet wiped off, and today was one of those days. Trip, towel in hand, had just wiped off Cash's left front paw when the Lab nosed the door open and ran down the hall into the kitchen.

"Trip McClure, I told you to wipe off his feet," she said, still out of sight, but not out of earshot. "Why Cash, how are you?"

All was forgiven, at least as far as Cash was concerned. In truth, Parker held Trip responsible for Cash's muddy paws, not Cash. Parker thought Cash's failure a reflection of Trip as a master rather than Cash's failure to do what he was asked.

Parker greeted Trip with her hands on her hips. Lunch with the missus had seemed like a good idea to Trip, too. Especially after Captain Arcenault's surprise visit had turned out so well. He hoped Parker would make him grilled cheese with hot peppers, and if he was lucky, maybe grits with Velveeta and onions.

"Mr. McClure, if you think for one minute that I'm about to make you grilled cheese with hot peppers, you can think again." She still had her hands on her hips.

It's never good when she calls me "Mr. McClure."

"You march right back there with your dog and wipe his feet off."

Trip started off.

"Never mind. His feet are wiped off on my floor." Parker started for the closet where the mop lived.

"Let me do that."

"You've done quite enough already." Parker mopped up Cash's tracks. "I might consider your grilled cheese." She opened the refrigerator door. "And I might have some cheesy grits."

Parker buttered the pan, sliced the cheese, picked the pickled peppers from the jar, then said, "What's this I hear about a smell?"

"A smell?"

"Captain Arcenault said he was here to investigate an odor from the woods."

"An odor? He said odor?"

"He said smell. Odor is my word."

Trip looked out the window away from his bride.

"It doesn't matter a never mind whether he said smell or odor." She put the sandwich together and slid it off the spatula into the frying pan. Trip breathed in the smell of the butter melting in the pan.

"What about this smell?"

"I took him out to the levee at Mama's Blind. We didn't smell a thing."

"He said it was foul. Like ammonia."

"Baby, I didn't smell anything."

Parker looked straight at him. "Trip, honey, a couple of times your clothes smelled like ammonia."

"Maybe it's from the farm chemicals I bought."

"Maybe." Parker flipped the grilled cheese.

She knows something's up.

After lunch, and much to Parker's surprise, Trip forsook his nap, a fixture in his schedule on days when there were no afternoon hunts. He had other business this afternoon.

The sky had clouded over, a gray blanket horizon to horizon. What wind there had been, wasn't. It was a good afternoon not to have hunters.

Trip drove to the duck shed. He pushed the couch a foot to the left, ever so carefully, so as not to leave a mark. He pried up a floorboard. The jars lay where he'd left them. The sample from Jake and three of his own, all in a row. The three he had somehow managed to make, despite all of the interruptions, each succeeding day's jar closer in color and texture to the one Jake had given him. The second split ended tomorrow. Then he could cook flat out. As long as no one got in his way.

After he moved the couch back, he took the four-wheeler out to the landing. He and Cash jumped into the johnboat. Trip ran it wide open. Cash's ears blew back against his head. He ran the boat hard all the way in and didn't cut the motor until he ploughed into Mama's Blind. Which was why he never heard the boat behind him.

Trip came alongside the levee, tied the bow line to a tree, and crabbed his way up. He stood there, hands on hips, looking into Bayou Meto, just like Captain Arcenault. He surveyed all that wasn't his, looking for the tape. Except there was no tape. No tape to be seen. Anywhere. No tape. He shook his head and looked again. There was no tape in sight.

He looked down at the boat he had hidden, the fourteen-footer he barged his chemicals with. The boat wasn't there, only brush.

The brush. That must be it. He'd brushed it so well even he couldn't see it.

Trip scuttled down the levee. This is where he had left it. He had tied it by the bow and the stern—there was no way it could have drifted off. He stood at the bottom of the levee and smoked. Then a branch cracked above him, from the levee. Like someone stepping on a branch.

He looked up. At Jake.

"Y'all right, Mr. Trip?"

"What are you doing here?"

"I left my bag hanging on that tree over there." He pointed to the Belle Oak side. "I wouldn't care except my calls are in it."

"What you doin' down there?"

"Checking the levee."

"Makin' sure we're still getting their water?"

"That's right."

"Drain's down that way, Mr. Trip." Jake pointed again.

Trip climbed up the levee. "You got your bag?"

"I put it in the boat."

"Let's go then."

"You goin' to check that drain?"

"I guess not." He slid down to his boat. "Let's go, Cash."

"Don't you worry, Mr. Trip."

Trip looked up at Jake again, this time from his side of the levee.

"About what, Jake?"

"Them tapes."

"Tapes?"

"And the boat. It's a hundred yards thataway," pointing yet again.

Trip had no idea what to say. He had no idea what Jake knew or didn't know.

"We don't want a ticket for carrying hunters into Bayou Meto," Jake said.

"No, we don't. We haven't done it."

"Not too much," Jake said. He grinned at Trip. The white line of his scar lit up.

Jake ripped down the tapes and moved the boat. Why?

"Don't you worry, Mr. Trip. I got your back." Jake skidded down the levee to his boat.

* * *

The sports limited the next morning. After the obligatory pictures with their ducks, they packed up and left, the second split over.

Trip had a week to cook up the recipe, and thanks to Parker, he was all booked up. If all that turned out, the money from the meth and the third split could hold off the foreclosure. He still had to figure out how to deal with Theo Boxwood and the crop loan that Big George had taken out.

If only I knew what happened to that money.

All he had to do now was finish painting up the stovepipe. He'd bought about forty feet. He was going to camo it and run it up the tree next to his cooker. He hoped the smell would spread out enough where no one would smell it. He'd made a sheet metal hood to go over the cooker to funnel the fumes up the pipe. As soon as he painted it, he'd carry it out to Snake Island. The guides were off and Arcenault would no doubt take a couple days off himself. He thought he could cook the recipe without being found out.

He'd finished painting the hood a flat muddy brown, and he had about half of the four-foot sections of stove pipe painted. They stood on the floor of the decoy shed like soldiers. He set his brush across the paint can and slid the couch away from the hide, waking Cash up from his nap. He pried up the floorboards and checked his jars again. No one ever came in here, and he was sure no one knew about his hiding place. He cradled a jar. Would this evil save him? Then he heard footsteps. Trip tucked the jar in his pocket and slid the couch over the hole in the floor.

Parker barged in. "Baby, what is that smell?"

"What smell?"

"What in God's name are you doing in here?"

"Painting." Trip sat down on the couch. The floorboard lay in front of his feet. When Parker looked at the hood and stovepipe, Trip scooted it under the couch. It scraped across the floor. Did she see it?

"Just what is going on here?"

"Just a little painting."

"Why aren't you painting in the shop?"

Parker stooped and picked up one of the freshly painted sections of pipe. Paint stuck to her fingers. "Damn it, Trip. I've got paint on my fingers."

Trip jumped up. "Let me get you some turpentine."

"What is this?"

"It's a hood. A hood for a cooker." Trip held the rag to the mouth of the turpentine and tipped the can upside down. He wiped the paint off Parker's fingers with the rag.

"Thank you, Trip." She let him hold her hand while he rubbed the paint off with the turpentine-soaked rag. "These fumes are making me dizzy."

Trip tried to ease her to the door, but she would have none of it. "Why do you have this stovepipe? And that thing there." She pointed at the hood.

"It's to fume off the crawfish. When we boil them."

"That's nonsense."

"The sports like to eat crawfish, but they can't stand the smell."

"There is no reason to paint any of this. Anyway, this is a project for the shop. Give me the rag. I'll take care of my own fingers." She rubbed the rag on her fingers. "The turpentine ate off my nail polish. Trip McClure, you have got some secret business going on, and I don't like it."

"Baby, I'm just trying to improve things for the sports."

"This farm and that damn duck woods aren't worth a single sin on your part. Not one sin. The only reason I even came out to your private little world was to tell you that Jude called. He's coming down for the last week of the season. Maybe he can straighten you out. Lord knows I can't."

I wish I could tell you.

Parker rubbed her fingertips with the rag. She studied her formerly red nails, now a drippy mess. "I'm going to fix my nails before I pass out." She threw the rag at Trip on her way out.

* * *

That night, long after Parker had gone to bed, Trip nursed a flat beer at the only table left at the Gator. Burt stared up at him.

Alligators are snakes with legs.

Why Bruno insisted on meeting here at midnight was beyond Trip. How did he even know the Gator existed? It was better than the farm, though, what with Parker on his trail and Jake showing up every time he turned around.

At one in the morning, Louis Bruno showed up. The gangster sat down and looked down at the alligator. "I wonder what that thing eats."

"Whatever falls in there."

"I guess he's not picky." Bruno smiled at him. "You got it?"

After Parker had left, Trip checked the baby food jars one last time. He'd picked the one with the whitest powder. Trip wished they had a baby to feed with the baby food instead of Parker's cats.

He handed the jar to Bruno.

"Be careful," Bruno said. "You want us to get caught?"

Trip raised his eyebrows.

This is probably the tamest thing going on in here.

Bruno grabbed the jar from Trip.

Bruno unscrewed the jar. He licked his finger, touched the white drug, then touched it to his tongue. "Now you're getting there." He slipped the jar into his pocket and stood up.

"Where's my money?" Trip said.

"Money?" He started to the door. Trip grabbed him by the shoulder. "Don't you ever touch me," Bruno said. "Ever."

"Where's my money?

"Five more of these jars and you're about even with the weed you never delivered."

"I want the money."

"You keep cooking." Bruno smiled sweetly at Trip. Bruno dropped Trip's glass through the bars. The alligator opened his jaws and crushed the glass in his mouth.

* * *

Trip slept until six the next morning. He hung around the yellow house as long as he could stand, trying to smooth things over with Parker. By eight o'clock he couldn't stand it any longer. He and Cash headed to the duck shed. He checked his cache one more time, then loaded the stovepipe and the hood into his truck. Cash ran in front on their way out. Frost sparkled on the weeds, falling off when Cash ran through it, the temperature right at freezing.

At the landing, a thin sheet of ice locked in the boats, but the ice broke up as soon as Trip stepped in with the first of the stovepipes.

This was the first closed day after the second split, and the ducks, as if aware of the armistice, had settled into the woods like fallen leaves.

At Mama's Blind, Trip hauled his cargo over the levee and into the hidden boat.

He cut west at the triple tape, the only tape Jake hadn't ripped off. Without the tape line, getting in and out would be dead reckoning.

As long as his shotgun was stuck in the mud at the Beaverkill, he knew the guides wouldn't use the hole. Whatever shortcomings they had, they would honor his lost duck bands. The Beaverkill, as far as the guides were concerned, was out of bounds until the woods dried out and Trip found his duck bands.

For the life of him, Trip couldn't figure out how Jake had had the foresight to pull the tapes off at the levee and hide the boat. He'd never demonstrated much in the way of foresight except his uncanny sense of when the husband of a married woman wouldn't be home.

Is it something else?

At Snake Island, Trip rigged the hood over the kettle. Then he drove spikes into the trunk of the nearest tree. He climbed the tree and strung the stovepipe together, link by link, until he had a chimney that stretched up into the canopy.

Trip slithered down the tree. At the lean-to, he admired his handiwork. He was sure this was the first ever camouflaged meth chimney, absolutely guaranteed to carry the smell away from the nose of the nosey Captain Arcenault, who by all rights shouldn't be anywhere near Bayou Meto when the season was closed.

Trip and Cash motored back to Mama's Blind. At the levee, he cut the motor. In the quiet of the woods he thought he heard an outboard in the distance. An outboard? Out here? When duck season was closed?

CHAPTER TWENTY-TWO

Celia sat across from Cullen Dubose at a Waffle House in Little Rock.

"Mrs. McClure, I do believe you are the first customer in the history of the Waffle House to order poached eggs."

"Fried eggs are unhealthy." Celia looked out the window at the parking lot. It was full of pickups and a few cars, mostly full-size cars, almost all of them old enough to be worth less than what the owner owed on them. The sky was so gray that even the red F-150 outside her window looked gray.

"You can get anything you want in here, as long as it's fried," the greasy man said.

Celia glared at him.

"Mrs. McClure, you are in no position to be rude to me."

"I am not being rude."

"Looking at me like that. That's rude." Dubose took a Marlboro from the crushproof red box and lit a cigarette.

"Smoking in front of me is rude," She waved the smoke away.

"That's rude. Telling me that smoking is rude."

Dubose made a show of blowing smoke away from Celia. "We're here about money."

"Mr. Dubose, the ten thousand I gave you when you were eating frog legs at Cothan's was the last of my money. I have no more to give you."

"I'm all done with 'no.' I need money."

"All God's children need money, Mr. Dubose."

The pasty face of Cullen Dubose turned red like a boiled crawfish. Before he could say anything, the waitress appeared.

"The cook says he can't poach eggs. He only poaches deer." She laughed out of the side of her mouth.

"Eggs over easy, with sausage and grits," Dubose said.

"I'll have the same," said Celia.

"That was accommodating." Dubose stubbed out his cigarette.

Celia glared at him again and resumed her study of the parking lot.

"What should concern you, Mrs. McClure, is not what's outside, but who's inside. Which is me."

Celia kept staring out the window.

I have no earthly idea what to do.

She'd caused the death of her husband. She'd taken money from Trip and lied about it. All she had managed to do was delay the inevitable. And here she was. No further ahead.

Lord, I don't know what to do, but I've got to do something.

Tomorrow was the one-year anniversary of the accident. She hadn't thought about it until now. New Year's Eve.

And Parker's birthday.

Forever ruined for her by what had happened last year. They didn't know about what happened. Not yet anyway. Nobody did. Nobody but Celia and the awful man sitting across from her.

Finally she said, "You're an awful man."

"And your husband was a murderer."

"He was not," Celia said, though, in fact, he was. And so was she. "As sure as I'm sitting here, you killed my husband."

"He pulled the trigger. Not me."

The plates arrived. Two white plates with two white eggs, fried, with just a hint of yellow where the yolks should be. A pile of white grits, buttered white toast, and three sausages lined up like logs at the mill in Pine Bluff.

Dubose studied his plate. He turned it a quarter turn so the eggs were right in front of him.

"Hot sauce?"

"Frank's," Dubose said.

"Be right back," the waitress said.

"Where were we?" Dubose turned his plate another quarter turn, the sausages pointing at him. "I remember. We're here to talk about money."

"You killed my husband," Celia said again.

"We're not here to talk about who killed your husband. We're here to talk about who your husband killed. Which brings us right back to where we started." Dubose smiled at her. "Money, that's what we're here to talk about."

"I don't have any more money."

"You got that farm and that duck woods. And that barge company."

"I told you. I don't have any more money."

"I guess we'll see what the state troopers have to say." He smiled at her. "Won't we."

"They said it was an accident."

The waitress dropped off the hot sauce. The blackmailer turned his plate again, this time a one-eighth turn. He poured the Frank's on his eggs and pricked the yolk with his fork, red and yellow running together.

"They haven't heard from the eyewitness." The greasy man tapped his chest and smiled again.

CHAPTER TWENTY-THREE

"Baby, why are you going there?"

"Because that's where the lobsters are," Trip said.

Parker finished her Veuve Clicquot. Trip hoped there was nothing prophetic in the name. It was four o'clock in the afternoon on New Year's Eve. They were in the library of the yellow house, Trip in the leather chair, Parker on his lap. Trip looked out the window. He watched the ducks circle into the flooded rice in the failing light, dropping right in. The season had been closed for almost a week now. The ducks had no worries, but that would change soon enough.

"How about it?" Parker held out her glass.

Trip reached into the ice bucket for the bottle and filled her glass.

"How about you, baby?"

"I've got to get those lobsters."

"Why are you going to the country club? You always get them at the Little Cajun."

"The country club got them in fresh today," Trip lied.

"Stay here with me. I don't need a lobster."

"We always have lobster on your birthday."

"Let's skip it this year. We can drink our dinner."

"I'll be right back." Trip picked her up and sat her back down in the chair. He emptied the bottle into her glass and jammed the dead soldier neck-first in the ice bucket.

The truth of the matter was that there were plenty of fresh lobsters at the Little Cajun, Stuttgart's finest, and only, seafood restaurant. The truth of it was Trip had an assignation at the country club, and in case it got back to Parker that he had been at the country club, he wanted to have a reason to be there.

Trip and Cash hopped into the white pickup. "Cash, this is getting complicated, but this ought to do it. This one time and we're all done."

It was dark now. The back tires spit out gravel on the way down the driveway. At the main road, Trip turned right, away from the country club. He had a stop to make, an important stop.

He wheeled into the driveway to the Club House and swung into the two-track that led to the duck shed. "This is going to do it with you, Louis Bruno." He unlocked the door and turned on the light. He had an empty cigar box, just the right size. He set it down on the workbench. Cash jumped up on the couch.

"You can sit there if you want, but I have to move the couch."

Trip pushed the couch away from the floorboard. Cash looked a little nervous, but he stayed on the couch. Trip opened the blade of his pocket-knife. It glinted softly in the light from the naked bulb. He got down on his hands and knees and studied the floorboards for the last time. For the past week, he had cooked and cooked and cooked up enough of the recipe to fill nine of Parker's baby food jars. Enough to fill up the cigar box and pay back the gangsters. Bruno be damned. The duck club money would take care of the rest. Planters Bank be damned. Theo Boxwood be damned. His brothers be damned.

Gently, ever so gently, Trip slid the blade between the floorboards hiding his hide. He pried up the floorboard and lifted it gently. He set it aside and looked down at his cache.

Gone. They were gone. The baby food jars were gone. What happened? Where were they? Trip knelt on the floor, like a dog on all fours, then rose to his knees and ran his hands through his hair. What happened?

Had he already moved them? That was it. He'd already gotten them. They were already in the cigar box. He ran to the workbench, ripped open the cigar box. Empty.

I knew it was empty.

Where were they? Had he forgotten where he put them? That was it. He'd already moved them. He had moved the baby food jars. In the heat of it all, he had hidden them. He had hidden them somewhere else.

But he hadn't hidden the baby food jars anywhere else. He'd thought about it, but he hadn't done it. He just wished he had.

Who could have taken them? No one came in here. Jude did. But he wasn't here yet. The guides? They hadn't been here since the end of the second split. Maybe Jake. What about Parker? She had seen him move the couch. It would be just like her. To save him from himself. That's what she'd think she was doing.

Parker. It had to be Parker. But it could be Bruno. He could have found them. Or Jake. There was always Jake.

Trip picked up the nearest decoy and threw it at the back window. The glass shattered.

* * *

The Country Club of Stuttgart was south of the bypass, just outside the city limits. The white pickup wound around the candy cane-studded driveway up to the clubhouse, not that there was any reason for a driveway to wind around anything here or anywhere else in Arkansas County, the ground so flat that the groundwater didn't know which way to go.

The country club was one story, just like everything else on the Grand Prairie. It had started out as a brick ranch house on a rice farm.

When the bank foreclosed on the rice farm, the members of the country club moved out of the house they rented and bought the house and farm. They turned the house into a club house and the rice fields into a golf course. The golf course started out with plenty of water hazards, but that meant plenty of snakes, so the grounds committee dried up the water hazards. The course played straight, flat, dry, and snakeless.

Trip pulled around the circle drive to the front door. There was nothing to do but show up. Nothing to do but see what happened with Bruno. The valet, a pimply-faced teenager, insisted on parking Cash and the truck. Trip gave him a ten to keep an eye on Cash, then kicked over the plastic Santa on the front porch.

There was a Christmas tree to his left in what had been the living room. The tree was at least twenty feet tall and stuck well up into the cathedral ceiling, an early architectural improvement by the building committee. The tree was decorated in white lights and duck ornaments of every size and shape. There were silver balls with painted ducks, ducks hanging on wires, miniature decoys, and a flying mallard on top of the tree.

Trip walked past the ballroom, filled with revelers, to the men's grill. It overlooked the eighteenth green, now a brown shade of brown.

He had no idea how Bruno could meet him here.

He's definitely not a member.

The McClures had been members for years. Trip rarely showed up for anything, but Big George and his mother had always come for the New Year's Eve lobster feast.

Bruno was sitting at a table by the window. He had his back to him and was wearing a Santa hat with a silver bell. The hat flopped over his left ear.

He's festive, but he won't be for long.

Santa gangster wasn't alone. Was he with Mrs. Claus? Trip thought about leaving before Bruno saw him. He'd just slide on over to the kitchen and fetch the lobsters for Parker's birthday dinner.

That will guarantee a visit from Bruno.

Trip teetered back and forth, heel to toe, neither in nor out of the men's grill. Mrs. Claus raised her hand and waved to him.

"Why, Trip McClure, it is you," said the voice. "Come on over. We were just talking about you."

Trip's every fear, Parker-wise, had just been realized. The beautiful Amelia Rademacher, realtor supreme, listing agent for Belle Oak, and would-be paramour, was none other than Mrs. Claus.

That explains how Bruno got in here.

He sat down at the table, the third of the Belle Oak triumvirate: one trying to sell it, one trying to steal it, and one trying to save it.

Amelia had pulled her hair back with jeweled combs. She had on a cheery holiday sweater. He could only imagine what he couldn't see beneath the table. He knew full well why Parker did her best to keep him away.

She stood, hugged him, and then stretched her neck to him and planted a very wet Happy New Year's kiss full on his lips.

"You two know each other?" Louis Bruno flipped his Santa hat to the other side of his round face.

"We surely do," Amelia said. "Trip, we were just talking about you and Belle Oak."

"Is that so?"

"Amelia wants to sell me your farm."

"Thank you for meeting me here, Mr. Bruno. You have a Happy New Year." Trip pulled out her chair. She kissed him again and left.

Oh, to be a beautiful blonde.

"She has her eye on you." Bruno unwrapped a cigar and bit off the end.

He stuck it in his mouth and lit it. "I thought she'd never leave." He rolled the cigar around in his mouth. "A lot of people have a lot of plans for that farm of yours." Bruno took the cigar out of his mouth and looked at it. "We can stop all those plans right now, can't we. You and me."

Trip didn't say a word.

"What you got for me?" Bruno lit his cigar.

Trip lit a cigarette.

"Do we have a problem," Bruno said, not asking. He studied the ash on the end of the cigar, then tapped it off and stuck the cigar back in his mouth.

"Not a problem," Trip said. "Just timing."

"Timing? Timing?" Then, "Timing." Not a question.

"Yes, timing."

"You mean timing, like now."

"Not exactly now." Trip shifted his weight from his left foot to his right then back to his left.

"Not now? That's the whole, entire reason I'm at this awful country club. If you can even call it that."

Trip didn't say anything.

"Where's the recipe?"

"It's not quite done."

"Not done?" The gangster turned red, matching his Santa hat. "What do you mean not done?"

"It didn't turn out quite right."

"The sample you gave me was perfect."

"The rest of it didn't turn out quite right."

"God damn it. I need that recipe. I'm supposed to bring it back with me. What am I gonna do?"

"I've got hunters coming in again, starting tomorrow. For the third split. It goes for another three weeks. I'll be busy. Real busy. As soon as it's done, I can get right back at it. By the end of February...."

Bruno shook his head. "I want it now."

"By Valentine's Day, I'll have it for you. All you do is give me the money tonight, and I'll give you the recipe by Valentine's Day."

Bruno erupted from his chair. "That's six fucking weeks. I need it now."

"It didn't turn out."

"Let me see what you've got."

"I didn't bring it."

"Where is it?"

"I threw it out."

Bruno's face turned redder. "God damn it, what am I going to do?" The gangster bit down on his cigar. "I can't wait until Valentine's Day."

"I just don't see how I can get it done any sooner."

"You get me that recipe in three weeks."

"That's the end of duck season. I don't have time."

"You make fucking time." Bruno shoved three fingers in Trip's face. As if he couldn't count to three. "One, two, three. God damn it. One, two three." He glared at Trip. Although Trip didn't think it possible, Bruno turned even redder. Then he clenched his teeth and bit through the cigar. All the way through. It fell end over end.

*　*　*

"Baby, will you just stick it in and get it over with."

Trip jumped. He'd forgotten where he was and what he was supposed to be doing. He turned the giant cousin of the crawfish toward his face and looked it squarely in the eye. The blue-black-green creature twinkled its antennae at him. Trip dropped the lobster headfirst into the boiling water, killing it instantly. He hoped.

He watched it turn red, just like Louis Bruno.

"The other one, too. So they're both done at the same time." A pause, then, "Baby, what is on your mind?"

Plenty.

How was he going to carry and fetch hunters in and out of the timber and brew the farm-saving poison at the same time? He dunked the second lobster in the boiling water alongside its dead friend.

"I swear, Trip McClure, you are someplace else. Get back here. It's my birthday." Parker had on a black cocktail dress and her Christmas pearls. She sashayed up to the stove where Trip was melting the butter. She nuzzled his neck, then backed up.

"Whose perfume is that on you?"

"What?"

"Whose perfume is that?"

"There's nobody's perfume."

"There is and I smell it. What have you been doing on my birthday? Of all days."

Is she going to cry or hit me? Or both?

"I bumped into Amelia at the country club."

"I knew I smelled something."

"Nothing happened."

"You don't smell like that when nothing happens."

Of all my sins, this isn't one of them.

He stepped toward Parker and reached around her waist. She stiffened.

"Get away from me."

"She saw me when I came in, and she gave me a hug. That's all."

"That's not all. She has eyes for you. And you have eyes for her."

Trip didn't want to fight with Parker. What he really wanted to do was to figure out how to get his hunters in and out of the timber while he made the meth. He needed Parker for the first part and most definitely not for the second.

"I only have eyes for you."

"Really?"

"You know that. Let's have some more champagne." Trip poured the last of the second bottle of Veuve Clicquot in her glass. "I'll get another."

Parker wasn't done yet. "What we have here, Trip McClure, is a triangle."

"What?"

"She wants you. I want you. You want the farm. You have to choose."

"Baby, I already did. It's you."

"You won't admit it, but it's true. You'd pick this farm and that damn duck woods any old day. You know you would." She glared at him. "I hate this farm. I hope you do lose it."

Maybe it was Parker who stole the meth.

Trip took another bottle of champagne out of the refrigerator. He unwrapped the foil and took the wire cage off the cork. Then he pushed the cork out. He knew better. He knew he was supposed to hold the cork and twist the bottle, but he pushed the cork out with his fingers. The cork exploded out of the bottle like a firecracker and shot past Parker's left ear.

"You did that on purpose."

"I'm sorry, baby." The champagne sprayed out of the bottle.

"You're going to have to choose."

"Maybe you already chose for me," Trip said.

"What does that mean?"

"You know what that means."

"I do not."

"You've been sneaking around the shed for weeks."

"My God, Trip McClure. You are paranoid. All you care about is this damn farm."

"It's not a damn farm. It's Belle Oak."

"It's possible to want something too much."

"What do you mean?"

"It will be our ruination. If it hasn't been already."

Trip turned toward the pot of boiling water. One of the lobsters stuck its head up. Its tail was fiery red, but its head was still brown. It waved its antennae at him. Trip held it down with the champagne bottle.

CHAPTER TWENTY-FOUR

Celia looked out the window of her sitting room. She poured herself another Manhattan from the crystal pitcher and thought about what happened exactly one year ago tonight. The night that had set in motion the downward spiral of McClure Tug and Tow, and through the transitive property of collateral, pledges, and guarantees, the soon-to-be demise of Belle Oak.

Celia and Big George had driven to the country club on the same route just driven by Trip. Big George took his time so the two of them could dally over their travelers, Veuve Clicquot, iced nicely by Tully and sitting between them on the console of the Benz. They finished the bottle just as they pulled up to the valet.

The two of them glided into the dining room for the lobster feast. Celia and Big George quite liked New Year's Eve at the black-tie Country Club gala. They feasted with Pig, his family, and the other well-to-do planters, the planters' well-to-do-ness a product of not so much farming acumen but of primogeniture and price supports for the rice. They ate, drank, and made merry—celebrating their good fortune, which to a man and woman they knew they deserved.

After dinner and one last New Year's toast, the tottering couple poured themselves into the Benz for the ride back to Belle Oak.

"Big George, you are tipsy."

"I'm just fine," he said.

Celia was right. She was more than right. Big George wasn't tipsy, he was drunk, having switched from Veuve Clicquot to Maker's Mark Manhattans about two-thirds of a fifth ago. Truth be told, Celia was drunk, too. Just not quite as drunk as Big George.

"Big George, you better let me drive."

"Celia, honey, you just pay attention to the road. I'll get us back in one piece."

The two of them were drunk enough that they made a wrong turn onto

Arkansas 165, heading due west on the road to Little Rock, although neither of them knew it.

The trouble really started when Big George started to hiccup. Celia reached over to loosen his bow tie. He looked down and didn't see they were coming up to the bridge over the Big Ditch. He knew it iced up this time of year, but he had no idea he was just about on it.

He wasn't looking at the road when the Benz ran onto the bridge. The car skidded on the ice and slid across to the other lane. He braked too hard, and the car started to spin in circles, around and around, and around again.

Celia gave up on the bow tie.

"Christ almighty. Where the hell are we?" Big George said.

"We're on the bridge over the big ditch," Celia said, fairly calm for someone in a spinning car.

"How'd we get here?"

Celia grabbed the steering wheel. Big George pumped the brakes. They stopped the car and saved the day. Almost.

Almost. They'd made it across the bridge, but the Benz was sideways in the middle of the road, and they didn't see the oncoming car, closing fast.

Big George took the wheel back from Celia. He drove into the wrong lane. It was too late when he saw the black Oldsmobile coming at them. It veered off the road and crashed head on into a cypress.

"What the hell were you doing back there?" Big George said.

"I was loosening your tie."

"My tie?" Big George felt around his neck and grabbed his bow tie.

"You had the hiccups."

"Did you see what just happened?" Big George pulled over to the shoulder. He turned the Benz around, then stopped. He turned the car back around and started off toward Belle Oak.

"What are you doing? We've got to get help," Celia said.

"Help? Did you see the crash? Whoever's in that car is dead."

"You don't know that."

"Hell, I don't. The only ones to help are us. We've got to get out of here."

"Big George, we've got to help."

"Celia, baby, he's dead. And I'll be in jail if we don't get out of here. Nobody saw us, and there's nothing we can do."

A year later, Celia chewed a maraschino cherry. She remembered slumping over in her seat crying. "It was an accident," he'd said. "Whoever was driving was probably drunk anyway. No one saw us." She remembered how Big George had driven them home. Out of harm's way. Or so they thought.

A year later, Celia thought that Big George had been right on two out of three. The driver of the Oldsmobile had been drunk, and he was dead. But someone had seen them. Someone coming up behind them had slowed down when the Benz spun and stopped when the Oldsmobile crashed. Then he followed the Benz back to Belle Oak with his lights off.

CHAPTER TWENTY-FIVE

The ducks had blown down like rain after the second split. When the third split opened, there were ducks everywhere. The first week of the third split went swimmingly, plenty of hunters and plenty of ducks. Trip managed the guides as best he could, duck hunting and duck guides being largely unmanageable. He took a few groups out on his own, but mostly he snuck out and cooked the recipe. He hadn't found the first batch or what had happened to it, and he didn't think it was smart to try and find out right now.

He had a dozen jars when the rain started. This time he hid them in the Crooked Tree, the twisted white oak three-quarters of the way to Mama's Blind. In the days of the first Archibald McClure, a thin, straight white oak snapped halfway up during a January ice storm. Unlike almost every other white oak that met this fate, this particular one didn't die. It started over where it snapped off, but it sent its new trunk off at an angle. It grew tall, thick, and crooked. In its old age, pileated woodpeckers pecked rectangular holes in the trunk about eight feet up. Trip hid the latest round of baby food jars in the holes.

Four straight days of rain stopped the cooking. He couldn't keep the fire going without so much smoke that anyone within five miles would surely see it or at least smell it, not the least of whom would be the good Captain Arcenault.

He hadn't been getting much sleep. For the last four mornings, he woke up at two and lay in bed, listening to the rain tap, tap, tapping on their bedroom window.

Now, with a week left in the third split, he woke up. What was it? It was quiet. The tapping was gone. The rain had stopped.

He fell back asleep. At 4 a.m. he drank coffee. At five, he got the guides going—all of them except Jake, who was "disappeared," no doubt in the bed of a fine young Arkansan lass.

He and Cash slipped past the Crooked Tree at six. He was cooking by seven. He had two jars by eleven. If he could keep it up, he'd be done in three days.

The clouds thinned out at dawn. When it cleared up, the ducks started to fly out into the timber. Ones, twos, and threes—all mallards. Now and then, a flock of twenty or more.

But with the ducks came the duck hunters. Shots rang across the timber. Outboards buzzed off in the distance. Bayou Meto closed at noon. As soon as the hunters got out, Trip would have the timber and the cooking to himself.

The wind came up about eleven. It started out in the southeast, clocked to the southwest, on its way to the northwest, freshening as it shifted. The smoke blew into Bayou Meto, a thin smoke at the treetops, running off in a flat trail. As the wind shifted, the smoke rotated clockwise, spreading the foul smell all over Bayou Meto.

Trip thought the smell would spread out and dissipate as it blew off the chimney. He was wrong.

By one o'clock, there was trouble brewing, and it wasn't coming from the cooker.

Trip heard an outboard off to the southwest, from the direction of the launch at Lower Vallier. He held his ground, but the sound of the outboard got louder and louder. He couldn't see a boat, but now it was so close he could hear the stroke of the engine each time it fired. His chest tightened. His breaths came in short strokes themselves. He had a plan for this, though.

He turned off the propane and pocketed the jars he'd made that morning. Then he motioned Cash to the boat and climbed in himself. He picked up the push pole and shoved off. He poled into the woods, gliding through the water. Quietly, ever so quietly. He lost himself in the timber, away from the sound of the outboard.

If nobody came, he'd go back. If it was the law, he'd keep going. Anything in between, he'd wait and see.

He watched. And listened. He heard the outboard get softer. Then nothing.

"Cash, I think it's going away." He listened. He listened hard. No sound at all.

"I think we're in the clear."

Then it was too late.

There he was, Captain Arcenault. Big as life. A hundred yards out, standing in a Game and Fish johnboat with a push pole. The Captain pushed the end of the pole, the boat gliding forward. He pushed again. The johnboat slipped silently to Snake Island, the engine tilted forward, the propeller out of the water. "So, that's what's going on."

He found the cooker.

Should he run? He didn't think Arcenault could catch him, but then again, Game and Fish had big motors. Just for this very sort of thing. Well, not exactly this sort of thing.

Trip decided to run for it. He pulled on the starter cord. The motor kicked to life, but then it was too late.

"Stop!" Arcenault said, shouting. "Stay right there." He took his service revolver out of its holster and fired a shot in the air. Arcenault boated the push pole, started his engine, and raced toward Trip.

Trip jammed the outboard in gear and started off toward Mama's Blind. He ran the engine as fast as he could, dodging between trees. The lower unit bounced off sunken logs. Branches ripped at his face.

Arcenault got closer and closer. Another shot. "Stop! Stop, I say."

Trip began to edge away from Arcenault, the fear of the pursued more reckless than the will of the pursuer. He turned away from Mama's Blind and ran through the woods. He headed north, then west. If he could make it to the main channel, where all the legal hunters came in, he could run wide open. His wake would leave a trail, but if he could mix in with the boats on their way out, he just might be able to lose himself in them and duck off into the timber and hide.

He was almost to the channel when he hit the log. The motor kicked out of the water, revved, then stalled. He yanked the starter cord. Again and again. It wouldn't start.

Then Arcenault was on him. "Stop right there," he said. "Hands up." Trip, his back to Arcenault, raised his hands, then turned slowly.

Trip broke into a wide smile. "Why, Captain Arcenault, it's you."

Arcenault pulled up alongside Trip. The two aluminum boats bumped against each other. Arcenault killed his engine. "Trip McClure, what exactly are you up to?"

"I came across that meth cooker. I thought you were the guy who had the cooker coming after me. So, I took off."

"What?"

"Who do you think I am?" Trip said, angry now. "I may have some money problems, but I'm not in drugs."

"Everybody knows you grow weed," Arcenault said. "We can get you for that any time we want."

Maybe I'm not as smart as I thought I was.

"That's for my personal use."

"Is that so." The boats drifted ever so slowly in the current. "Let's go back and see if we can figure out who that contraption belongs to." Arcenault waved the revolver at him. "You thought I was the bad guy."

"I surely did."

"What were you doing out there in the first place?"

"Scouting," Trip said.

"Scouting?"

"That's right."

"You know you can't cross that levy and hunt without a permit."

"I wasn't hunting. I was scouting."

Arcenault holstered his revolver and started his engine. "What say I follow you back to that cooker, and we'll have ourselves a look-see."

Trip pulled the starter cord. This time the engine started. He headed back in the general direction of the cooker.

"I'm not sure I can find it," he said over his shoulder and over the whine of the outboards.

"I suspect you'll find it all right."

Trip steered through the flooded timber.

I just might make it through this.

Getting caught by Arcenault wasn't his biggest problem. Arcenault would surely break up the cooker. How would he finish the recipe?

"Damn it, Cash. Damn it to hell." He lit a cigarette, looked back at Arcenault who smiled a law-enforcement smile at him.

Trip had the makings of another plan. He headed a bit east of the direct route to the cooker, not that there was a way to go anywhere in a straight line through the timber. He dodged around trees, high spots, low water, tangles, taking the most circuitous route he could, always further from Snake Island and the cooker.

"I think we need to go a bit more back to the west," Arcenault said.

"I think it's the other way."

Arcenault pulled alongside. Trip put the outboard in neutral.

"Back this way," Captain Arcenault said.

"No, it's this way," Trip said pointing to the east.

"You know exactly where it is. You've been hunting here your whole life." Arcenault looked up at the sun through the trees. "It's just west of the way we've been headed. If I didn't know better, I'd say you were heading us the wrong way on purpose. Not too much wrong. Just enough wrong so we miss it."

To which Trip did not reply.

Arcenault pointed to his right. "Now you just head that way. I'll be right behind you."

Trip put the outboard back in gear and off he went. He knew exactly where the cooker was. This time he steered too far to the west.

Arcenault waved him back on course. Ten minutes later and there it was. Snake Island. In all its glory. The bow of Trip's johnboat nudged the seasonal island. Cash sprang out. Trip stepped into the water, waded ashore, and pulled enough of the boat on the island so it wouldn't float away.

Arcenault beached his boat and climbed to the bow, then out. "For the life of me, I can't see how you could mistake me for a criminal. Not with this." Arcenault took off his flat-brimmed trooper's hat.

"I couldn't see you through the trees."

"I guess not." Hands on hips, the Captain surveyed Trip's drug factory. He studied the cooker hidden in the lean-to with tree trunks for corner posts. He looked up, sighting along the camouflaged stovepipe that disappeared up in the trees. "This here is one clever son-of-a-bitch." He shook his head. "Can't even smell it unless the wind is just right."

"I guess not."

"How long you been makin' this stuff?"

Trip's chest tightened and he had trouble breathing. He tried to focus on sucking air in through his nose. His chest began to heave, but he didn't think Arcenault could see it underneath his parka.

"Cat got your tongue?" Arcenault took a step toward Trip. "First thing to do is to see if you got any on you. Then we'll just bust this up."

Trip shut his eyes and blew out what little air he had in his lungs. When Arcenault found the baby food jars, it would surely be over.

"All right, then," Arcenault said, face-to-face with Trip. "Raise up those arms, and let's see what you got." Trip raised his arms. Arcenault took a half step, then he smiled at Trip.

"Come on now, Trip. Did you really think I was going to search you?" He laughed. "Let's take some pictures. Then we'll get out of here. Get the state police back here to check it out." Trip stood, arms still in the air, speechless.

At that moment, there was a blur from behind the lean-to. Someone swung a branch the size of a baseball bat at Arcenault's head. He saw it and ducked, but it hit Trip in the temple, knocking him down.

Trip lay on the hummock. He was seeing double and couldn't get himself to move. It was Jake. He had Arcenault by the throat.

The duck guide and the warden were locked together. They wrestled toward the water, then Jake had him down. He dunked him in Bayou Meto and held him there. The warden's arms thrashed like a chicken having its neck wrung.

Trip's vision cleared. He staggered to his feet and stumbled to Jake. He tried to pull him off Arcenault. Jake pushed him away.

Trip hit Jake square in the jaw. Jake shook it off and kept Arcenault down.

"God damn it, Jake!" Trip screamed. "You'll kill him."

"I believe I did," Jake said, smiling.

* * *

Trip and Jake sat in the muddy water of Bayou Meto, the water not quite over their waders. Arcenault floated between them, face down. Jake got to his feet and pulled Arcenault by the straps of his waders.

"You might as well give me a hand." Jake got Arcenault's head in the Game and Fish boat and pulled his shoulders again. He lost his grip on the dead man, and Arcenault's head bounced on the gunwale then fell in the boat. The boat started to drift away dragging Arcenault's body through the muddy water.

"His waders are filled up," Jake said. "He must weigh an extra fifty pounds."

"He's dead," Trip said.

"We been through that. Now we got to get rid of him."

"Why did you kill him?" Trip said, still sitting in the water.

"I saved you man. I saved your sorry ass."

"I had it taken care of."

"Then why was your hands up?" Jake lit a cigarette. "He don't look too good hanging there by his neck. Kind of like a duck on a game strap."

"Jesus Christ, Jake. He's dead." Cash waded out to the dead man, sniffed him. "God damn it, Cash, get away from there." Trip walked over to the boat and kicked at Cash.

"But for me, you'd be in jail," Jake said.

"I told you, I had it taken care of."

"Then why was your hands in the air?"

"He was playing with me."

"Like hell. The least thing that would've happened is the cooker would have got busted up." He crushed out the cigarette on Arcenault's neck.

"Somebody drowns out here every now and then. Give me a hand. We got a drowned man here. That's all we got."

Trip looked down at Arcenault.

How does Jake know about this place?

"Help me get him in the boat," Jake said again.

Trip lost his breath again. He turned red. He tried to take a deep breath.

Jake sloshed over and hit Trip on the back. "You don't look quite right to me."

Trip sputtered. Spit bubbled at the corners of his mouth. His knees buckled. Jake hit him on the back again. Trip fell forward. Jake caught him by the scruff of his neck.

"Don't you worry, Mr. Trip. Just help me get him in the boat."

Trip started breathing again. He looked over at Arcenault. The bow swung away from Arcenault's feet. The dead man's head snapped back. His head bounced on the gunwale. The good, but dead, Captain splashed face first in the floodwaters of Bayou Meto. The boat drifted away.

* * *

Under Jake's leadership, they wrestled Arcenault into the Game and Fish boat. Jake retrieved his own boat, and they towed the Captain and his boat southeast into a tangle of underbrush. Standing in waist-deep water, Jake unscrewed the drain plug on the Game and Fish boat, waited for it to fill, then screwed the plug back in.

The swamped boat hung at the surface, then the outboard dragged it down.

Arcenault floated on the surface above his sunken boat. Jake dragged him by his hair to an oak that had fallen across the tangle. Jake stuffed Arcenault under the trunk. The boots of his waders floated to the surface.

"That won't do." The murderous duck guide yanked him out, reached into his parka, and came out with Arcenault's service revolver. "Look here. A souvenir."

"You can't keep that."

"You worry too much." Jake pushed the warden further under the tree. Seeing no more of Arcenault, Jake smiled at Trip again.

* * *

Trip told Jake to follow him back to Mama's Blind, and Jake did, for a while. Trip disappeared into his own thoughts. When he looked behind him, Jake was gone. Trip cut his engine and listened. He heard the sound of an outboard off in the distance. It might not be Jake, but it surely wasn't Arcenault.

"My God, Cash, what have I done?"

Trip didn't want to stay in Bayou Meto any longer than he had to. He ripped on the starter cord and ran back to the levee at Mama's Blind. He hid the boat and scuttled over the levee to the relative safety of Belle Oak.

When he slithered down the Belle Oak side of the levee, he saw a baker's dozen mallard decoys in the hole in front of Mama's Blind.

"Damn it. Damn it to hell."

The decoys were motionless, in the still air. No ducks overhead. Nothing moved inside the blind. There wasn't supposed to be anyone out here. What if they'd seen something or heard something?

Trip sat on the bank of the levee, his feet in the water. Nothing moved. Finally, he dug out a small rock from the levee and threw it at the stake blind. He heard boots scrape. Then a head popped up.

"Trip. It is you."

"Damn it, Jude. What are you doing out here?"

"Big John dropped me off. Your boat was here, so I knew you'd be back. Nothing flying."

What am I going to do with you here?

The Yankee stood up, stretched, and grinned. His smile lit up the entire hole.

* * *

At 11:30 the next night, long after Trip's duck season bedtime, he sat across from Louis Bruno at a sticky table in the Gator.

They had been sitting there for the better part of an hour. There had been a fair amount of talking, but not too much listening. A dozen baby food jars sat in front of Louis Bruno.

"Louis, I'm all done."

"You're all done when I say you're all done. You just take these back with you. I'll see you when you have another dozen." The gangster slid the jars back to Trip.

"You might just as well take what's here." Trip pushed the jars back to Bruno. "Because what's here is all there's ever going to be here."

"You can't pay off your debt with these." Bruno picked the jars up, one at a time, and set them in front of Trip.

"This pays off part of it," Trip said. "I'll have the rest of the money when duck season is over." Trip had another dozen jars hidden in the Crooked Tree, but he was damned if he'd tell Bruno about them. Not yet anyway. The reverse tug-of-war continuing, he pushed the jars across the table.

"I don't want cash. I want meth." He started with the jars again, then stopped. "How about this. We'll just leave these jars in the middle right here." Bruno moved them halfway to Trip. "Until you get it figured out."

"I got it figured out."

"You'll lose your duck woods."

"I'll pay the rest of what I owe you in cash," Trip said.

"Young man. I don't want cash. I want meth, and I want you to make it for me," Bruno smiled at him.

"I told you. I'm all done."

"I don't know what's got into you. We're partners."

CHAPTER TWENTY-SIX

Trip slept in until four the next morning. He let Cash out, made coffee, and smoked his first cigarette while he made himself a fried egg sandwich. He went outside and threw his waders in the pickup. The moon hung just above the tree line. The wind had picked back up, still from the northwest. Today would be a good day to kill ducks in the timber. Today would also be a good day to cook the recipe. This wind, a bright, hopeful wind, that would blow away the smell of the recipe. He'd told Bruno that he'd quit, but he was going to make more.

Just in case.

Trip lit another cigarette and waited for Cash. Then, "Cash. Cash, come." Trip climbed into his truck and rolled down the window. "Cash, come." He drove down the driveway with the window open. There wasn't any heat from the heater yet, and the Arkansas winter blew in through the open windows. He called again.

"Damn that dog."

It wasn't like Cash not to come when he was called. He never strayed too far, especially during duck season.

Trip turned toward the Club House. He crawled along the road and called for Cash again.

He'll meet me at the Club House. He's done this before, run the path through the woods.

Trip pulled off the shoulder of the road and stopped the truck dead in its tracks. He killed the lights and rolled up the window.

"My God," he said out loud, as if to Cash. Trip hit the steering wheel with his fists. "My God. What have I done?" He fell forward against the steering wheel. "The Captain's dead, and I killed him." He sat up and pounded the steering wheel with his fists. "I didn't kill him. Jake killed him. Jake did it. He didn't have to kill him. There was another way. Jake didn't have to do anything. I had the Captain convinced it wasn't me." He looked out the window. "How did Jake know?

It was Jake. You can never trust Jake.

"But Jake was trying to help. That's what he was doing, but I should turn him into Sheriff Dewitt. I didn't kill the Captain. Jake did. I didn't kill him." The cold blew into the truck. Trip rolled up the window. "I'll turn him in. That's what I'll do. I didn't kill him. Dewitt will think it's Jake's cooker. It's something Jake would do." Trip smiled. "That's what I'll do. But as sure as there's ducks in the timber, Captain Arcenault died at my hand." Trip slumped over the steering wheel again. "And Sheriff Dewitt may have a thought that all this might go farther back than Captain Arcenault and the cooker. I played a part in all this. A big part."

Flashing lights pulled up behind him.

Trip sat straight up. He looked in his rearview mirror, but the lights blinded him. He couldn't see a thing. He heard a door open, shut, then boots on gravel.

How could anyone know? It's too soon.

There was a rap on his window. A flashlight in his eyes. He raised his hand to block the light. He squinted around his hand, but he couldn't see into the darkness behind the beam.

"Roll down that window," said a voice on the other side of the window. "Roll it down."

Trip rolled down the window and cold, clammy air blew back in.

"What's goin' on here?" said the voice.

I know that voice.

"I said, what's goin' on here?"

"Church, is that you?"

"Course it is, Mr. Trip. You know that. Now, what's goin' on?"

Trip leaned back on his seat. "Church, what in God's name are you doing with those damn lights?"

"Those are my new fireman's lights," Church grinned at him. "I thought you might be in trouble, pokin' along like that, and I sure didn't want anybody running up our backside here in the dark."

"You put a fright in me."

"Why would that be?"

"Put that light down. I can't see a thing."

"Yes, sir. Sorry, Mr. Trip." The light went out. "But what exactly are you doing stopped on the highway, halfway between the yellow house and the Club House?"

Trip leaned toward Church. "I'm looking for Cash."

"Where'd he get off to?"

"If I knew that, I wouldn't be looking for him."

"I guess that's so."

"I let him out this morning, and I haven't seen him since."

"He's surely at the Club House." Church smiled at him. "He knows there's a duck hunt today." He started off toward his flashing truck. "Let's get over there, and that's where we'll find him." The volunteer fireman climbed in his truck and roared off, lights flashing.

Trip swung back onto the highway and drove to the Club House. He climbed out of his pickup, fully expecting to see Cash.

"Cash," he said. "Cash, here."

Church appeared beside him. "Where can that dog have gotten to?"

"Lord if I know." Trip stepped up on the porch and walked in. Cigarette smoke hung in the air. Underneath that, the smell of ashtrays and burned coffee. Big John snored on the lower bunk, his chest rising and falling. He had his headphones on, the Walkman on his chest, also rising and falling. Cad sat at the kitchen table.

"You seen Cash?" Trip said.

"Not since yesterday," Cad said.

"What about him?" Trip asked, pointing at Big John.

"Been sleeping since I got here," Cad said.

"Damn that dog," Trip said. "Where's Jake?"

"Haven't seen him," Cad said.

Trip pulled the earphones off Big John. "You seen Cash?"

"No, sir," said the big man.

I've got to get on with it.

Trip lit another cigarette. "Boys, we got ourselves a full house today. Four groups of four." He looked at the cigarette and crushed it out in the overflowing ashtray. "You boys figuring on emptying this, or are you waiting for the maid?"

"It's Jake's turn," Big John said.

I'm sure he'll do it when he shows up. If he shows up.

Trip looked at his watch. "Let's go get the sports." Trip stood at the open door as the guides shuffled out. There was a glow in the southeast, but no Cash.

* * *

Jude showed up just as they piled into the trucks. Jake was still missing, just like Cash. Trip took Jake's group, four boys from Montgomery, plus Jude. The only thing Trip liked about Alabama was Parker.

Trip called them in that morning. He called them like he called in the late season, by hardly calling at all. These ducks had been shot at from Saskatchewan to Stuttgart. They were spooked by just about everything, and they didn't want to hear very much.

He called them in. The sports killed them. Trip retrieved them. They had their limit by 10:30, then Trip and Jude took the four-wheeler and drove all the levees. Trip called for Cash. Again and again. They ended up at the shop.

"Damn that dog," Trip said.

"He's around here somewhere," Jude said.

"Just where would that be?" Trip walked around the edge of the shop where the concrete pad met the dirt. When he got to the driveway, he got down on one knee and studied the dirt. He brushed his hand over the dirt. Then he traced an outline with his finger.

Jude came up behind him. "What is it?"

Trip stood and followed whatever he was following. Then he stopped. "What is it?"

Trip knelt again and placed his palm on the gravel.

Jude started to walk toward Trip. "Stop. Stop right there."

"For God's sake, Trip, what is it?"

"Cash's footprints are here," he said, kneeling again.

"That's not too surprising. He's here every day."

"These are fresh."

"He was probably here this morning."

"He was. And there's boot prints right next to them."

"What difference does that make?"

"They're not mine. And right here," Trip said, pointing, "somebody picked him up right here."

"How do you know?"

"There's more boot prints but no more dog prints." Trip stood up and kicked at the gravel.

They ate lunch in the yellow house. That is, Jude ate. Trip picked at his gumbo. He spooned the rice in the roux, but he didn't eat.

"You can't be sure somebody took Cash," Parker said.

"He's gone. And somebody took him." Trip splashed hot sauce on the gumbo.

"He'll show up any minute," Jude said.

"Only if he's delivered in somebody's trunk." Trip squashed the rice down in the gumbo.

"Baby, eat something," Parker said. "Why would anyone want to take Cash?"

"I have no idea," Trip said, who had a few ideas who might want to take Cash.

"Is there something going on around here?" Jude said.

"Nothing that a couple hundred thousand dollars wouldn't take care of," Trip said.

"We'll just wait on him. He'll be back," Parker said.

Trip took his bowl to the kitchen counter. It perched on the edge of the sink, teetered, then pitched in. It broke in two pieces. The gumbo drained out like muddy water when a levee board was lifted.

It turned out that they didn't have to wait long. Just as Trip dropped the broken bowl into the trash, Jake came crashing through the door.

He took two steps into the kitchen. Jake, unlike Cash, had never been invited inside the yellow house. Trip glared at him. Jake returned the look. Then he took two steps back, his bravado leaking out his boots.

"Jake," Trip said.

"Mr. Trip, I got a message for you."

"What is it?"

"Mr. Trip, do you know where Cash is?"

"What do you know about Cash?" Trip started toward Jake who backed up into the door.

"There's a man at the Gator. He said if you want Cash, you best come see him straight away."

"What were you doing at the Gator? You had hunters this morning."

Jake cocked his head. "I thought I had the morning off."

"You didn't."

"I had a fuzzy head this morning, so I thought a short one might be just what I needed. Anyway, this guy came up to me, the guy I brought out to you at Mama's Blind. He said to tell you, you best come meet him at the Gator, right away, if you want Cash back."

"What's his name?" Trip said, knowing the answer.

Jake stuttered, then, "He didn't say, but he looked Italian," pronouncing it "eye-talian."

I'll deal with you later.

On the way into Stuttgart, Trip looked over to the passenger seat at least half a dozen times, each time expecting Cash to be riding shotgun, each time finding the seat empty. Finally, he willed himself not to look. He looked straight ahead at the white line on the two-lane highway, then up. There were high cirrus clouds off to the west. "Cash, the weather's about to change." Trip pounded the steering wheel with his fist.

The parking lot at the Gator was almost empty. Trip parked next to Bruno's Fleetwood. He opened his door on the Cadillac and dinged the gangster's door.

Jake knew damn well who the Italian was.

The bar was dark even at two in the afternoon. Cigarette smoke and flat beer hung in the air. Trip saw Bruno by himself at a table next to the gator pit. Trip sat down across from him. The gangster smiled his yellow teeth at him.

The waitress arrived, a puffy haired, twentyish woman with too much eye makeup. She raised her pencil-thin eyebrows at Trip.

"Nothing for me."

"You can't sit here 'less you order," she said, her eyebrows collapsing.

"The boy will have a Maker's Mark on the rocks." Bruno was drinking something clear from a rocks glass.

The waitress arched her left eyebrow.

She has a gift.

"Bourbon," Bruno said.

"We don't have that." She actually spoke.

"Nothing for me," Trip said again.

"Make it a Jack Black then," Bruno said.

She shook her head no.

"What do you have?"

"We have Kessler's. Smooth as silk," she said, smiling. "That's what the billboard says, at Christmas."

"A double," Bruno said. "And one more of these."

"Yes, sir."

Bruno looked at Trip. "They don't have Stoli either. This is Popov's." He drank a little and made a face. "What is it that you want?"

Trip stared at him.

"I know why you're here. You're here because you want to make more meth."

Trip didn't say anything.

"I wonder what it could be." Bruno took out a cigar from the pocket of his sport coat.

I've never seen anyone with a sport coat in the Gator.

The gangster unwrapped the cigar. He bit off the end and spit it into the gator pit. There was a slithering sound and then the sound of jaws snapping shut. "That must be one hungry alligator." He lit his cigar.

Trip stared at him.

"Why is it that you're here?"

"You know why."

Bruno poked the cigar into his mouth, struck a match, and lit his cigar. He threw the match into the gator pit. Trip watched the flame drop out of sight. More slithering and snapping.

"Lord knows what they feed that thing," Bruno said.

The waitress dropped off the drinks. Bruno handed her a twenty. She reached into the pocket of her apron for change.

"Keep it."

The waitress smiled at the gangster with her eyebrows.

Bruno took a swallow of his drink. His hand was so big it looked like he was drinking from it. He shook his head. "Popov's is the vodka equivalent of Kessler's. Maybe a notch below."

Trip didn't touch his drink.

"Now, then, where were we?"

"You know where."

"No, son, I don't. And if I did, I'd still want you to tell me. Have a little sip. Then tell me." Bruno pushed the glass of whiskey toward Trip. "What is it that you want?"

Trip felt himself losing control. His chest tightened again, like it had in the timber. He stared at his drink, then at Bruno. "Where's my dog?"

"Your dog? What kind of dog is it?"

Trip glared at him.

"What's his name?" Bruno asked.

Trip stared at the gangster. He gripped the edge of the table.

Bruno chewed on his cigar. "Oh, I know. You mean the black one. That's right. The black one. What's his name?"

"Cash."

"Cash," Bruno said. "It's funny how that's what you need, cash, and that's the name of your dog." He took the cigar out of his mouth. "Cash," he said again. "I know right where he is." Bruno smiled at him with genuine concern. "He's close. Very close. Bring me all the jars you've got. And then I'll tell you." Bruno sucked on his cigar. "I think you've got more than those six jars." Bruno took the cigar out of his mouth and looked at it. "And you make more jars. You make them until I say you can stop."

"Where's Cash?"

"Do you agree?"

Trip stared at the gangster. He had a death grip on the table. He could hardly breathe his chest was so tight.

Trip nodded.

"That's a good boy," Bruno said. "Now, go get me what you've got, and I'll meet you back here tonight." He stuck the cigar back in his mouth. "Say, ten o'clock."

"Where's Cash?"

"You're a broken record." Bruno's cigar tipped up and down as he spoke. "Why he's right here. He's been here all along."

"Where is he?"

"Come over here, son."

Trip stood and walked over to Bruno.

"He's right down there." Bruno pointed down in the gator pit.

Cash sat on a ledge halfway up the side of the gator pit. The alligator stared up at the dog.

"Burt just ate so he's not too hungry. But he will be by tonight."

Cash looked up at Trip. The dog's left front leg trembled.

Trip ran out of the Gator and raced back to Belle Oak. He skidded out the levee to the landing. He jumped in the johnboat and busted out to the Crooked Tree.

He got the rest of the baby food jars. Another dozen and a half. Enough for Cash's ransom, plus a few spares.

Maybe it was a good idea to keep cooking.

There was no hurry, though. Ten o'clock was hours away, but he wanted those jars in his pocket. The clouds had thickened from the west while he was in the Gator and now they filled two-thirds of the sky.

Jude was waiting for him at the dock when he came back. "What's up?"

"Scouting," Trip said, sitting in the stern of the johnboat.

"What about Cash?"

"I'm picking him up at ten tonight. At the Gator." Trip wrapped the stern line around the post.

"Why didn't you get him while you were there?"

"The guy didn't have him with him."

"Who?"

"The guy who found him."

"And who was that?"

"The guy who found him."

"Jesus Christ, Trip. What's the mystery?"

Trip looked down at his boots.

"What's going on?"

"With what?"

"With you. You've been acting funny ever since you started this duck club."

"I'm just tired is all."

"You never drive your truck out here during duck season."

"Quad wouldn't start," Trip lied.

Jude stuck his hands in his pockets. "Funny thing about friends. They talk things out, help each other."

"I don't need any help." When Trip stepped onto the dock, the boat started to drift away. Jude grabbed him by the arm and pulled him on the dock.

"I'd have made that," Trip said.

"I know it."

CHAPTER TWENTY-SEVEN

The parking lot at the Gator was full at ten, unusual for a Wednesday night, except for the last Wednesday of duck season. The last week of duck season was like seven national holidays in a row.

Trip had convinced Jude not to come to the Gator with him. If he could just get Cash back, he could figure out the rest. He couldn't see any reason to bring anyone else in, least of all Jude. Yankees had no idea what went on down here.

I can do this on my own.

He knew he'd been slow. Jake was in this up to his eyeballs, and Trip was in it, too—way over his head.

Trip put the baby food jars in the pockets of his coat and walked into the bar. He pushed his way through the smoke and the crowd, men outnumbering women at least ten to one, the odds even greater if the barmaids were subtracted. The Duck Masters hurt Trip's ears, but they drowned out the improbable stories, the tall tales, and the outright lies.

He slithered through the standing-room-only crowd, past the locals, the guides, the public ground hunters, the leaseholders, the duck club members, the planters, and the out-of-towners. This was just about the only time that all the classes of hunters would ever be together in a place totally without class.

The gangster sat at the table next to Burt, a plastic glass of vodka in front of him. The waitress with the pencil-thin eyebrows set a double Kessler's down in front of him.

Trip slid the baby food jars across the table. Louis Bruno unscrewed the top of the jar closest to him. He dipped a wet finger into one of the jars, tasted it, and screwed the top back on.

"This will do. This squares you with the weed." He put the jars in the pockets of his jacket.

"That more than pays for the weed," Trip said. "Where's my dog?"

"He's all right."

"I didn't ask if he was all right. I asked where he was."

Bruno took a swallow of his vodka. "I never knew duck hunting was so popular."

Trip didn't say anything.

Bruno took another swallow. "Where were we?"

"Where's my dog?"

"That's where we were. Your dog. You know, this has worked out so well, I've decided to keep him for you."

"You said . . ."

"I changed my mind."

"I want my dog back. Now."

"Make me another dozen jars and then we'll see." Bruno took a cigar out of his pocket and rolled it around in his fingers. "I'll take good care of him for you. You just go cook me up some more recipe."

Trip lunged at Bruno. The gangster pushed the table at him. It caught him in the belly and sat him back down in his chair. Trip started up again. The gangster pulled the nine-millimeter out. He slammed it on the table next to the plastic glass of cheap vodka.

"This thing isn't much good on ducks, but it will work on a dog," Bruno said.

Trip clenched the edge of the table with both hands. "Where's my dog?"

"You just don't get it. You and your farm and your precious duck woods. Your high and mighty family. And your old money. It's over son. You work for me now." Bruno unwrapped his cigar. He bit the end off and shoved it in the corner of his mouth. "I think I'd rather smell my own smoke." He lit the cigar. "Your dog is right where he was."

Cash sat on the same ledge, the gator closer than before. Not a soul, save Trip, gave the dog so much as a glance.

* * *

Trip climbed in his truck and backed up. Then he threw the truck in park. He sat in the cold, the engine idling. The clouds had moved in, and the night sky was starless, dark except for the red neon alligator above the door of the roadhouse.

He reached over and opened the glove box. The pearl-handled Colt that Big George had done himself in with filled up the glove box, except for the pint of Maker's Mark next to it. He took a pull from the bottle.

Trip took the Colt out of the glove box. He fondled the gun and felt the cold luster of the pearl handle. His fingers found the spot worn down by Big George. He ran over it with his finger.

How long had it taken to wear down the pearl?

He sat in the truck and held the pistol. He checked to make sure it was loaded, then he put the barrel in his mouth, just like his father had done. He took the gun out of his mouth and took another pull on the bottle. He sat in the truck and rubbed the handle, just like his father must have done.

The parking lot had started to empty. As soon as a few more cars left, he'd make his move. He didn't know if Bruno had left and he didn't care.

I'm going to get Cash back. One way or another.

There were only a handful of cars left in the parking lot. It was time. He took one more pull on the bottle. He tried to open the door to the truck, but it slammed back in his face. He pushed on the door, but it wouldn't budge. There was a face against the glass, but he couldn't make it out. The face had a hand that rapped on the window.

Trip rolled down the window. It was Church. Church, the duck guide, pastor, and fireman.

"What are you doing here?" Church said.

"I'm going to get Cash."

"Not with that, you ain't," Church pointed at the pistol.

"Cash is in the gator pit."

"I know it. You either give me that gun or put it back in the glove box. I don't care which."

"I'm going to get Cash." Trip swung the pistol toward Church.

"Mr. Trip, you just stop right there. You know that whiskey and guns don't mix. I'm here to help you get Cash." He held his hand out for the pistol.

"We might need it," Trip said.

"No, we won't."

"What are you doing here?"

"Mr. Jude sent me to look after you."

"I don't need any looking after."

"I'd say you do. You more than most. Hand me that pistol and we'll go fetch Cash."

"How?"

"I have a plan."

Trip studied the Colt, then he handed it to Church. The fireman opened the gun and shook the bullets into his free hand. Trip put the gun back in the glove box.

Church led Trip to the back of the Gator. A lean-to hung onto the back of the building. Church opened the door. "We got to be quiet." He clicked on a flashlight and pointed it down at the floor. "The kitchen is right through this door. They're cleaning up in there. There's a few boys still drinking in the bar."

Church played the flashlight around the room, on a lawnmower, a gas can, a rake, shovels, a pickaxe, paint cans, a pile of rags.

Church stooped and picked up the gas can. He unscrewed the cap and poured gasoline on the rags.

"What are you doing?"

"Not so loud, Mr. Trip." He poured more gas on the rags. "What we have here is an accelerant."

"A what?"

"That's fireman talk." Church struck a match and dropped it on the rags. The rags caught fire, not a raging fire but a small, soothing fire. "We'll just let this burn a minute. I'll run in the kitchen and holler 'fire.' I'll get everybody out the front. You sneak in and get Cash."

"This is arson."

"Mr. Trip, this is just a little friendly spontaneous combustion. No one should leave rags in a pile like this."

The flames licked a little higher. "You'll burn the place down."

Why should I care?

"Soon as I get everybody out, I'll call the firehouse. We'll have it out in no time." Church beamed. "There hasn't been a fire around here in a long time. They need the practice."

"There's ways of finding out how fire's start," Trip said.

"That's right, Mr. Trip, except I'm the arson investigator in Arkansas County." Church started for the door to the kitchen. "You just wait right here."

Church burst into the kitchen. "Everybody out," Church yelled. "There's a fire out back. Everybody out."

Trip heard voices, but he couldn't make out what they were saying. Then, "Mr. Slick, you can't go back there and put it out. It's too far gone. You got to go out the front. Right now. I radioed for the fire truck." More voices. "You can't go back there, Mr. Slick. You got to go out the front."

Trip waited while Church got everybody out. He thought it would have been easier to pretend there was a fire than to start one, but then Church must like fires, or he wouldn't be a fireman.

The line between a fireman and a firebug is blurry.

The fire took hold of the rags and licked up the wall. The shed was hot now—Trip couldn't stay in here much longer. One of the paint cans blew. Trip ducked. The lid flew off and bounced against a wall as the paint can tipped over, spilling paint on the floor. When it reached the rags, it lit up. Trip had to get out. As soon as the rest of the paint caught fire, the shed would become a furnace. Another can blew. When he cracked the door to the kitchen, the fresh air stoked the fire. He opened the door a little further.

Then he heard Church. "I said you can't go that way, Mr. Slick. We got to go out the front."

Trip shut the door and waited inside the lean to. But the heat was too much. He opened the door to the kitchen and stepped in.

"Out, Mr. Slick," Church said.

Trip ducked behind a cooler.

"I've got a fire extinguisher. I'll put it out," Slick said. He opened the door to the shed. Flames shot out at him.

"God damn it, Mr. Slick. You can't put that fire out with that little thing."

Slick's back was to him. Trip ducked out from behind the cooler. Church saw Trip and winked. "All right, then, let's give it a try. I got one here, too." The two men sprayed a suffocating white foam through the door.

Trip bolted through the kitchen into the bar. There was no sign of Bruno or anyone else. He ran for the pit. There was Cash still sitting on the ledge, under the watchful eye of Burt whose interest in his next meal was growing. Trip lifted off a section of the grate and jumped into the gator pit. The gator started toward Trip. Trip boosted Cash out of the pit and climbed out.

They made for the front door. Trip peeked out, but everyone who had run out was watching the Gator burn. Trip found an emergency exit on the side. He cracked the door—no one on this side of the building. He took Cash outside and stood in the shadows and waited. He bent down and hugged his dog. Cash licked his nose. Trip had never been so glad to see anyone, two-legged or four-legged.

When the fire truck roared in, the two of them bolted for the pickup. Cash rode shotgun.

* * *

After he sent the guides, once again sans Jake, to the timber, Trip stood in the driveway of the Club House and looked up through the live oaks. The moon had set, but Orion was low in the sky. The giant's sword sparkled at him.

He needed a new plan. He'd have the money from the third split, but without any money from the jars, that wouldn't be enough. And there was unfinished business with Bruno. And Jake.

An Arkansas County police cruiser roared up to the Club House, its lights flashing.

One more set of flashing lights will be the end of me.

Sheriff Dewitt lumbered up to Trip. "Trip," Sheriff Dewitt said.

"Sheriff," Trip said back

They both looked at their feet. Neither spoke. The cruiser's lights kept flashing.

I didn't think anyone had seen us sneaking out of the Gator.

The two of them stood there saying nothing, there being an unwritten rule in the south that the first one who spoke, lost.

Cash wandered over to the right front tire of the sheriff's cruiser and lifted his leg on the tire.

"What the hell," Sheriff Dewitt said, the spell of unspoken words now broken.

Cash looked back at the sheriff and smiled a dog smile at him.

"That was uncalled for," the sheriff said.

"Cash, come," Trip said without conviction. Cash, understanding the non-command command, ignored his master and continued around the car, marking as he went.

"Cash, you cut that out," Trip said, still not really meaning it. The dog kept going.

"Get that dog to stop."

"How about you turn off those lights? They'll scare away the ducks."

"Not from here they won't."

"Cash, come," Trip said again. This time he meant it, and this time, Cash came.

The sheriff turned off the lights. "We got ourselves an issue."

"What's that?" Trip knew the issue all too well. Sheriff Dewitt was about to arrest him for the fire at the Gator.

"Captain Arcenault is missing. Been missing since Monday."

Trip's chest tightened again and he lost his breath. He hoped the sheriff hadn't noticed.

"What happened?" Although he knew all too well what happened.

"His wife called in from Pine Bluff. Sometimes he stays up here during duck season, but he always calls her."

"And?"

"First she called Game and Fish. They said he'd been trying to find a meth plant in Bayou Meto. They said he'd been over here at Belle Oak."

"He was here. At the end of the second split. I took him out two weeks ago. We looked around at the levee."

"See anything?"

"No."

"They found his truck and trailer at Lower Vallier, so that's where they figure he went in. They got me checking on this side."

"What's with the lights?"

"Fired 'em up just to make sure they was working."

"Why here?"

"It scares everybody if I do it in town."

"I see," Trip said.

"Plus, it's kind of fun."

"I guess so. Depending on where you sit."

"You ain't seen him?"

"Not since we rode out to the levee."

"How about we go out there again as soon as it gets light?"

"All right by me. You seen Jake?"

"I thought he worked for you."

"He does when he shows up."

"Saw him last night. At the Gator. At the fire. You know anything about that?"

"Fire?"

"Seems there was a dog in the gator pit and now there ain't."

"Really?"

"Really. How about some breakfast?" said the man who never missed a meal.

"Come on in."

The sheriff sidled by him and slipped inside the Club House.

* * *

Trip and Sheriff Dewitt bounced along the levee on the four-wheeler. The sheriff sat behind Trip and held on for dear life. Cash, none the worse for wear, trotted ahead, looking back every now and then, annoyed that the quad ran along the levee so slowly.

Trip had fed the portly sheriff steak and eggs with grits and toast. He had hoped that the oversized breakfast would make the sheriff sleepy, but it only seemed to further his resolve.

At the landing, Trip fired up the outboard and the three of them set off. The sheriff had put on his waders and parka. Except for his hat, he looked like a hunter. He'd even brought his shotgun, although the law enforcement model had a ten-round magazine.

Trip lit a cigarette. In the cold, he couldn't tell the difference between the smoke and his breath.

Trip shook his head when they passed the Crooked Tree.

What was I thinking?

They made it to Mama's Blind just before eight. Trip killed the motor, and they drifted up against the levee. "This is the end of the line."

If I can just keep him here, I'll be all right.

"Tie the boat here, and let's have a look." The sheriff climbed out of the boat and crabbed to the top of the levee. Trip stayed in the boat. The sheriff disappeared.

"Get on up here," Sheriff Dewitt said.

"Damn it, Cash." Trip tied the boat and climbed up.

"Over here," the sheriff said.

Trip joined him fifty yards to the south.

As long as he doesn't find the boat on the Bayou Meto side, I'll be all right.

Trip met up with the sheriff where the levee jogged slightly to the northeast. He had hidden the boat another twenty yards down the levee.

If I can just keep him here.

"There you are," said the sheriff, puffing.

Trip answered with his patented silence.

"Let's get out there and look around." He pointed into Bayou Meto.

"How so?"

"In your boat."

"My boat's back there," Trip said. "You want to haul it over the levee?"

"I want you to take me out in the boat that's just down the path."

"What boat?"

"The boat you hid down there."

Damn it. Damn it to hell.

"It's not my job to bust you for sneaking in from this side. There's some damn fine holes in there, and I expect you know right where they are." The sheriff waddled down the path in his waders.

Sheriff Dewitt slid down the bank and eased himself into the boat. The bow dipped when he sat down. He settled himself next to a bag of decoys. Trip passed him the shotguns. Cash jumped in.

"It don't take much of a thinker to figure you'd want to hunt from this side." The sheriff kicked the bag of decoys away from his feet. "Only a fool would hunt on your side with all this in your backyard."

Trip pushed the boat off the bank and started the motor. "Where to, Sheriff?"

"You tell me."

"I'm sure I don't know," Trip lied. He hated himself for his part in Arcenault's murder, but he didn't see how finding him would help.

"I bet you know something. I heard there was a powerful smell of ammonia coming from somewhere over here. We'll just look around and see if we can't find some sign of the Captain or the smell."

"Which way?"

"Damn it, Trip. You know these woods, not me." Dewitt loaded his gun.

"Sheriff, you can't ride around with a loaded gun."

"This is police business, and I've got the safety on. Let's get. You take me out to your favorite holes and we'll see what we can see."

Trip started out northeast, then cut west. He'd stay as far away from Arcenault and Snake Island as he could. He took the sheriff on a circuitous route. He wound around trees, through channels, in and out of holes, hoping to disorient the lawman. The ducks had begun to fly, flying just above the treetops, looking for a place to land. After fifteen minutes, Trip guided them into Blackwater, just about as far he could get from Snake Island. When he nosed the boat in the hole, four dozen mallards exploded into the air.

"Damn, that's about as fine a sight as I've seen. We get a chance, I may shoot one."

"You'll have to plug your gun."

"This is a police gun. It's legal for ten shells."

"Not for duck hunting."

"I won't shoot more than three times. Not that I can't, but I'm a sportsman."

They kept going west through Woodpecker Channel, then south. Trip kept them well east of Snake Island. They puttered around for the better part of an hour, zigzagging back and forth out of harm's way. By nine a.m., the ducks were really flying.

They turned back. When Trip pulled back into Blackwater, they spooked more mallards. Dewitt told him to shut off the engine.

What in God's name for? We're almost out of harm's way.

"Slide us up against that tree and call me in a few."

"Shouldn't we get back?"

"I got all day."

"I've got hunters coming in," Trip said.

"Call me in a couple and we'll go. Call 'em in like your mama says you do. She always tells me you call so sweetly." He took off his sheriff's hat and set it down next to him. "You got a spare hat? One that's not so shiny?"

Trip fished around in the toolbox and came up with a soggy camo hat that said "Mack's." He handed it to Dewitt.

"Call 'em in. I'll sit here and watch." He put the hat on.

Trip, not accustomed to doing what he was told, did what he was told. He called them, cajoled, begged, pleaded. He wooed them. He called, ever so sweetly, and in they came.

Half-a-dozen mallards fluttered down through the trees. Sheriff Dewitt picked out a drake and missed. Three times. He didn't say a word.

He missed again on the next two groups. "Damn hard from the boat. Can't you get them any closer?"

If they were any closer, they'd be landing in the boat.

Trip called in a fourth group. Dewitt crippled a drake on his fifth shot.

So much for sportsmanship.

"That's more like it." The sheriff beamed. The flightless mallard swam to the edge of the hole.

"Cash, fetch," Trip said. The dog was locked on the duck and jumped in.

The sheriff raised his gun at the duck.

Trip pushed the barrel up in the air.

"He's getting away."

"You'll shoot my dog."

"Hell, I will."

Just then, in an exquisitely quiet and unfortunate moment, the whine of an outboard motor.

"What's that?" the sheriff said.

"I didn't hear anything," Trip said, who had.

"That's an outboard."

"I don't hear anything."

"Hell, you don't. It's over there to the west." The sheriff wasn't as lost as Trip had hoped. "Let's go see who it is."

"Cash isn't back yet."

"He can wait here for us," the sheriff said, all thoughts of his mallard now forgotten.

"I'm not leaving without Cash." The retriever swam after the mallard, who ducked in and out of the trees just beyond the hole.

"Damn it, Trip. I want to see who that is."

"I know it, Sheriff."

"Tell him to hurry up." At that very moment, the mallard picked a most opportune time to dive. Cash lost him. The dog stood on his hind legs, chest out of the water, and pirouetted.

"That duck dove. He's going to hang on down there and drown himself."

"Give him a minute. He wasn't hit that hard."

Dewitt scowled at him. Sure enough, the duck surfaced. Cash had his back to him. The duck, with only its head above water, snuck off to the north.

"He's gone for sure," Dewitt said. "Call off your dog."

The outboard whined, further off now.

Take your time, Cash.

The dog turned, spied the duck, and chased after him. The duck dove three more times. The third time Cash pitched his head underwater. He came up with the duck and started back to the boat.

"He's got the damn duck. Go over there and pick him up."

"There's too many logs."

"Damn it, Trip. I can't hear it anymore."

"It's probably just hunters."

"Probably don't cut it in police work. Get that dog in here."

Cash swam back to the boat a bit too promptly for Trip. The dog presented the crippled duck to Trip. It flapped its one good wing. "Fine bird, Sheriff."

"Wring its neck and let's go."

Trip pulled Cash in. He shook himself off on the impatient sheriff. Trip wrung the crippled mallard's neck. The whining outboard had faded into nothingness.

"Let's go," the sheriff said.

"Which way?"

"That way." The sheriff pointed west.

Trip's chest tightened. That way was the way to Snake Island.

Damn it.

Trip started off the way the sheriff had said, then veered slightly to the north, hoping the sheriff wouldn't notice.

"Not that way. That way." The sheriff pointed right toward Snake Island. "If I didn't know better, I'd say you were trying to take me in the wrong direction."

"It's hard to keep on a line in here."

"Not for you." Sheriff Dewitt pointed to the west again. "That way."

They motored to the west.

"Cut the motor," the sheriff said.

Trip pushed the kill button and the engine stopped.

Voices. There were voices close by.

"Sheriff …"

"Shush. I hear somebody talking. Don't start that motor." Trip thought real hard about pulling on the starter cord but didn't.

Sure enough, there were voices. They were too far away to hear what they were saying. Sheriff Dewitt listened. And listened.

The sheriff whispered at him. "Get your push pole and pole us in. Quiet."

Trip took out the push pole. Slowly and quietly, he poled them through the flooded timber toward the voices.

He hoped they were hunters, but this close to Belle Oak, he had his doubts. If they were hunters, they were probably lost hunters. He banged the push pole on the side of the boat.

Dewitt hissed at him. "Quiet. You'll wake the dead."

Too late.

A hundred yards. Another hundred yards. Still another. Then the johnboat nosed out of the timber. There it was, fifty yards dead ahead. Snake Island. In all its infernal glory. The voices had faces. They weren't lost hunters. They weren't hunters at all.

There was a johnboat beached on the Belle Oak side of Snake Island. And who should be sitting in the stern? It was Jake. What was he doing here? Someone else poked around the cooker. Trip couldn't make out who it was. He was bent over the pot, his back toward them. Jake saw Trip and the sheriff. He tried to wave them off.

The sheriff whispered at him. "Move in, Trip,"

"I'm not so sure this is a good idea."

"We just found ourselves that smell."

Trip poled them in. The sheriff reached for his shotgun when they were thirty yards out. At twenty yards, he told Trip to stop. "Right here, son." The portly lawman stood up in the boat, his gun out of sight.

"I wouldn't stand up if I were you."

"Hush up." The sheriff put his hands on his hips. Trip had a pretty good idea who was at the cooker. He pulled the bill of his cap down in front of his face.

"Stand up and turn around," Sheriff Dewitt said, shouting. The hunched figure didn't move. "I said stand up and turn around."

Louis Bruno stood up and turned around. He pointed the nine-millimeter at the sheriff.

Dewitt hollered at him. "Put that gun down."

"Get the hell out of here," Bruno said.

"Put that gun down. I'm the sheriff of Arkansas County."

"And I'm Santa Claus."

Trip looked over at Jake who, like Trip, was doing his best to disappear.

"You've got one more chance to put that gun down and put your hands up," the sheriff said.

"And you've got one more chance to turn your fat ass around and get the hell out of here."

Sheriff Dewitt stooped to pick up his shotgun.

"Don't move, mister," Bruno said.

The sheriff moved and the gangster fired a shot over the boat.

"Sheriff, let's go," Trip said.

"You know who that is?"

"I sure don't." As hard as Trip had tried to stay ahead of it, this whole mess always got in front of him.

The sheriff raised up his shotgun. "Drop the gun."

Bruno fired again, not as far over Dewitt's head.

Not to be outdone, Sheriff Dewitt clicked off the safety and shot off a branch above Bruno's head. The branch fell, glancing off Bruno's shoulder. Bruno fired again, this time at the sheriff. The bullet pierced the side of the boat.

The sheriff racked the shotgun and fired at Bruno's feet. He missed.

Bruno fired again and missed again.

The sheriff took aim at Bruno's chest. He lost his balance when he fired and fell back on the seat. The blast blew over Bruno's head. The sheriff scrambled to his feet still holding his shotgun.

"I don't know much about hunting, but I know those things only hold three shells."

Bruno held the pistol in both hands. He aimed at the sheriff's chest. "I won't miss you this time, fatso."

Just as Louis Bruno was about to squeeze the trigger, the sheriff aimed at Bruno's chest. The gangster laughed at him. "You're empty."

Sheriff Dewitt fired his fourth shot. Trip thought he saw a surprised look on Louis Bruno's face just before the 870 police model blew twenty-five holes of number one buckshot through the gangster's chest.

* * *

Sheriff Dewitt stood over Louis Bruno, now deceased, his giant hands still wrapped around his pistol. Bruno's face had twisted into a wry grin, staring up at the sheriff through lifeless eyes. Bruno looked just fine above his neck. From his neck to his waist, blood leaked out of his waders like water draining through a strainer.

The four of them—Sheriff Dewitt, Jake, Trip and Cash—stood in a half-circle around the recently departed gangster.

"You got a tight pattern on that gun, sheriff," Jake said.

"Full choke," Sheriff Dewitt said.

"Didn't open up much. But then again, it was only twenty yards," Jake said. "If that."

The sheriff looked at his shotgun.

"You two sure didn't shoot very straight," Jake said.

"I wasn't trying to hit him until the last shot," the sheriff lied.

Cash walked up to Bruno and sniffed him.

"Get away, Cash," Trip said.

"He thought you were empty," Jake said.

"Must have known something about hunting," the sheriff said.

"He didn't believe you were a lawman," Jake said.

"I told him," Sheriff Dewitt said.

"Yes, you did. You surely did, but you don't look like one, not with them waders and the parka. And that hat."

"What hat?" Sheriff Dewitt said.

"Where's your sheriff's hat?" Jake said.

"It's on my head, you fool."

"You just don't look much like a sheriff. Not with that Mack's camo hat."

Sheriff Dewitt reached for his head and pulled off his hat. He studied the hat Trip had given him. "I guess so, but I identified myself."

"You did, Sheriff," Jake said.

"That right, Trip?"

"That's right, Sheriff."

Dewitt went back to the boat and came back with his sheriff's hat squashed on this head. "Must have sat on it, but this is what I had on the whole time. You boys got that?"

"Yes, sir," Jake said.

Trip nodded.

"There will be an investigation," the sheriff said.

Dewitt poked around the cooker. Trip lit a cigarette. "This looks to be what Arcenault smelled, all right. Jake, boy, how'd you get mixed up in this?"

"He drug me out here. Made me bring him."

The sheriff looked at Jake.

I wonder what he's going to say next.

"He knew right where it was," Jake said, lying again. "He was getting ready to fire it up, I think," he said without being asked.

Jake wouldn't know the truth if it bit him on the face, but that probably helps me.

"What's his name?"

"Said it was Bruno. Louis Bruno. From New Orleans."

"That figures. He looks Italian." The worldly sheriff also pronounced it "eye-talian."

"Let's see his I.D.," the sheriff said.

Trip found Bruno's wallet in his parka. The wallet bulged. Trip opened it. It was full of cash, mostly hundreds. He turned away from Dewitt and stuck most of the money in his parka.

"What you got Trip?"

"Here's his wallet." Trip lit another cigarette.

"Lordy, Lordy, Lordy," Sheriff Dewitt said. "There must be at least a thousand dollars in here." Dewitt stuck some of the money in his own pocket. Then he studied the dead man's driver's license. "This here is Louis Bruno all right."

"You know him, Trip?"

"I took him hunting. Once. Maybe twice."

"Where?"

"Mama's Blind."

"I thought you said you didn't know him."

Trip flicked what was left of his cigarette into the water. It hissed when it hit the water. "I didn't know him from his backside."

"Jake, how'd he find you?"

"I got to the Club House about eight and there he was. Said he wanted a hunt."

"Pretty late start."

"He said he'd give me a thousand for a hunt. We got to Mama's. That's where he told me to take him. Then he had me haul my boat over the levee. And here we are." Jake smiled at the sheriff.

"I guess so." The sheriff shook his head. "You two drag him over to Jake's boat. We got to go in. I never killed no one before. I never even shot at no one."

Jake took one of Bruno's arms, Trip took the other. They dragged him to Jake's boat. When they threw him in, they banged his head on the gunwale.

"That makes two," Trip said, under his breath.

Sheriff Dewitt bent over at the waist and threw up his breakfast.

CHAPTER TWENTY-EIGHT

Trip hitched the little John Deere onto the trailer that he'd hauled the dove hunters in back in September. He threw a decoy bag in the trailer for tomorrow's hunt.

It was the last weekend of duck season, and it was for family and friends only. It was the best time of the season. All over southeast Arkansas, family and friends showed up at their favorite places for the last weekend of duck season. It wasn't always the best hunting. By this time the birds were call shy, decoy shy, and just plain scared, having been shot at since September all the way down the flyway. On top of that, the ducks had started to turn their attention from food to mating. It was tough to get underneath them when they had love on their minds.

No matter, though. This was a time-honored tradition to celebrate the end of another duck season, see the people you cared about, rejoice at the prospect of ten months without a four a.m. wake-up call, and maybe, just maybe, shoot a duck or two.

It should have been the best time of the season at Belle Oak, too. But not this season. Not with the sports, the foreclosure, and certainly not with two dead men. Even if one of them was Louis Bruno. Trip hadn't heard anything from DeMarco, but he thought it was just a matter of time. Unless they wanted to stay as far away from Bruno and the meth as they could.

This year, Trip dreaded the last weekend. Would it be the last weekend ever, the last family and friends weekend at Belle Oak? It just might be.

He threw another bag in the trailer. Just then, his mother barreled up to the shop in her Benz. He didn't expect her until cocktail hour, and he certainly hadn't expected to see her in a black dress and diamonds.

There's only one reason for her to be here early.

"Trip, honey," she said, shivering in the cold, "I hate to ask, but I am a little short."

"Mama, you'll catch your death," Trip said. "Come on inside." He turned to the door.

"I've only got a minute."

"At least put your coat on." He opened the door of the silver Benz and reached in for her full-length mink.

"Hang the cold." Celia stood there like it was a fine spring day, not the dead of the Arkansas winter.

"How much, Mama?"

"Fifty thousand," she said, without flinching.

"Did I hear you right?"

"If you heard fifty thousand, you heard me right."

"You must be feverish."

Celia took two steps toward him. She stood right in front of him. "Trip, I need the money."

"Is it for the barge company?"

"It is."

She's lying.

He backed up a step. "I don't have it," he said, also lying.

"How much do you have?" She took a step toward him. "You put a lot of hunters through here."

"I've been paying Theo on the crop loan," Trip said, extending his lie.

"You must have something. I told Little George I'd come early so we could get the unpleasantness done before the hunt," Celia said, continuing her own lie.

"I'm sorry, Mama, but I gave it to Theo." Trip fished in his pocket, pulling out a wad of cash. "Here," he said, "you can have all I've got." He handed her the ball of money. "I think it's about two thousand."

"This will never do," Celia said, but she took the money. She kissed him on the cheek and scooted around her youngest son. She slid into the Benz and raced off.

At the end of the driveway, she turned toward Stuttgart. Trip gave her a one minute head start, then he and Cash followed her in the pickup. He stayed as far back as he could. The two-lane road was filled with pickups, SUVs, cars, and just about anything that could tow a duck boat. This was duck season's grand finale, and the hunters were out in force.

Trip knew full well that the fifty thousand wasn't for the barge company, and he knew full well that his mother knew full well that he had the fifty thousand.

When he made it to Stuttgart, he saw the Benz in front of the Mallard. He squeezed into a "no parking" parking spot next to an overflowing dumpster. He spied on his mother primping herself in her rearview mirror. She got out and walked into the restaurant. Then he saw Jake meet a greasy-haired man with glasses and a pasty complexion in front of the restaurant. The two of them talked for a couple minutes and then the greasy-haired man went inside. Jake got back into his truck and watched what was going on inside.

Trip cracked his window and Cash's. The fortyish weather leaked into the truck. Cash stuck his nose out his window. Trip lit a cigarette and flicked the ash out the window.

"Cash, old pal, I think that little greasy-haired man followed Mama inside, and everywhere I turn, who should I see but Jake."

Trip waited as long as he could, which was about five minutes. Then he backed out of the parking lot, staying away from where Jake was parked. He drove around to the back of the diner and let himself in through the door where the help went in. He nodded at the cook and peered out into the dining room. Celia sat across from the greasy-haired man. She looked like she'd lost her best friend, which of course she had. She also looked like she'd been crying which she never did.

"That's just about enough," Trip said out loud.

"Enough what, Mr. Trip?" the cook said.

"Enough of this namby-pamby bullshit." He stormed over to the table and sat between the two of them. "Is this man bothering you, Mama?"

Celia jumped in her chair.

The greasy-haired man looked at him through his glasses. "Can I help you?"

"If you are the cause of Miss Celia's tears, you best leave."

"Your mother is the cause of her own tears," Cullen Dubose said.

"What's that?"

"Once she pays her debt, her tears will dry once and for all." He smiled knowingly at Trip.

"What's this all about, Mama?"

"It's just some unfinished business," Celia said bravely, her best foot forward. "With your father and me."

"What kind of business?"

The weak-eyed man smiled. "Monkey business," he said, also bravely.

"What exactly is going on?"

"I think it best if your mother tells you."

"Mama."

Celia looked down at her hands. "There was an accident. With the car. Last year. On New Year's Eve."

Cullen Dubose smiled at Trip. "A man was killed. At the big ditch."

"Did you see it?"

"I did."

"And now you want to get paid," Trip felt his chest tighten.

"It's a fee," Cullen Dubose said.

Trip set his hands, palms down, on the table. It was his turn to smile. He smiled at Celia, then at Cullen Dubose. Calmly, very calmly, he peeled the glasses from Cullen Dubose's face. His pupils shrank before Trip's eyes. He folded the bows of the glasses in, then folded the glasses over again at the nosepiece, then he folded the bows over each other. He passed the perfectly useless glasses back to Dubose. Still smiling, Trip hooked the greasy-haired man by the collar of his coat and jerked him out of his chair. "If I ever see you again, I'll kill you."

Cullen Dubose seemed to believe him and started for the door. Trip grabbed him by his coat and threw him out.

Trip walked back to the table and sat down across from his mother. None of the patrons would look at him. Trip pried the tale of woe from his reluctant mother. She took a cigarette from Trip and lit up in the middle of the nonsmoking section. This drew more looks than the bum's rush Trip had put on Dubose.

"Mama, he was blackmailing you."

"I know what it's called."

"How much have you paid him?"

"Nothing." She took a drag on the cigarette. "Not too much."

"Mama, those are two different answers."

"He said he'd go to the police."

"If he went to the police, then he'd never get any money," Trip said.

"Then where would I be?"

"Is that why Big George killed himself?"

"Don't talk that way about your father."

"Is that where the crop loan money went?"

"No," Celia said. "Well, some of it."

"How much?"

"Twenty, maybe thirty thousand."

"Where's the rest of it?"

"For the life of me, I don't know."

"Mama."

"Truly."

A twentyish waitress with bad teeth arrived. "This is the no-smoking section," she said.

"I know it," Trip said.

"Then …"

"Two timber specials," he said.

"What about the cigarette?"

"It's just about burned out," Trip said.

The waitress picked up the menus and left.

Trip didn't know who was more foolish. His mother for getting sucked into this blackmail or himself for cooking meth in the heart of Bayou Meto.

"Mama, where's the rest of the two hundred thousand Big George borrowed from Theo Boxwood?"

"Trip, honey," Celia squashed out her cigarette. "I don't know. I surely don't."

"That money would have straightened things out. And then, I wouldn't have …"

"Wouldn't have what?"

"Nothing."

"You were about to say something."

"No, I wasn't."

"Trip McClure."

"I thought better of it."

"Are you mixed up in something I should know about?"

"No, Mama. I'm just carrying sports into the timber."

"So you can save the farm," Celia said.

"That's right, Mama."

"Maybe you should use the money for the barge company."

Trip felt his chest tighten again. "So those two idiots can lose it again."

The waitress with the bad teeth showed up with the timber specials. Eggs over easy, sausage, biscuits, and grits.

"Trip, but for the barge company, there never would have been a Belle Oak."

"And now, but for Belle Oak, there's no barge company."

"You're going to have to make a decision," Celia said.

"About what?"

"There's not enough money to save the barge company and the farm and stop the Memphis bankers from foreclosing on the farm. Not to mention Theo Boxwood." Celia stuck her fork in one of the egg yolks. It spilled over onto the grits. "And I don't think we've seen the last of Cullen Dubose."

"What should I do?"

"I don't know, Trip." She ate a forkful of the egg soaked grits. "There's at least three places for whatever money you've got. Maybe four. I think we might ought to move on. We just aren't who we once were." Celia wolfed down the grits, then started on the sausage.

I don't think she's eaten in days.

"What's Jake got to do with us?" Trip said.

"Jake?"

"Jake Lawless, our farmhand."

"Why would Jake have anything to do with this?"

"I saw him talking to the blackmailer," Trip said. "He's everywhere I've got trouble."

"What trouble are you in?"

"It's nothing, Mama. Guide stuff."

Trip didn't like the way any of this was headed. He felt like he'd been backed into a corner. Two men were already dead. He didn't kill them, but he just as well might have. He pushed his plate away.

"You didn't touch your breakfast."

He lit a cigarette. "Do Little George and J.D. know about Cullen Dubose?"

"No." Celia finished her sausage and started in on the biscuits. "And there's no need for them to know. We might just as well have ourselves a good old-fashioned last weekend. It might be our last one."

"Don't talk like that, Mama."

The waitress came over. "There's no smoking in here." Trip handed her a twenty.

"Be right back with your change."

"Keep it."

"You got ten coming back, and there's still no smoking." She ran off with the twenty.

"That's a big tip," Celia said.

* * *

Trip marinated the medallions in jalapeño juice, then he washed them in a ginger and whiskey bath. He wrapped them in bacon, then he grilled them for three minutes on a side. Tully watched over the crawfish boil. They'd come in season in Louisiana a week ago, and finances notwithstanding, Trip had twenty-five pounds driven up from the Gulf. Hush puppies, greens, and gumbo. Pouilly-Fuissé for the crawfish and Bordeaux for the duck.

After an extended cocktail hour where the Maker's Mark poured into the McClures like Bayou Meto poured into the timber, the McClure clan took their places in the dining room of the yellow house.

Trip sat at the head of the table. Parker, in a little black dress, sat at the other end. They had all dressed for dinner. Jackets and ties for the men. The brothers McClure, their wives, the children, the widow McClure, and Jude. Thirteen in all.

"Lord," Trip said, head bowed, "bless this family, bless this meal, and bless tomorrow's hunt. Amen."

A chorus of amens.

A clink of wine glasses.

"We might have prayed for a bit more than that," Little George said, puffy looking in his blue blazer.

"Don't start, Little George. Sometimes it's best not to ask for too much," Celia said. She drank her Bordeaux.

"We have bigger things to worry about than tomorrow's hunt," Little George said.

"I thought I'd pray for something that actually has a chance of coming to pass," Trip said. He heaped his plate with crawfish. He picked one up and broke off its tail. He gouged the meat out of the tail and poured Frank's on it. He chewed it, then sucked the brains out of the head.

"Must you do that," Little George said.

"Mind your own crawfish," Celia said.

"Mama, the barge company is in default and the farm is in foreclosure," J.D. said.

Celia picked up a piece of the duck by the toothpick and bit off the end as ladylike as she could. "We'll have ourselves a fine hunt, and the rest of it will have to take care of itself."

"This is just about the end of life as we know it," Little George said.

"That's all the more reason to celebrate the weekend," Celia said.

"Well said." This from Trip.

"That's a cavalier attitude from somebody who's going to hunt from the other side of the levee next year, and do God knows what for a living," J.D. said.

"Unless you made more money than you're letting on," Little George said.

The truth was that Trip didn't have enough. He had the money from the sports and he had the money from Louis Bruno's wallet, but that wasn't enough. Without the money from the meth, there wouldn't be enough to go around. He was out of ideas. Even bad ones.

"What kind of hunt are we going to have with all these sports running all over the place?" Little George said.

"Don't you worry, Little George," Trip said. "Jude, the guides, and I are going to take them out. You won't even know they're here."

"I better not," Little George said.

"You're pretty uppity for a half-sunk bargeman who wants the sports' money," Trip said.

"How much do you have?" Little George asked, suddenly interested and almost as smooth as the Pouilly-Fuissé they served with the crawfish.

"You behave yourself and we'll see." Trip sucked the brains out of a crawfish.

* * *

Trip met the guides Saturday morning at five. Cad, Big John, Church, and the formerly missing Jake, found once more. The stars were fading and the clear sky promised ducks in the woods.

Trip sent the guides out to the best spots he had, except the two he had reserved for his family and Jude. He had some unfinished business with Jake, but that would have to wait until after the season. Just to be safe, he kept Jake in close where he could keep an eye on him.

The ducks flew that morning, flew like they'd flown all season.

If I make it until next year, I just might make a business out of this.

After the morning hunt, Trip, Jude, and the guides gathered at the shop. Forty degrees and clear, a fresh wind from the northwest. Trip had brought a case of Dixie, but they weren't going to get in much trouble splitting a case six ways.

"One more day, boys. We'll sleep in Monday and pick up on Tuesday," Trip said. "Final wages paid when the last decoy is picked up."

This didn't go over well with the guides. They finished the beer and drifted off, all except Jake who edged up to Trip on the way to his truck. He kicked at the dirt with his boot.

"Mr. Trip, I know I been a bit of trouble this year."

"That's about right."

"I haven't meant nothing by it. Just circumstances."

Where is this headed?

"How about we meet at Mama's Blind at eleven. The sports will be in by then. We can pick a hole to hunt across the levee."

"The ducks will all be shot up by then."

"Not on the Game and Fish side. The ducks drop in there all day," Jake said. "I'll meet you at Mama's Blind at eleven. We'll go have ourselves a hunt." The guide with the scar gouged an *X* in the dirt with his boot heel.

CHAPTER TWENTY-NINE

Sunday morning, the last morning of the last day. They were all in the woods, the guides and the sports, Trip's brothers, his mother, and Jude. Trip and Cash sat in the dark in the johnboat at the landing, the last ones to leave.

Saturday night had been quiet. Trip had grilled steaks. There hadn't been much drinking. They were all tired from Saturday's hunt, and they all had their own worries.

Trip had sent them all out ahead. He told them he'd stay behind to make sure everybody got to the right spot. He told Jude he'd catch up with him and the others as soon as he could. He waited until they were all in the timber, then he and Cash took off down the ditch.

He stopped at the Crooked Tree to make sure the baby food jars he had hidden in the old tree were still there.

I don't see how I'll ever get anything for them. Just as well.

He tied off the boat at Mama's Blind. He made sure he left it where Jake could see it. Trip climbed over the levee to the other boat. At the triple tape, he turned south, cut his speed and ran dead slow through the timber. He took a compass course just east of south, past Snake Island, then on to the Beaverkill.

He'd meet Jake here at eleven. By that time, the ducks, if they were coming into the timber, would have already come and gone. These weren't midday holes. Jake knew it, and Jake knew Trip knew it.

He'd been a fool. It had gone too far. It had gone bad, and one way or another, he was going to finish it at eleven. First, though, he was going to have the last hunt of the season with Cash.

"Damn every last one of them."

He cut the engine back at the Beaverkill. They drifted over to the fallen tree. "Cash, kennel." The dog jumped from the boat to the log and sat.

He poled into the woods and tied the boat to a tree. He slid into the water, covered the boat with burlap, grabbed his shotgun and shooting bag, and slipped into the water. He waded through the woods, the smell of wet timber and rotting leaves all around him. Cash wagged his tail when he got back to the fallen log.

Trip leaned against the tree closest to the fallen log. There was some daylight in the woods, but the sun was still below the tree line. It was too dark to see the shotgun, the Parker over/under he'd stuck barrel first in the mud the last time he was here.

I'll get it later.

Trip reached into his pocket for the Ziploc bag that kept his cigarettes dry. His fingers found the joint in with the cigarettes. He rolled it in his fingers. His ears had a powerful ring to them, but this wasn't the time to smoke a joint. He took out a cigarette and lit it. He smelled the burning tobacco and watched the smoke trail off.

Trip heard wings over his head, looked up and saw silhouettes above the trees. He took out his duck calls and called at them. Sweetly, ever so sweetly.

He landed the first bunch. Cash didn't break but it was all he could do to stay on the log. His leg shook.

Trip shot two drakes out of the second bunch. Cash fetched them both.

More ducks flew over the hole. Trip heard the wind rush over their wings as they circled the hole, a low whistling, like wind through bare branches. The circle grew tighter. Then it was a spiral, a swirling spiral. A hen dropped below the treetops and landed in front of them. Three more splashed down on the other side of the hole.

Trip heard another splash, but it wasn't the splash of a duck. He didn't turn toward it.

Trip heard the splash again. Cash turned his head to the sound. Trip didn't turn, not yet. He blew the call softly and landed the rest of the ducks. He heard the click of a safety. Cash's ears pricked up.

Trip turned, but he had turned too late. He had turned right into the barrel of Jake's twelve gauge. Jake was much closer than he'd thought, barely fifteen yards away. There was no time to shoulder his gun, much less fire it.

Jake dropped the barrel down and pointed it at Trip's chest.

It wasn't going to end at eleven. It was going to end now.

"Cash, fetch," Trip said. The dog leapt in the water. The swimming ducks took flight. Wings beat against the water. The ducks exploded into the air. Three-dozen pair of wings erupted out of the hole. They swarmed up and out of the hole blocking Jake's shot. Trip hid behind a big white oak.

"Cash, come." The dog turned and started swimming toward him.

Once the ducks cleared, he'd have a shot at Jake. One shot, before Jake shot him.

The last of the ducks cleared. Cash was still twenty feet from him. Where was Jake? He hadn't figured on Jake moving.

"Drop your gun in the water, or I'll blow your head off."

Trip spun around. There was no one behind him. He couldn't tell where the voice came from, but it wasn't Jake.

"Drop it," said the voice. "Drop that shotgun in the water or I'll blow your head off."

Trip stayed behind the tree. Who was it? He couldn't see anyone. He heard the splash of a gun.

"Take three steps into the hole. Turn away from me. Put your hands on your head."

Cash swam up to Trip. He couldn't touch bottom, and he swam in lazy circles. Trip had no idea what had just happened or what was about to happen, but he knew he didn't want Cash anywhere near it. He grabbed the dog by the collar and yanked him over to him. He lifted Cash by the collar. The Labrador stood next to him on his hind legs.

"It's all right, Trip. You can come out," the voice said.

"Who is it?"

"It's me, Jude."

Jude? How did Jude get here?

"It doesn't sound like you."

"It's the mask."

"What's your father's first name?"

"Cassius."

"Take the mask off."

"Not while I've got this twelve-gauge trained on Jake."

Trip peeked around the tree. Jude, if it was Jude, had his shotgun aimed at Jake, who had his hands on his head.

Trip took a half step from the tree and pointed his gun at Jake. "I've got Jake. Take off your mask."

The masked man held his gun in one hand and pulled off the mask.

"Damn it. Damn it to hell."

"I told you it was me," Jude said.

"You should have shot him."

"There's already one dead and one missing."

"This one here is the cause. Put your gun back on him." Trip started toward Jake. "Stand right there and don't turn around. I'd just as soon shoot you as look at you." Trip waded over to Jake who still had his back to Trip. He grabbed the guide by his shoulder and spun him around.

Except it wasn't Jake.

Cash swam up to Trip and circled him again. Trip pointed to Cash's former perch. "Cash, kennel." The dog wasn't too happy, but he swam to the fallen log and climbed up.

"This isn't Jake," Jude said.

"I know it."

"Who is it?"

"His name is Cullen Dubose."

"What's going on?"

"Nothing."

"You know what you are? You're a prisoner of your secrets. They'll eat you up if you don't tell somebody."

This is no time for a sermon.

"Who's Cullen Dubose?"

"For the better part of a year, he's been blackmailing Mama."

"About what?"

Trip looked at Dubose. "Where's Jake?"

"Who's Jake?" Cullen Dubose said.

Trip stared him in the eye, then looked away. He turned back and smashed Cullen Dubose in the head with the butt of his shotgun. The greasy-haired man staggered, then fell face first into the water.

"Get him up, or he'll drown."

"If he doesn't drown, I'm going to kill him when he gets up."

"I got your back but not if you kill him." Jude waded over, reached down, and pulled Dubose to his feet.

* * *

Trip, wearing Cullen Dubose's parka and hat, motored slowly through the woods. The triple tape was a hundred yards ahead.

Jude was behind him in the johnboat with Cash and a trussed-up Cullen Dubose who had a bruise the size of a grapefruit on the side of his head and a powerful headache.

Dubose had told them that Jake had dropped his hunters off with Big John. Then they each took a boat to the triple tape and hid in the woods, waiting for Trip. When Trip turned off to the Beaverkill, Jake had given Dubose a compass course to the Beaverkill. He'd used a push pole when he got close. Trip never heard him come in.

Jude said he'd heard more outboards than he thought he should. He'd followed Jake and Dubose into Bayou Meto. Jude followed Dubose into the Beaverkill. He didn't think Jake had seen him.

Dubose said he was supposed to meet Jake at the triple tape. He was to bring the dead Trip with him.

Trip and Jude's plan, such as it was, was for Trip, masquerading as Dubose, to surprise Jake at the triple tape.

Trip didn't know how Jake would react if he only saw one person in Dubose's boat, but he hoped Jake would think Trip's body was out of sight.

Trip saw the triple tape fifty yards ahead. It flashed in the sun as he motored through the trees. Jude was supposed to be fifty yards back, engine off, poling. Ducks flew at the treetops, silhouetted against the blue sky. There were a few shots off toward the Government Addition. Nothing from the Belle Oak side of the levee.

Trip cut the motor about ten yards from the triple tape and coasted in, hood up, hiding his face.

He was going to end it with Jake. Here and now. Jake had been in on it with Bruno. He was also in on the blackmail with Dubose. Why hadn't his mother told him about Dubose? Why didn't he see it before? And why hadn't he figured out what Jake was up to?

Trip checked Dubose's gun. It was loaded with buckshot. He checked his own gun, hidden next to the gunwale, loaded with BBs.

Trip lit a cigarette. He blew the smoke out slowly through his nose, like a dragon, he thought.

A shot rang out. His ears rang when it pierced the hull of his boat.

Trip looked at his cigarette. He must have given himself away. Did Dubose smoke?

There was no spray of pellets, no thud from a slug.

Jake was close by. Close by with a deer rifle. Out of range for a shotgun. Trip dove to the bottom of the boat.

The rifle spat again. The bullet buried itself in the transom. Jake would kill him if he stayed here. He'd kill Jude, too, but so far Trip didn't think Jake knew that Jude was back in the timber.

Trip reached up and jerked the starter cord of the engine. He shifted into gear and peeked just above the hull. He made for the ditch. There were more shots, but they were off the mark. When he got to the ditch, he opened the motor up and ran wide open toward the Belle Oak levee. The shooting stopped. Trip sat up on the stern seat, bent over as low as he could.

He ran the boat through the ditch, ran it hard until he reached the levee. He scrambled up the levee and then jumped into the johnboat on the Belle Oak side.

He'd thought about waiting for Jake at the levee, jumping him there, but he decided it was too risky.

Trip raced down the ditch toward the farm. He thought he heard a boat behind him, but he wasn't sure. If he could make the landing, he could jump on the four-wheeler and get help. It was one o'clock, and everyone should be in.

Jude has his hands full with Dubose so it's just Jake and me.

Trip rounded the last bend and saw the landing. He eased up on the throttle and let the surge of the wake carry him in. He jumped out and tied the boat off at the bow. As he climbed up the bank, a bullet spit into the mud, six inches from his right boot. He slipped on the levee and fell to his hands and knees and belly crawled up the levee. There was another shot, but he didn't hear it hit anything.

Jake is behind me, and he's still in his boat. I've got a little time.

He made it to the top of the levee and crawled to the four-wheeler. Where the four-wheeler should have been.

Gone. It's gone.

Someone had taken it. He'd have to run to the shop, but he'd be a perfect target when he stood up. Jake could land the boat anywhere along the levee. He could hide anywhere.

Trip crawled south along the top of the levee for fifty yards. Then he ducked down the bank into the flooded rice stubble. He edged his way further south along the base of the levee. He'd be safe as long as Jake didn't walk this levee. At the end of the field, he climbed up the levee, then down into the next field. At the end of this field he could turn east and head to the shop. He bent over at the waist and crept through the field. His boots stuck in the mud with every step. They stuck just enough to make the going slow. He smelled the wet rice stubble and the ooze from his footprints. The temperature was up to fifty. He started to sweat.

He reached the end of another field, climbed up the levee, and peeked over the top. There was no one in sight. He stood up next to the power unit. The shop was a mile to the east.

Trip stood, just for a moment, but a moment was all it took. The bullet spun him around and knocked him flat on his back. There was another shot. It slammed into the power unit. Trip rolled to it and crawled to the west side, away from the shooting. Jake was between him and the shop.

He was safe here, at least for a few minutes. He sat up against the power unit. Another shot rang off it. Jake meant to keep him here while he worked his way in.

Trip ripped open his parka and peeled his waders down. Blood leaked out of his side just above his hip. It was a crease. The bullet had ripped through his parka, his waders, his shirt, and creased his side.

There was a gouge, a gouge about six inches long just below his ribs, but that was it. It bled like hell, and it hurt worse. He had to stop the bleeding and get away from here. And he had to do it now.

He folded one of his gloves in half and put it on the wound. Then he took off his belt and wrapped it over the glove and around him. He pulled it as tight as he could stand. Then he pulled up his waders and put his parka back on. If that stopped the bleeding, and if he didn't pass out, he thought he had a chance.

He'd left both shotguns in the boat. He had to get away. He rolled down the levee away from Jake. He crabbed west a hundred feet, then up to the next north-south levee behind a clump of willow saplings. Down again, then up, then down. Heading west.

He didn't have a plan. His only thought was to get away from Jake. No one knew where he was or thought twice about it. His brothers and the guides were all having lunch. Then they'd pack up and leave. They wouldn't pay any attention to the gunfire, if they heard it all. And Jude had his hands full with Dubose.

Trip had to find a place to hole up while he figured out what to do. He kept on going. He'd lost track of where he was. All he knew was that he was on the west side of the farm.

Then he was at the end of it. The last levee. There was nowhere else to go. The buckbrush on the other side of the levee was too thick, and the flooded timber was past that.

He crawled over the top of the levee and slid down to the buckbrush. He heard the quail whistle behind him. He had to rest. Just for a little while.

* * *

The sound of the quad woke him up. He sat up with a start. How long had he been out? He looked at his watch. It was two-thirty. He'd passed out for half an hour. His wound burned. He laid back down and rolled over on his good side.

He couldn't just lie here, but he didn't know if he could walk. He sat back up. His side burned, and there was blood oozing through his waders. He sat there for a couple of minutes then he crawled up the levee and peeked over.

There was Jake. He was crisscrossing the levees on the quad, the rifle slung over his shoulder.

Hunting him.

He was two levees east of where Trip was hiding. Jake would find him here. He couldn't stay where he was, but he couldn't get away without Jake seeing him. Trapped. He was trapped.

Then he saw it. A chance.

It might be my only chance.

Two quarter sections over, due south. Hangman's Blind where Big George had shot himself. It had been off limits all season—not that anyone wanted to go near it. Especially Trip. He didn't think anyone had been there except Thanksgiving night when he'd found Mama there.

If he could make it there, he'd at least be covered up. Covered up until he figured out what to do. He didn't think the plywood walls would stop a deer rifle but they'd slow it down.

First, though, he had to get there. It was two fields over, each one half a mile square, and there was no cover.

Trip peered over the top of the levee again. Jake was one levee to the east. One more and he'd find him.

Trip skidded down the levee into the tangle of weeds, thorns, and buck-brush. He fell off the levee. A burning pain shot through his side. He got to his feet and made his way south, slowly, painfully slowly. One step after another.

He was on the outside boundary of the farm. He limped through the tangles, stumbled and fell. In and out of the buckbrush. In and out of the mud. In and out of the tangles. All the while, he could hear the droning of the quad. Jake was getting closer and closer.

It took him half an hour to make it to Hangman's Blind, a four by eight rectangular box with a half roof over the bench seats. The blind was open at eye level all the way around, the roof on posts. It looked east, facing the flooded rice stubble.

Trip snuck up the levee. There were at least two hundred ducks—mallards, gadwall, teal, and spoonies—in the flooded rice stubble. He cracked open the door of the blind. A snake the size of a baseball bat sunned itself on the bench. It looked at him with soulless eyes. Trip slammed the door. The ducks busted up in the air.

"Damn it. Damn it to hell." Trip thought Jake must have heard that, and if he hadn't heard it, he must have seen the ducks fly off.

Trip opened the door again. He had to get inside, no matter where the snake was. It was a bull snake, perfectly harmless, but he didn't care. He didn't want to be in there with it, but he didn't have a choice. He climbed in the blind and crouched in the northwest corner, the snake out of sight. He watched the ducks circle above the muddy water. They drifted back in.

Maybe Jake didn't think anything of it.

If he could just catch his breath, he'd figure something out. He thought he'd be safe here, at least for now. The corner posts were two by fours and the sides were half inch plywood. He didn't think the rifle could kill him in here, but he didn't want to find out.

Trip didn't have to wait long. The rifle cracked again. The bullet pierced the north side of the blind about a foot from his chest. It blew right through the plywood and out the south side. The ducks jumped up and scattered.

Another shot. This one lodged in a two-by-four about a foot from his head. Another shot blew all the way through the blind about eighteen inches from his chest.

He couldn't stay here, but there was no place to go. Jake would shoot him as soon as he opened the door. He was closing in, and he wouldn't keep missing.

Maybe I can climb over the back side. No, he'll shoot me when I climb over.

Trip dropped to the floor of the blind and crawled under the bench. He couldn't see Jake, but he'd be safe here, at least until Jake got into the blind.

Trip lay on his good side. The pain was still wicked. He fished his pocket knife out of his parka and fiddled with the blades until he found the biggest one. Two and a half inches. It wasn't big enough unless he got right up to Jake, but it was all he had.

He'd lie here and wait it out. Jake would have to come into the blind. The rifle wouldn't be much use this close. That was his only chance. Not a good chance, but a chance. Unless Jake got him with the rifle first.

Another shot slammed through the blind right where he'd been sitting. Then another. This one buried itself in the two-by-four right behind his head. He heard the quad roll up the levee to the blind. The engine idled.

"Mr. Trip. Mr. Trip, you in there?"

He didn't answer.

"You in there?" Jake shut off the engine. "I think you are. But you may be shot up. Why don't you call out? We got a few things to work out. Then we can move on."

Trip stayed where he was. He turned a quarter turn so he could lie on his back. He'd have to turn back on his side when the time came, but it wasn't time yet, and it hurt too much to stay on his side.

"Look here, Mr. Trip. You just come on out and direct me to that money you got. I seen you take money off of Mr. Louis. Just tell me where you got it hid, and I'll be on my way. You'll never see me again."

Trip didn't say anything.

"You hear me, Mr. Trip? I know you have money. Mr. Louis was to give me some for helping him with you. And you got money from the sports. You got money for Dubose. Did you kill him, too?" There was another shot. This one kicked in the dirt in front of him.

Trip heard Jake climb off the quad. "I found out all about Mr. Louis and Dubose, too. I ain't the dumb farmhand you think."

There was another shot. This one kicked in the dirt in front of him.

"Hear that, Mr. Trip? Did you hear it? That's my six-shooter. There's five left. And if you're in there, I won't need but one."

A pistol. Jake has a pistol.

He hadn't figured on that. What could he do? There was nothing he could do. There was nothing he could do but wait.

Trip looked at the underside of the bench, up at the planks above him. They were six inches above him. There was something taped to one of the planks, right over his head. It was a piece of brown cardboard that blended in with the plank. Maybe four-by-five-by-eight inches.

He peeled it off the plank. It was damp but not soaked through. There was a Ziploc bag taped to the other side of the cardboard. There were hundred-dollar bills in the bag. It was full of hundred-dollar bills.

It was the missing money. Big George had had it all along. He'd hidden in the blind before he killed himself. But why?

There were footsteps outside the blind and a hand on the door. Then the sound of the quad. Had Jake left?

What was going on? Was there someone with Jake? Trip didn't have time to figure it out. He turned back on his side. He'd have one chance.

"Jake. Hey, Jake, what in God's name are you doing? Shooting off a rifle like a crazy man." It was Parker on another quad.

"You say one word, and I'll kill her," Jake said. "Varmints, Miss Parker. Varmints."

"What kind of varmints?"

"You stay quiet, Mr. Trip. You hear me," he said under his breath. Then, "Snakes, there's snakes, Miss Parker."

"Since when do you shoot snakes with a deer rifle?"

"Miss Parker, you just go on back to the yellow house. I'll be there directly."

She turned the engine off. "Have you seen Trip?"

"Last time I seen him he was in Bayou Meto. Said he was going to have one last hunt at the Beaverkill."

"When was that?" Parker was close to the blind.

"She's gone too far now, Mr. Trip. One step too far."

Trip sprang out of the blind. He slammed the door into Jake and knocked him down. Trip was on him with the knife. He slashed at Jake's throat with the open blade. Jake rolled to his left. Trip sliced off the top of Jake's right ear. Blood spurted everywhere. Jake threw Trip off and came at him.

Parker picked up the rifle by the barrel and swung it at Jake. The stock hit him square in the back of the head and knocked him cold.

"Baby, I think there's a few things you need to tell me about," Parker said.

CHAPTER THIRTY

The rain started the day after duck season ended. The heavens opened, and it rained for seven days straight. Game and Fish pulled the boards at Lower Vallier, but the water in Bayou Meto rose and rose. The floodwaters covered up Snake Island and washed away the meth cooker.

Trip took the johnboat to the Crooked Tree. He took the baby food jars out of the woodpecker holes and poured out the recipe.

Sheriff Dewitt never went back to the little drug factory where he'd killed Louis Bruno. The floodwaters of Bayou Meto were a perfect excuse.

Game and Fish searched for Captain Arcenault by boat. When the woods dried up, they searched by foot, but Bayou Meto never gave up its secret.

Jake and Dubose both went to jail, Jake longer than Dubose. Dubose got a year for reckless endangerment with a firearm. Jake got five years for assault with intent to do great bodily harm. Jake was mum about Captain Arcenault. So was Trip.

There was no word from the New Orleans gangsters. Trip decided not to go back to Le Pavillon.

As for Big George, they were never really sure what happened. Celia was sure it had been an accident. She thought he'd hidden the money and had meant to come back for it. Trip didn't think so.

Trip used Big George's money to pay off the crop loan. He took the money from the sports and paid enough on the loan with the Memphis bankers to stop the foreclosure. He gave some of the money to his brothers for the barge company.

He took the rest of it over to Pine Bluff and left it in Captain Arcenault's mailbox.

They didn't sell the farm. Amelia was brokenhearted.

Trip told Jude the whole story.

He didn't tell Parker about the meth. She knew there was something. What he didn't tell her made a wall between the two of them. A wall that grew higher and higher. A wall of secrets. Of lies, told and untold. Jude had been right about secrets.

When he could bear it no longer, he told her the whole story. She said she forgave him, but he wasn't sure.

There would be at least one more year at Belle Oak and the duck woods. He'd call so sweetly, but he had fences to mend.

THE END

Acknowledgments

To Ellen Jones, my longtime, part-time, long-suffering assistant for her typing, copy editing, sage advice, encouragement, and endless patience.

To Bruce Stickle, Jesse Melcher, Mike Murphy, Diane Newman, Mark Lewison, Steve Spencer, and Charlie McLravy for reading the manuscript. They made many story suggestions and helped me correct countless factual, contextual, and typographical errors.

To John Wickham for his cover design.

To Mission Point Press for all their help in producing *The Hangman's Blind*. They have been spectacular: Hart Cauchy for his editing and insight, Misha Neidorfler for being a great team leader, Sarah Meiers for interior design, Darlene Short for proofing, Jen Wahl for her direction and leadership, Tricia Frey for her great work with publicity and marketing, Tanya Muzumdar for her evaluation, Chris Jones for marketing, and Doug Weaver for his firm but steady hand as he passed the torch.

Finally, thanks to my wife, Christi, for her unflagging support during the writing of *The Hangman's Blind*.

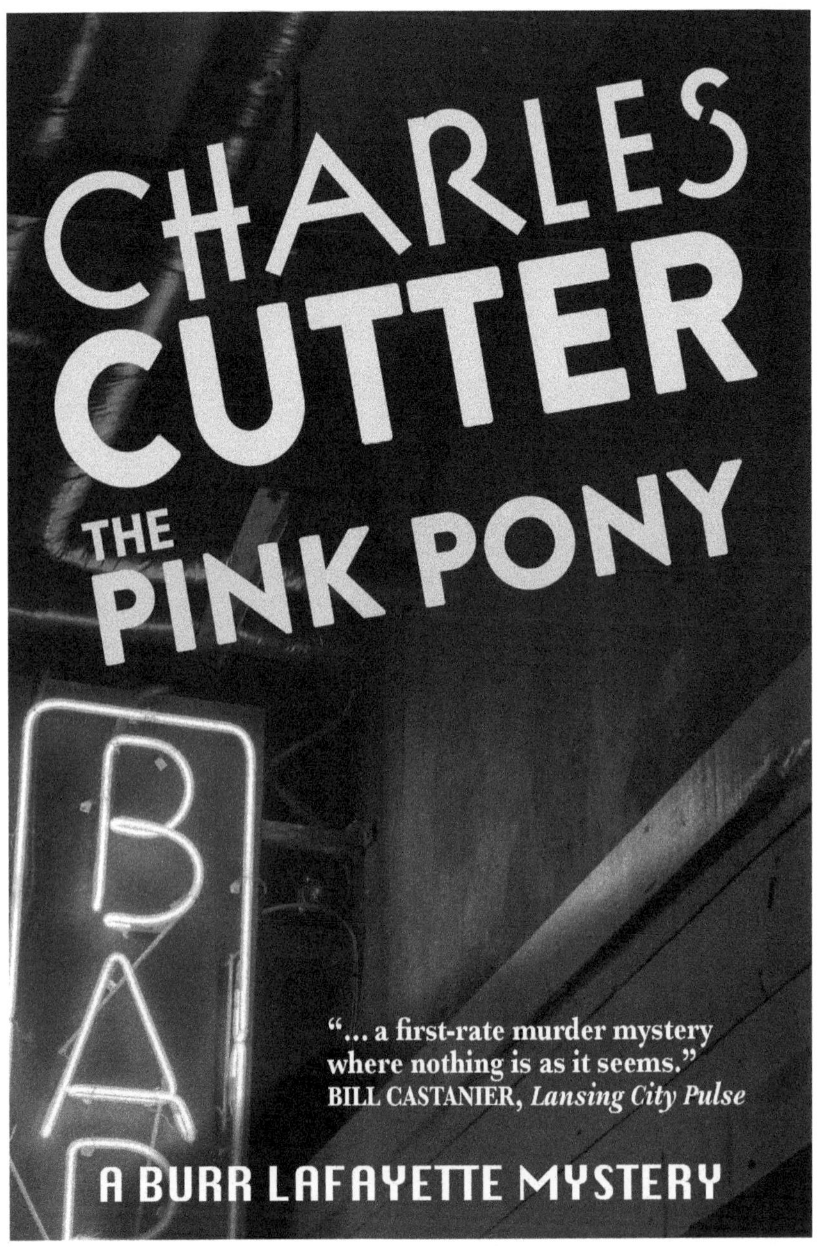

"If you can't make it to Mackinac Island this summer, it's not too late to escape through the pages of *The Pink Pony*. It's a fast-paced, highly entertaining mystery that uses Mackinac Island as the backdrop for a criminal trial."

Ray Walsh, *Lansing State Journal*

"A smashing murder mystery featuring a quick-witted protagonist... Cutter's razor-sharp dialogue in the courtroom [is] truly unforgettable."

Kirkus Reviews

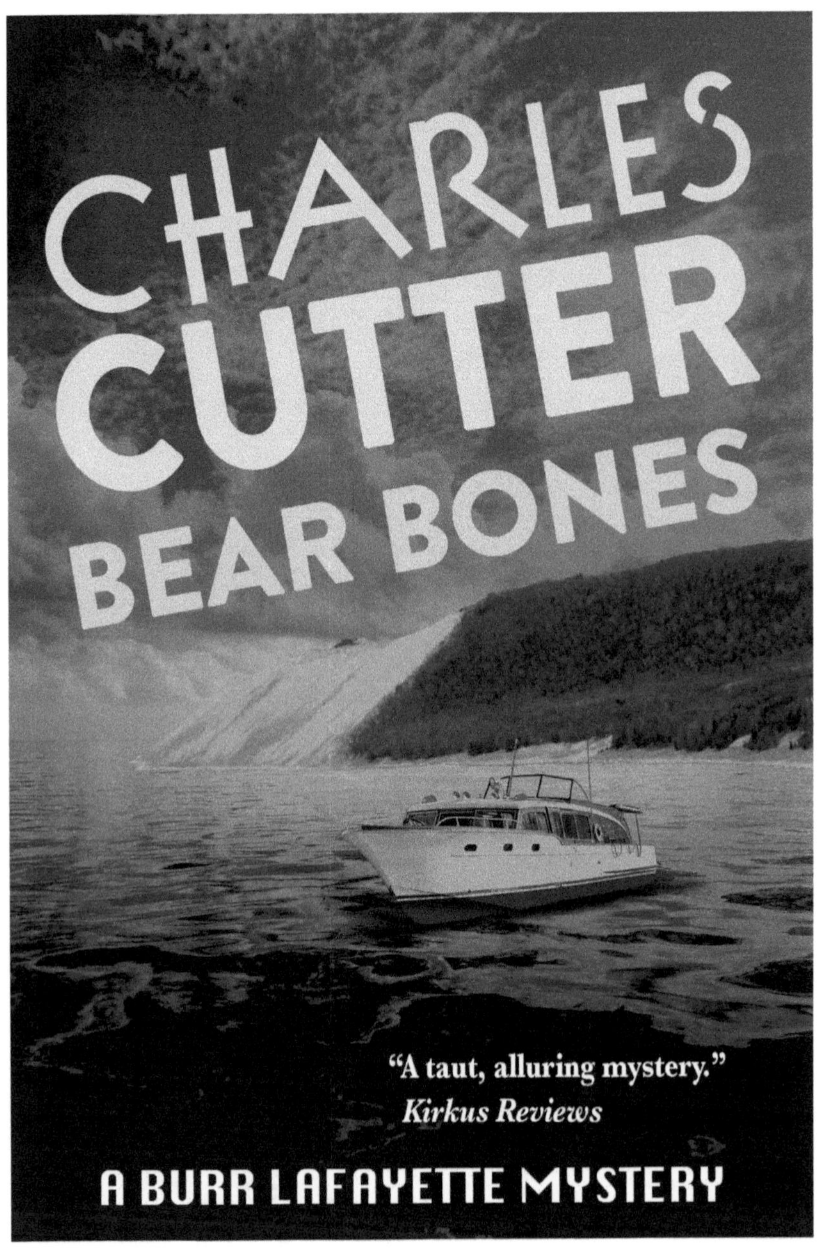

"*Bear Bones* and Burr Lafayette remind us of what we have and why we love where we are. Part mystery, part ode to the last best places, Cutter's prose captures the best of what is always slipping away. A page turner of a mystery."

Glen Young, *Bear River Literary*

"Cutter's narrative maintains a relentless edge; numerous characters lie; and an unsettling ambiguity hangs over everything. Another superb, realistic installment of this Midwestern legal thriller series."
Kirkus Reviews

"*Under the Ashes* is like a good gin and tonic:
clean, crisp, and with a bite."

Steven Pruett, *Executive Chairman,*

Cox Media Group

About the Author

Charles Cutter is the author of the highly acclaimed five-book Burr Lafayette legal thriller series. *The Pink Pony,* the first book in the series, recently won First Prize in the Global Book Awards.

Cutter is a cum laude graduate of the University of Michigan Law School and a graduate with highest honors from Michigan State University. Before his writing career, he was in the media business and was a practicing attorney.

Cutter is active in conservation, most recently serving as chairman of the board for Pheasants Forever and Quail Forever, the largest upland conservation organization in the United States. He lives with his wife, two dogs and four cats in East Lansing. He has a leaky sailboat in Harbor Springs, and a leakier duck boat on Saginaw Bay.

Books in the Burr Lafayette series include *The Gray Drake, Bear Bones, The Pink Pony, The Crooked Angel* and *Under the Ashes.* They are available at Amazon and your local bookstore. Cutter has also written literary fiction, short stories and screenplays. He is currently at work on the next book in the Burr Lafayette series.

For additional information, please go to www.CharlesCutter.com.